DESIGNS

BOOK TWO IN THE TAPESTRY SERIES, FIRST BOOK WAS THREADS

MARY HOWARD WRIGHT

DESIGNS

BOOK TWO IN THE TAPESTRY SERIES,
FIRST BOOK WAS THREADS

Copyright © 2023 **Mary Wright**

All rights reserved. No part of this publication may be reproduced, distributed, or transmitted in any form or by any means, including photocopying, recording, or other electronic or mechanical methods, without the prior written permission of the publisher, except in the case of brief quotations embodied in critical reviews and certain other noncommercial uses permitted by copyright law. For permission requests, write to the publisher, addressed "Attention: Book Rights and Permission," at the address below.

Published in the United States of America

ISBN 978-1-962110-90-7 (SC)
ISBN 978-1-962730-28-0 (Ebook)

Mary Wright
222 West 6th Street
Suite 400, San Pedro, CA, 90731
www.stellarliterary.com

Ordering Information and Rights Permission:

Quantity sales. Special discounts might be available on quantity purchases by corporations, associations, and others. For details, contact the publisher at the address above.

For Book Rights Adaptation and other Rights Permission. Call us at toll-free 1-888-945-8513 or send us an email at admin@stellarliterary.com.

Sometimes you find yourself in the middle of
nowhere and…
Sometimes, in the middle of nowhere
you find yourself

—Author Unknown

Contents

1 Reunion 1
2 Dining at the River 9
3 Rachel's New Friend 14
4 A Matter of Trust 19
5 Changing Times 26
6 Clyde's Dilemma 31
7 Clyde's Family 36
8 Expectations 42
9 Double Trouble 45
10 Front Porch Chats 50
11 Decade of Love 56
12 Amos 65
13 A Sign 72
14 More to Love! 74
15 Lightning Strikes Twice 85
16 Polecat Poultice 92
17 Hilda's Christmas Surprise! 96
18 Building a Sears House 102
19 Puppy Love 107
20 Karen's Discontent 111
21 Fire! 116
22 Lola's Lament 124
23 Mothers Know 131
24 Child Bride 135
25 Blessings of Family 141
26 A Knock at the Back Door 147
27 Dotty's Big News 151
28 Dotty's Sorrow 155
29 Stranger in Town 158
30 Sixth Sense 164
31 Close Encounters 169
32 Taking Advantage 177

33 Lost Innocence 182
34 Looking for Trouble 186
35 Decisions... 193
36 Mountain Justice? 204
37 The Prodigal Hobo.. 208
38 A New Job Opportunity 212
39 Working on the Claytor Dam.. 215
40 A Lost Community, Mahanaim 220
41 Floodgates... 223

Reunion

The sun blazed warmly in the late April sky of 1921. The weather was chilly as the gentle spring season pushed away the remnants of a harsh winter. The mountain air was fresh and softly scented by the wildflowers and blooming trees. A late morning shower made everything outdoors glisten. The wet earth gave off a woodsy aroma.

The slow-moving locomotive called the Huckleberry lumbered into the bustling town of Blacksburg Virginia. Fletcher Broce, along with his much-awaited family, stepped off the train at the railroad station. First came his wife, Rachel, carrying the squirmy Dotty, who was nearly a year old, followed by her energetic older brothers, six-years old Joseph and Arwood, who was four. Next came Fletcher's brother and sister-in-law, Peter and Karen. She held their sleeping infant, Andrew, in her arms. Most of them were catching their first glimpse of their new hometown. On the trip from Roanoke, Rachel marveled at and remarked to her husband about the soft Southern accents of the fellow passengers. It was so different from the New York dialect and rapid speech pattern her ears had become accustomed to this past year. Somehow, these voices seemed easier to understand, perhaps because of the more even cadence.

Rachel's eyes searched for Mama and Papa in the waiting crowd. She quickly located them. *What dears they are,* she thought. John and Hilda seemed so much more relaxed and yes, happier than when she had last seen them on the passage over from Germany to New York.

Joseph and Arwood both quickly caught sight of their grandparents too. "Hey, Mama, Papa, here we are!" Arwood shouted. He and his brother ran to give them a hug.

Rachel thought, *I wonder if they realize that now they will have to share Mama and Papa with two new babies.* She knew the grandparents' hearts would always have a special place for their first grandchildren.

John and Hilda hugged the little fellows. Mama planted a big kiss on each boy's rosy cheek.

"Oh, Mama, I'm getting too big for kisses now!" Joseph said as he rubbed his face vigorously to brush away the offending smooch.

Hilda laughed and said, "Don't do that, Joseph. You'll just rub it in. You can't rub off Mama's kisses because they go straight to your heart!"

Joseph made a resigned face. Four-year-old Arwood watched his big brother. He was wondering if he also would get too big for Mama's kisses. *I hope not. I like kisses*, he decided.

Peter and Karen stood back expectantly. They were excited to show off their little man to Mama and Papa. Taking the infant in her arms, Mama hugged and kissed Peter and Karen and told them how happy they all were to have their family together again. She lifted the soft blue baby blanket so they could see him and revealed a tiny red sleeping face. Papa beamed with almost as much pride as the young couple when he looked at their sweet new grandchild. His and Mama's eyes met as they welcomed the new child. They both felt love flowing into their hearts for this newest family member. They studied Andrew's features. He opened his eyes and blinked long dark lashes at the bright sunlight and cool air. He stretched his tiny body slightly and grunted as he shut his eyes once again.

"He looks like Peter did when he was a baby! I'm so happy for you both," Mama exclaimed. "I never thought this day would come."

Papa patted her on the back as her eyes filled with tears and brimmed over. She hugged Karen and Peter tightly. Mama reluctantly handed Andrew back to his mother and dabbed at her eyes to blot the tears.

"I've prayed and prayed that the Lord would be merciful and give you a healthy child to love. How was your labor, Karen?" Mama asked.

Karen lowered her eyes and felt them burn with unshed tears. She didn't like the deception and felt uneasy answering the question. Rachel felt her own breath catch. Peter quickly came to Karen's rescue. "Mama, she was a trooper. This little guy didn't waste any time making his appearance. You know how badly we've always wanted a child. Our son, Andrew, was worth the wait."

Karen shot her husband a grateful glance. Hilda thought there was something odd about the eye contact they exchanged. Karen had never before been shy around her mother-in-law.

Hilda recalled that time in New York when she had walked over to the window at the boardinghouse to get a little fresh air. Their sons and their wives were sitting on the porch talking quietly. She could hear their voices, but couldn't hear what they were saying.

Not that she had been trying to eavesdrop, she was just curious about what they could find to talk so long about, she told herself. Peter and Karen had acted strange when they came into the room and saw her standing there, almost like a cat that had swallowed a canary. If she had to name their expression, *guilty* would be a good description, but that didn't make any sense, so she'd quickly dismissed it.

She glanced at her other daughter-in-law and son. Fletcher and Rachel were sitting close together. Fletcher had his arm around his wife as they played with their little girl. *They look like teenagers in love*, Hilda thought. She studied Rachel's face. The girl looked happy, if not a little frail. *After the ordeal she had gone through on the ship last year and then having to stay away from her family to help Karen, what can I expect?*

The menfolk gathered the bags and got everyone loaded into the wagon. Mama had brought along a couple of quilts for Karen to sit on so the long ride wouldn't jostle her and the new grandson too much. Karen winked at Rachel as she lowered herself onto the cushy seat. The two sisters of the heart shared a secretive smile. Karen offered to spread the quilts out for her and Rachel to share. Hilda didn't think that would be wise. She knew she was probably being overly protective of the new mother. They had waited a long time for this baby, and now that he was here, she didn't want Karen taking any chances with her health. Who knew, she and Peter might be able to have another child someday if she was careful.

Mama exclaimed over baby Dotty, "I declare, Rachel, she is a real beauty. She certainly has the Broce family's pretty blue eyes. Dotty reminds me of Arwood when he was a baby except that she is so dainty and ladylike. I can't get over how she has grown since I saw her last. How very nice to have a little granddaughter here to spoil!"

Mama held out her arms and beckoned Dotty to her. She winningly toddled over to her grandmother. She planted a big sloppy kiss on Mama's cheek and tightly hugged her soft wrinkled neck. She unceremoniously plopped herself down in Mama's lap. The active little girl decided it would be great sport to try to remove Mama's spectacles. Fletcher seized the moment to give his wife another soft kiss. They had missed each other's company.

Fletcher's father, John, glanced over his shoulder at his rapidly expanding family. He caught Hilda's eye. His old girl was happy now. All she ever wanted was to have her family close by.

They were a source of great joy to them both. It seemed like no time at all before they reached the home place. The house was down a short winding drive. Part of what attracted Papa and Fletcher to the property was the privacy. They couldn't see other neighbors' houses from theirs, but knew they were fairly close by if they needed them.

The young ladies, Rachel and Karen, loved their new home at first sight. The charming old country farmhouse was well maintained. It appeared to have been whitewashed. Rachel wondered if that was Fletcher's and Papa's doing. It looked like something straight out of a storybook with its bright red metal roof. It was strategically situated among huge pin oak trees that appeared to be at least fifty years old.

Once inside, Mama enjoyed her role as tour guide and showed her girls around. They couldn't help but admire the gleaming hardwood floors, the good-sized bedrooms with spacious closets, the soaring ceilings, and the large kitchen. Rachel adored the sprawling front porch.

"It's perfect for all of us, Mama!" Rachel said. "I can't wait to get settled in, and hopefully, Karen and I will be a big help to you and Papa."

Rachel wondered where the men had disappeared to. She looked out the window, and there they were, outside, of course. They were all admiring the huge vegetable garden Fletcher and his dad had planted earlier that spring. It looked full of promise. She and Karen went out to the front porch for a better look. They sat there for a while, resting and watching father and sons catching up with one another. They were going to enjoy relaxing on this lovely porch with the swing and sweet sky-blue ceiling. Suddenly, as if Fletcher was aware of her eyes watching him, he turned and waved at his love.

The screen door slamming startled them. Mama came bursting on the scene with a big platter of salt-cured Virginia ham sandwiches slathered with mustard. She placed them on the picnic table that sat under one of the big weathered oak trees. John had made the table and benches with his own hands.

Joseph came out right behind Mama with a pitcher of lemonade sloshing precariously close to the spout. Rachel ran to his side to rescue the full container before disaster struck.

"I can do this Mommy," he protested.

She watched her big boy continue to the table. Next in the parade was Arwood with a brimming bowl of brownies. Rachel noticed telltale crumbs on his lips and a suspicious bulge in his left cheek.

She had to smile. She tousled his hair as he scooted by, not meeting her eyes. Apparently, Mama had been training her young guys to be more helpful around the house. Karen and Rachel offered to help, but Mama assured them she and the children had everything under control.

The men joined them for the hastily prepared but tasty dinner. They all laughed and conversed as they enjoyed the food. Baby Andrew was sleeping in the wooden cradle a friend of Fletcher's had made for him. Rachel remembered Fletcher talking about his friend Clyde's accident in the mines and the loss of his leg. They had agreed to have him make the cradle as a surprise for Peter and Karen. Peter had proudly carried it outside. He admired the nice cherry finish and ornate headboard. Mama had made a perfectly sized thin blue pillow for Andrew to sleep on and a calico infant quilt to keep him warm. Of course, she had sewn one for baby Dotty too.

Fletcher studied each face seated around the table. His heart was bursting with affection for his family. He stood and pulled Rachel up by his side. She looked at him uncertainly, not knowing what to expect. He looked into his family's happy faces. "First of all, I want you all to know that I love every one of you. Yes, even you, Peter!" Everyone laughed. "I can't believe we are all together again, at long last. This feels like a dream come true. What an incredible blessing. I thank God for each one of you."

Turning to his mother and father, Fletcher said, "When I first came to the United States, my heart was broken thinking that I would never see either of you again. I was overjoyed when your letter arrived telling me that not only were you both joining me, but so were Peter and Karen. I couldn't wait to get Rachel and the children here with me. Then as fate would have it, my sweet wife, Rachel, stayed in New York to help with your first baby." He smiled at Peter and Karen. "We've all had to make sacrifices."

"I could never have managed without Mama and Papa here to help me with the boys while I slaved away in the mines. And I give God all the glory for giving us such good children. Joseph and Arwood, you have always been the delight of my life. I'm so proud of how well you behaved for your mommy when I was away. Then you were both so brave, coming to Virginia without your mommy. You've been such wonderful helpers for Mama and Papa."

Looking at Rachel and pulling her closer to him, he continued, "I have loved this woman from the first moment I saw her, even before we met or said the first word to each other. I don't know how that happened, but it did. She has been my anchor and my great encourager. I am incredibly proud of the woman and mother she has become. I couldn't ask for a better wife or friend." Bending over, he kissed her softly on the cheek. He noticed her watery eyes.

There was scarcely a dry eye at the table. Everyone clapped and cheered Fletcher's impromptu speech. The sudden noise woke up the sleeping baby, Andrew. He wailed, showing his displeasure at the rude awakening. They all laughed. Karen scooped him up and carried him inside. She thought the air may have gotten a little cool for the baby. She went into the kitchen. Hilda followed her inside to see if she could help. Karen asked her to hold him while she prepared his formula.

"Oh yes, I certainly will hold him," said Hilda. "It has been a while since I held such a little baby, but I think I remember how it's done." She winked. She admired her newest grandson and chuckled at the cute baby sounds and faces he made. His little mouth formed an *O*, and he was making sucking sounds. "Looks like someone's getting hungry," she told Karen.

Hilda watched Karen measuring out the ingredients for Andrew's formula. This was something new for her. She had always nursed her babies, as had Rachel. She couldn't help but wonder why Karen wasn't breast-feeding her baby. She asked her why she was giving him that formula concoction. Karen explained that she wasn't able to produce breast milk.

Hilda thought that was very odd, but then the girl always had so much trouble with her pregnancies. *Well, maybe next time will be easier*, she thought. Karen handed Mama the warm bottle of milk. Andrew greedily latched onto the nipple and began to suckle. She walked into the living room and sat in the rocker with him. This would be something new for Hilda to learn, but it pleased her that she would be able to help feed him if need be. She cradled his warm little body close to hers.

Rachel relished giving her children their baths and having snuggly time as she read their bedtime stories that first night back together. Dotty had insisted on being in bed with her brothers while Mommy read to them. The little boys were tired after their exciting day, which involved two train rides on the Huckleberry and most importantly, getting their Mommy back home with them. They quickly fell asleep, and there was Dotty, wide awake between her older brothers.

Rachel gently lifted her from the bed without waking the boys. Dotty smiled and placed her head on her mother's shoulder, nestling her pudgy cheek against her mom's neck. Rachel loved that. She took her to the nursery, changed her diaper, and nursed Dotty until the child drifted off to sleep. Rachel almost fell asleep too. It was nice being in a home again instead of that boardinghouse, but it had served its purpose. Dotty had always slept in the same room with her mom. Rachel wondered how she would do sleeping alone, but was certain she'd be able to hear her daughter if she woke up during the night. The good Lord attuned a mother's senses to her children, especially to their distress calls.

Earlier in the evening, Karen and Peter placed the cradle and baby Andrew in their room. They couldn't imagine having him out of their sight. Rachel smiled to herself. She remembered those days with her children. When he got a little older, they'd look forward to having him in another room. The light beneath their door was already out. It had been a long day for them all. Everyone was weary.

Rachel and Fletcher's room was at the back of the house near the nursery. When she got to her room, Fletcher surprised her with a new soft pink nightgown with matching robe that he had ordered from the Sears, Roebuck & Company catalog. Rachel had to smile. He was always romancing her, whether with a smile or a look and now with a pretty gown. She ran her fingers over the cool satiny fabric. She had never worn anything store-bought. She worried that he may have spent too much money on the items. When she glanced at him, he had an anxious, inquiring look on his face. She wouldn't dare ask him about the price. She hugged her husband and thanked him for her gift.

"Is it for me to wear tonight?" she asked him.

"Of course, Rachel. I thought you'd like something special to wear for our first night together again," Fletcher told his bride.

Rachel took the gown set and slipped downstairs to the bathroom to freshen up. The gown fit perfectly. Fletcher had ordered the smallest size they had without buying her something from the girl's section.

She quickly climbed the winding staircase, softly closed their bedroom door, and fell into her husband's embrace.It seemed like a lifetime had passed since they'd been together. Rachel ran her fingers longingly through his curly dark hair. She stared into the eyes of the sweet man she loved with all her heart. She wanted to have a normal life with him once again.Fletcher lovingly traced the shape of her face and gently kissed her lips, leaving her breathless.

He carefully removed the hairclips from her long wavy locks. He stood back and admired her. She was even more beautiful with her hair cascading down her back. He held her as tightly as he dared, and this time, she didn't pull away. She slept peacefully in her husband's strong arms. For the first time in a long time, she felt safe again.

Dining at the River

Rachel thoroughly enjoyed that first glorious weekend in Virginia with her young family. She felt so alive and happy. They had a lot of catching up to do, not counting all the missed hugs and kisses to make up for. Understandably, the boys demanded her attention. Nearly a year was entirely too long for the children to be away from their mother. She assured them that she was here to stay.

She sat quietly with her sons and played with their hair or rubbed their backs while Dotty explored her new surroundings. They told Mommy about the friends they had made since their arrival last year. They talked excitedly and both at once, constantly interrupting one another. It was impossible for Rachel to catch every word. She had to remind the boys that they would have plenty of time to tell her all about their adventures; she wasn't going anywhere. She knew it wouldn't be long before her novelty wore off, so she reveled in every minute of their attention.

When the boys went outside to play, she walked out to the garden and helped pull weeds. It was nice spending an hour working shoulder to shoulder alongside Fletcher. Their time together right now was precious. Sadly, she reminded herself that he would have to return to work in the mines the next day. Rachel wanted to stretch this time out as long as possible. She actually knew very little about his job. When she quizzed Fletcher about it, he didn't seem overly anxious to discuss work. He'd quipped that Monday would come around soon enough.

While they were working together in the garden, Rachel hatched a plan to surprise her husband. She'd put together a picnic basket so they could have dinner by the river when he got off from work the next day, just the two of them. He had spoken often of the beauty of the New River. Rachel was anxious to see it for herself. She could carry an old quilt to sit on. Almost as an afterthought, she decided to take along a change of clothes for Fletcher in case he felt like cleaning up before their meal. She'd get Papa to help her hitch up the horses tomorrow.

She pictured herself sitting in the wagon, out of sight until she saw Fletcher coming out of the mine. Later tonight, she'd talk to Peter and have him suggest that the brothers go fishing after work. That way, Fletcher wouldn't ride back on the wagon with the rest of the fellows like he usually did. It was a foolproof scheme. Rachel delighted in thinking how astonished Fletcher would be to see her instead of Peter picking him up tomorrow evening.

She drifted through the next day. It seemed to drag as she anticipated spending some quality time with her husband in such a beautiful setting. She and Karen helped Mama around the house. Rachel played with the children. She tried to put all three of them down for an afternoon nap. Joseph and Arwood protested that Mama didn't make them take naps anymore because they were big boys now.

Rachel fought back tears. Her boys had grown so much this last year without her there. It made her understand how important it was to establish new routines more befitting their ages. Maybe just to humor their mommy, they agreed to take a nap. She sat in the room with her two big boys and watched them sleep. Rachel realized with a start that Joseph would be starting school in the fall.

Baby Dotty seemed especially clingy to her mother today. It would take her a little time to get accustomed to everyone and to adjust to her new home. Her routine had certainly been turned upside down with all their travels and being around her extended family. Her big brothers thought she was wonderful. They constantly chased after her, and she squealed in delight. The little thing must've been exhausted because she had slept soundly both nights this weekend. She didn't seem to mind waking up in her own room. She was a good baby. Rachel and Fletcher loved hearing the baby chatter when Dotty awoke in the mornings.

Rachel removed a soft rose-colored dress from her closet. She had made it to wear on the train for their reunion. She had wanted to look pretty for her husband, but realizing how long the train trip would be, she decided to keep it in reserve for a special occasion. She studied the dress and smiled to herself. What better time to wear it than today when she and Fletcher had their romantic riverside picnic?

She left the house about a half hour before the mine whistle was due to sound. Pulling the wagon and horse over to the side of the road, Rachel found a choice vantage point to watch the men as they exited the mine. She judged that she was far enough away to be out of view. The shrill signal rang out like an alarm, startling Rachel. She knew it had to be a welcome sound to all the tired workers.

Rachel studied the faces of the men as they emerged from the dark hole. She couldn't figure out why there were so many black men working as miners. She would have to ask Fletcher about their nationality. She had yet to see a white face. What was taking Fletcher so long? She hoped some problem didn't delay him.

After a while, everyone seemed to have left except for a couple of men waiting near the end of the road, and then there was a lone black fellow standing there. Rachel decided to walk down and ask him if he could help her find her husband. The man was facing away from her. He was whistling and appeared to be whittling on a stick. She started, "Excuse me, I'm looking for my husband, Fletcher Broce. Could you— "

The man whirled around and flashed her a big friendly smile, his bright eyes dancing mischievously. "Rachel, it's me!"

She felt light-headed and feared she was going to faint. Fletcher ran over and reached out his hands to steady her. She bucked back. "Oh my God, don't you dare touch me with those dirty hands, Fletcher Broce! Let me catch my breath. I swear you scared the daylights out of me! I came over here to surprise you, and I'm the one surprised instead."

"Just look at me! I feel so foolish all dressed up," Rachel stammered. "I thought it would be fun for us to go down by the river for a picnic supper together. Oh, Fletcher, it's ruined. You look a sight!"

Fletcher didn't say a word. He stood there with that big good-natured grin on his face. He didn't miss the tears of embarrassment shining in his sweetheart's eyes. "Ah, Rachel, it *is* a surprise for me. Don't think I'm not grateful. I'm sorry. I know my appearance is shocking for you. I guess I've gotten so used to coal dust that I forget how I must look to someone who hasn't been around the mines."

Rachel looked uncertain. "Fletcher, I brought you a change of clothes. I thought yours might be dirty, but…" Rachel felt the laughter welling up inside her. "I had no idea you'd be such a mess!" She burst out laughing at him and herself.

Fletcher joined her and laughed at the funny situation. "Now, pretty lady, may I accompany you to this romantic supper you've planned? It's a warm day, and I can wash off in the river."

Fletcher offered her a hand up into the wagon, but Rachel shook her head and grinned at him. "No thank you," she replied. When they got down to the river, Fletcher quickly washed his face, hands, and arms and dried them on the towel Rachel had packed with his clothes. He went behind a bush and changed into the clean duds.

They savored their peaceful meal and watched the sunset together, just like old times. Despite the funny happenstance, Rachel was right. They had needed this getaway to reconnect the threads of their life again, Fletcher concluded.

After the simple meal, they talked of the events of the last year. Rachel voiced her anguish and nightmares about the trip from Germany. Rachel shed tears as she recounted the painful journey. She told Fletcher that she prayed constantly that the Lord would show her how to forgive that wretched man who had raped her. Fletcher's eyes darkened, and she saw him visibly tense up.

"Rachel, I cannot even begin to forgive that horrible excuse for a man for what he did to you!" He held her close and felt her tremble. She knew only time and his sweet love could heal that terrible wound. Fletcher vowed to her that he would keep her safe. He commented that he was relieved that she seemed so much stronger than the last time he had seen her.

"Fletcher, I think things are back to normal between Mama and me. I don't sense that she is treating me any differently now. That is a relief. Have you talked with them anymore about what happened on the ship?" She stared up at him imploringly.

"No, Rachel. We don't ever bring it up. I think they both feel guilty that something that horrific happened on their watch. I think its best that we leave it be, don't you?"

Her eyes met his, and she simply nodded her agreement. She wanted that night to be put behind them—forever.

They talked about her and Dotty living in New York with Peter and Karen. She discussed her labor with the baby and how easy it had been this last time. They agreed that Peter and Karen were the ideal parents for baby Andrew.

Fletcher caught her up on the boys. They were learning more about farm life. He talked of his dad's plans for the land. Many of those plans required cash to complete, so for the time being, he would need to keep working in the mines. They daydreamed about building their own home someday. They knew they wouldn't be able to afford anything as grand as his parents' house, but that didn't matter to them. They had each other and their precious children. That was enough.

They were sitting on the soft homemade quilt and leaning back against a big stone. Fletcher had his strong arm around her and cuddled her close to him. They listened to the river rushing over the rocks. Here, the water was almost shallow enough to wade across.

"Rachel, I know it'll be an adjustment for you getting used to us all living under one roof. I want you to think of it also as an enormous blessing. I'm glad we can be together as a family so much sooner than I ever imagined possible," Fletcher told his bride.

Rachel marveled at how the Lord had brought them through so much.

He leaned over and kissed her as the last little patch of daylight waned. Rachel melted in his arms. It had been a delicious little slice of heaven for them despite its hilarious and awkward start. They packed up their things and headed home to continue their life together.

3

Rachel's New Friend

The mining families were keyed up about the upcoming spring picnic. This was the first year for the community social event. They looked forward to a day of good food, fun, and relaxation. Each family was asked to bring a stuffed picnic basket. The basket was to contain enough food, including dessert, for their family. If everyone cooperated, then when they spread it all out to share with each other, there would be plenty to go around.

The date was set for Saturday, May 28, 1921. The men picked the location. To absolutely no one's surprise, they selected a big field near the river. The women planned to have games for the kids such as sack races, jump rope, leapfrog, and hide-and-seek. Of course, the men needed to enjoy themselves too. For the bigger boys and men of all ages, there would be horseshoes, footraces, baseball, and more likely than not, a little fishing. They left it up to the women to come up with prize ideas for the victors. The judges would be a handful of chosen men. If the weather cooperated and was warm, the kids could also splash and play in the water.

The women had no need for additional physical entertainment. They were content to visit with each other and meet any newcomers. They planned to carry along their sewing to work on and demonstrate for their neighbors. Between minding the younger children, preparing, and serving the food, their day would be full. The big but unspoken competition for the women was the delicious dishes they brought to the table. They would be unofficially sized up by their peers on everything from food taste to presentation. No prize, just bragging rights.

Obviously, the women and daughters would have to have a new dress, hat, or at a minimum, a flouncy new apron. No need to fuss too much with the men and boys, simply get them out the door wearing clean shirts and pants that didn't need any mending.

A well-known fact, though seldom articulated, was that *women dress for other women more so than for the men.*

Many different nationalities were represented by the miners. The women looked forward to sharing recipes and learning about new dishes to try on their families. It wasn't uncommon for the men and boys to seek out their own family's cooked food at church gatherings. This probably wouldn't be any different. The women would busy themselves by sharing home remedies for sickness, parenting tips, and occasionally, gossip, if it was juicy enough.

Rachel and Karen were looking forward to the big day. Even though it was a couple of weeks away, there was plenty of routine work to do around the farm until then, plus all the preparations for the picnic. It added an extra element of excitement to have something to look forward to. Their days, like everyone else's, were filled with childcare, gardening, and housework, especially laundry with their houseful of adults and children. Babies generated additional soiled garments, mostly in the form of bottom covers.

Karen went down to the kitchen the next morning to fix Andrew's formula. She was surprised to find Mama already up and bustling about. "Good morning," she told Hilda, giving her a little hug. "You certainly are awake early today. What time is it anyway, 5:30 or 6:00 a.m.?"

"It's 5:00. I can't sleep. All I can think about is the big job I have to do today. I'm going to need both of you girls to help me. We're going to make lye soap. Papa and I used to be able to make it ourselves. He stays so busy on this farm trying to get everything just the way he thinks it should be. I fret that he will wear himself out. I think he does too much," said Mama worriedly.

"He's always been a hard worker. I guess it's hard to slow down," Karen said. "I warn you, I don't have any idea how to make lye soap, but you know Rachel and I are always ready to help you if we can."

"It's high time you both learned how to make soap. I won't always be around to do it for you. Don't worry, there's nothing to it, but it's time-consuming," said Mama.

"I've got to go back upstairs to get Andrew. I know he's awake. I heard him in there making his sweet little baby noises. I'll give him his bottle while you tell me all about it," said Karen as she walked out of the kitchen.

When she returned with the infant, Hilda explained how to make the soap.

"Last night, I had Peter and Fletcher set up the big soap kettle we got at the general store. I miss mine, but we couldn't bring everything over on that boat.

Anyhow, they put together a wooden frame to suspend the kettle over the fire. Fletcher has already put the wood under the kettle, so all we have to do is light it up when we're ready."

"What goes in your lye soap?" Karen asked.

"Well, for months now, I've been adding whatever leftover scraps of fat or grease we had to the kettle with plenty of lye. You have to cook the fatback before you put it in there, or it would stink to high heaven," Hilda explained. "I keep the kettle out behind the house, so it's out of sight but can get plenty of sunshine. Papa covers it up at night or if it looks like rain. The pot is about half full now, so it's time we got busy with our soap making."

"Do we make it only once a year? I've always gotten my supply from you since Peter and I got married. I'm so ignorant about this," said Karen.

"You'll learn. I used to only make it in the fall, but I declare, Fletcher's clothes get so filthy in that coal mine, it has taken every bit of my reserve for his laundry. We'll probably end up making two batches a year now," Hilda told her daughter-in-law. "Here, let me take Andrew off your hands. I can tell he wants to talk to his mama this morning, don't you, big fellow?" Hilda put the baby on her shoulder and was rewarded with a noisy burp for the gentle back rub she gave him. She smiled warmly at Karen. "I'm so happy for you and Peter, Karen. Andrew's such a sweet, sweet baby. And he's very handsome too, just like his daddy. Here, I'd better give him back to you so I can get breakfast started."

Karen smiled at the doting grandmother. "How long will it take us to finish the soap, Mama?"

"We let it boil for a few hours and then stir it with a big wooden paddle. I can usually look at it and tell if it's ready. The proof of the pudding is when we put a little bit of the concoction in a cup and add about a spoonful of water. If it stays thick like molasses, it's good. If it still looks runny, we boil it a little more until the soap thickens and then try again. The tricky part is getting the grease and lye proportions right." Mama explained all this while mixing, shaping, and cutting her dough for that morning's biscuits.

Mama continued, "I guess all that cooking and the animal grease gives the lye soap its nice yellow color. We can't use it right away. We have to take it off the heat, cover it with a lid, and let it sit until the next day. It'll get even firmer. Next, we shape it and let it age a few months.

After that, we'll cut it into good-size bars and spread them out to dry. It's hot work, so that's why we normally made it in the fall when it's cooler. Well, as you can see, we're going to have our work cut out for us today."

"I like learning how to do things like that. Andrew is asleep. Let me put him down in his cradle, and I'll come back down and help you with breakfast," Karen said.

The next couple of days of making lye soap were rewarding, but tiresome. Both Karen and Rachel enjoyed acquiring the new skill. It seemed like they were particularly busy with the children and other household matters this week. Of course, there was the matter of planning a trip to town to buy fabric for their new dresses for the picnic. The men of the family were busy with makeshift tables that the womenfolk would cover with tablecloths. Each family would bring blankets for their family to sit on.

The Broce family menu was selected by the ladies. Karen was looking forward to baking her famous German chocolate cake with the delicious coconut topping. Rachel decided to make her German potato salad with the tangy sweet-and-sour sauce. Mama would carry a jar or two of her home-canned dill pickles as a side dish. She was cooking her salty pan-fried fish, fried cabbage with onions prepared with plenty of salt and pepper, and a cake of corn bread. The men thought the menu sounded delicious. John Broce suggested that maybe the women should do a trial run of their fixings over the weekend so the men could make sure everything was seasoned just right. He was promptly shooed from the kitchen.

On Friday, Rachel and the other ladies made a trip into town to plan their new dresses. It was an adventure for them and the children. They looked over the many bolts of fabric and made their selections. They met other mining families with the same thing in mind. The women laughed and talked of nothing but the upcoming picnic. Each described the dishes they were bringing. One of the ladies ventured that if the men sampled even half of the food being served, they would pop. Laughter rang out. The hardworking housewives were excited about having a day away from chores.

One lady, perhaps a little younger than Rachel, seemed magnetically drawn to her. They conversed over the material and helped each other select thread and buttons. Mostly, Rachel had grown up surrounded by family. She had never had a friend to share things with. It was nice carrying on an easy conversation with a lady friend.

Rachel learned that the girl had come to America with her sister's family and still lived with them. She wasn't married but told Rachel she had her eye on a certain handsome young fellow. They talked about her nephews, and Rachel told her about her children. Rachel invited the young lady to come to their house for dinner that night, if she could. She accepted the invitation right away.

The women bought the children a scoop of ice cream and began the journey home. Hilda and Karen talked animatedly about the people they had met. Normally, the ladies were confined to the friendships they made at church because of the rural area. Each of them looked forward to making new friends. Hilda didn't know who had come up with the idea of the picnic, but it certainly was a good one. Rachel told them that she had invited a young lady she met at the store to dinner tonight. Everyone agreed that was fine.

When Fletcher arrived home right before supper, he was surprised to see someone sitting on the front porch with Rachel. She looked slightly familiar, but he couldn't make out exactly who it was. She had her back to the road. He could hear faint traces of conversation and laughter ringing out. It was unusual for them to have company, especially on a weeknight. Oh well, he'd find out who was visiting soon enough. He was starved, and he could smell the wonderful aroma of supper wafting out the kitchen window.

As usual, Fletcher was covered in coal dust. He headed around to the back of the house to scrub off the day's labor in the little bath/laundry shed. His dad constructed the building because his mother was so particular about keeping her house clean. Coal dust settled on everything and was nearly impossible to clean. He used the homemade lye soap even though it stung a little. With his brisk scrubbing technique, he had to be careful not to get it in his eyes.

Either Rachel or his mom had put a change of clothes in there for him. He always felt like a new man after his bath. It was a nice transition from work to home. As instructed by the ladies of the house, he left his dirty clothes in a basket in the corner of the shed. He knew they always washed his mining garb separately from the rest of the family's clothes.

He didn't blame them. They were filthy.

A Matter of Trust

Going around the house to the front porch, he glanced up at the mystery guest. His heart nearly stopped. He couldn't believe his eyes. His mind raced. *What is she doing here?*

Noticing him approaching, the young lady sprang to her feet and gave him her most dazzling smile. Fletcher blurted out, "Anna Leigh, what the devil are you doing here?"

Rachel had an appalled look on her face. "Fletcher, how rude! Anna Leigh and I met in town today. She is our guest. I invited her to have dinner with us tonight."

As Fletcher reached the top step, Anna Leigh came over and took him by the arm. "Oh, honey, don't mind him.

Fletcher and I go way back, don't we, Fletch?"

Rachel looked shocked. Her eyes flashed. Had Fletcher been unfaithful with this young lady while she was apart from him? Her heart told her *no*, but her heart and mind began a tug-of-war about the situation. Her array of emotions and torment reflected on her face. Bright tears stung her eyes, but she tried her best to maintain her composure. She had always trusted him. How could this be? She felt sick at her stomach.

Fletcher rather roughly peeled Anna Leigh's hand from his arm as if he were loosening a viselike grip. He went to Rachel. His eyes searched hers and begged her to believe in him and see the sham for what it was. As Rachel struggled to size up the situation, Anna Leigh's musical laughter rang out like a shrill crow's caw in Fletcher's ears.

"Oh my, I hope I haven't let the cat out of the bag. I thought you would've told Rachel about our, uh…little friendship. She can surely understand how a grown man needs a little companionship? She's been gone a long time!" said the heartless young woman.

Fletcher was holding both of Rachel's hands. She jerked free and ran off the porch toward the back of the house. Fletcher heard her cry of despair. He turned ferociously toward Anna Leigh. He had never struck a woman in his life, but he wanted to kill this one. At that precise moment, Hilda and John came to the door to announce that supper was ready.

Hilda could feel the tension in the air. "Is everything all right out here?" she asked her son. She glanced from him to the smiling young lady Rachel had met at the store earlier that day. She hadn't paid much attention to Rachel's guest. Now she knew *who* they were dealing with.

Well, she has some nerve coming here and trying to stir up trouble between Fletcher and Rachel! Hilda had ignored the rumors about this girl pursuing Fletcher because she had never seen any direct evidence of it. Hilda was not one to gossip about unfounded suspicions.

Fletcher looked frozen in his tracks and furious. His mother spoke to him, trying to break his icy stare at Anna Leigh. "Fletcher, why don't you go check on Rachel? Your dad said he saw her running towards the woods in back of the house." Fletcher didn't budge. Hilda could feel him seething. He was about as mad as she had ever seen her youngest son.

Hilda turned her attention to Anna Leigh. "I'm not sure what's going on here, but I think it's best we cancel this little supper party. I guess it was your brother-in-law who dropped you off? Well, don't you worry, John will give you a ride home."

Anna Leigh turned to Fletcher with a smile as she daintily dismounted the steps and said flirtatiously, "See you around, Fletcher." She sashayed toward the wagon, fully aware that all eyes were on her, probably not in the way she expected however.

Fletcher started toward her. His dad caught his arm and steadied him with his eyes. "Son, you need to go after your wife. Don't leave her back there alone."

Hilda stood on the porch thinking, *Well, isn't this a fine state of affairs!* She knew this would all get sorted out, but what kind of person would put on that kind of show? It was entirely self-centered and hurtful. She knew one thing for sure. Fletcher and Rachel were innocent victims. *How unfortunate that their happiness should be marred by suspicions raised by that heartless girl!*

In the Broce household, the next week flew by for some, for others, it was the longest week of their life. In no time at all, the ladies were packing up their baskets and getting everyone and everything ready to go out the door to the picnic. The children were overjoyed and could hardly contain themselves.

Even Papa, who wasn't overly sociable, seemed to be looking forward to the festivities. His world was limited to the few folks he met when he took Hilda into town or at their church; he didn't get out much. Hilda loved to read and wanted to find more friends to exchange books with. Peter and Karen hoped to meet other young couples with children so they could socialize. Everyone seemed to have a reason for going. Only Fletcher and Rachel seemed unaffected by the excitement of the big day.

Relations between Rachel and Fletcher were still tense, with no sign of improvement. Their hearts ached, and emotions were raw, but for different reasons. Fletcher had backed himself into a corner where he didn't feel like he needed to defend himself. Rachel felt emptied of trust and more than a little naïve. She was conflicted and almost sick from the strain. Fletcher's silent treatment felt like sandpaper on a wound to her hurting heart. They were both functioning by rote, and nothing was right in their universe.

Soon, it was time to go. The children helped carry out the blankets and the feed sacks for the sack races. Peter and Papa had loaded the wagon and gotten the horses hitched up. They were a fine-looking pair of geldings. The horses were tame and healthy. Papa and Peter took the boys on horseback rides down to the river from time to time.

At the last minute, Mama had decided to take her brewed sweetened tea. She was getting it ready to go. Papa used to get so frustrated with her for keeping them waiting for one reason or another. Over time, he accepted that was just her way. She had placed the tea bags in the hot water to steep and was busy adding sugar to the jug of water. In about fifteen minutes, she'd be ready to leave.

Fletcher hadn't seen Rachel in the last half hour or so. He went looking for her and found her sitting on the back stoop. "Hey, Rachel, the wagon is packed, and everyone is ready to go," he reported.

She looked at him with the most sorrowful expression on her face. He would never be able to find the right words to describe the impact that look had on him.

Without even turning to look at him, Rachel said, "Fletcher, I can't- I just can't go and pretend that I'm having fun. Everyone has been looking forward to this day. I'd be a wet blanket, robbing them of their joy today. You go ahead.

Tell everyone that I'm not feeling well. That is the truth." Rachel sat forlornly staring off into space.

"If you're not going, then, neither am I.

Let me tell them to go on without us," Fletcher told her.

Rachel nodded numbly, already lost in her own dark thoughts again. She was too weary from the emotional toll of the last week to even muster a response.

When Fletcher went back through the house, he saw his mother still doing last-minute things in the kitchen. That was so typical of her. He told her that he and Rachel were staying at home. He asked if she minded keeping an eye on the boys. Fletcher said they would keep little Dotty with them.

Mama immediately crossed the kitchen to reach Fletcher. She hugged his neck hard for a very long moment. "That's fine, dear. Don't worry about your children. And I'm taking Dotty with us, no argument. I'll feed her Andrew's formula if she wants her milk. Today, I'm worried about *my child*—or should I say, *my children*, because I think of Rachel like one of my own too."

His mother told him, "I know you and Rachel are dealing with too many hurt feelings this week. I've been praying for the good Lord to intervene. Promise me, son, you two will pray about your situation. We don't always have all the answers, but we know Someone who does."

Fletcher *was* a praying man. He gave his mother a strange look. "You know, I have *not* prayed about Rachel and me and what we're going through right now. I've been so down in the dumps that I didn't even think about it."

He went over and hugged his mom around the shoulders. "Thanks, Mom, I'm going to ask for help from above."

His mother patted him on the arm and winked at him as she headed out the door. He knew she would cover for them with the rest of the family.

When Hilda reached the wagon, the children asked where Mommy and Daddy were. Hilda told them, "They have a few things to work on, so they're staying home, but we're all going to have fun, aren't we?"

The children cheered in agreement.

Peter and Karen held hands and silently hoped their best friends in the world would work things out and be happy once more. John patted Hilda on the knee to reassure her. His sweet girl could pretend with everyone else, but he knew when she was concerned.

When Fletcher went back around the house, he saw Rachel walking slowly through the garden with her head down and her back to him. She had on a soft-looking white hat, and her long wavy hair flowed down her back. She'd had her hair pinned up earlier.

He felt like he was looking at a fine oil painting. His heart felt like it would burst with love for her. For as long as he lived, this picture of Rachel would be indelibly imprinted in his mind.

Her petite figure looked so pretty in the newly made yellow cotton dress with small purple flowers on it. She had sewn tiny white buttons down the front and added a narrow white collar to the round neckline. How he wished he could turn back time and make all the pain disappear. He wasn't sure if it was best to leave her alone with her thoughts or go to her. Torn, he stood watching her for what seemed like an eternity but might have been a few minutes.

It was a lovely spring day and partly cloudy, but not in an ominous way. If he had to guess, he'd venture the sky looked more likely to be sunny than stormy today. Fletcher looked up at the heavens, tried to organize his thoughts. It alarmed him to realize he couldn't even voice his prayer. His heart throbbed in misery.

The strangest thing happened next. Instead of feeling frustrated or defeated, he suddenly felt blanketed by the most incredible, peaceful, warm sensation. It seemed to begin at the top of his head by stilling his mind, rendering it blank, and making his tongue incapable of speech. When it reached his heart, Fletcher very physically experienced his bruised spirit being lifted, healed. If his heart was beating, he couldn't feel it.

Never in his life had something like this happened to him. It was as if he had been in a trance. He had no idea how much time had transpired. *Had time been suspended?* While these thoughts played through his mind, they were not worrisome to him in any way. He knew it had to be the work of the Holy Spirit.

The dark cloud that was covering the sun at that moment seemed to magically evaporate. Rachel was illuminated in the garden. He could only describe her as a human ray of sunshine, reflecting light. Fletcher didn't walk. He ran to her as quickly as he could. He didn't call out her name, but she turned around at the same instance as if he had spoken to her. To the delight of his heart, she held out her arms to him, her face radiant, and began softly running in his direction. Had she experienced the same healing transformation he had?

They united at the edge of the garden. Fletcher and Rachel embraced and clung tightly to each other as if their life depended on it. They seemed to share one common heartbeat.

In complete weakness and submission, they'd found each other again. Their sweet, endearing love came flooding back like ocean waves, sweeping away all the misery.

He looked into her eyes and saw a thousand shimmering sunrises and the reflection of their shared sunsets. He picked her up right there in the garden, held her in his arms, and kissed her so profusely, it left them both breathless. It was as if they were trying to pour their hearts back into one another.

He slowly lowered her feet back to the rich black soil in the garden. Today, love had grown there. Rachel felt so lighthearted that she wondered if she might float away. She couldn't understand what had just happened between them. Incredibly, it was all gone—all the doubts, suspicions, distrust, and yes, the fear of loss. It was as if they had been purged of all the negative energy that had sapped them and made their world seem very small and very ugly. All that had been accomplished without a single word being spoken. Neither of them wanted to sully the experience by talking about it.

They walked hand in hand to the front porch. They settled on the swing and tucked pillows around them for comfort. Rachel pulled a soft lap blanket over them. The soft breeze blowing hinted of summer's approach. They heard the wind rustling in the trees, the birds singing, and the soft creaking of the metal chains on the swing, complaining. It was around midday. The extraordinary transfiguration had exhausted them. They fell asleep in each other's arms.

When they awoke about an hour later, they looked at each other to make sure what they had been through was real.

Fletcher said, "Rachel, I love you more today than I ever have in my life. I don't know how that is possible, but it is true. There will never be a time when I don't love or need you. My life wouldn't be worth living if you weren't a part of it. It would be like having my heart taken away from me. I couldn't survive!"

Rachel pulled his head toward her and smothered his face with kisses. She ran her fingers through his curly hair. Their arms interlaced around each other, they went inside. It was so quiet in the house with everyone out. It was as if the doors of paradise had been flung open for them. It was such a luxury to be alone, to have their faith in each other restored and their love rekindled.

Changing Times

Over the next twelve months, Rachel began to meet the many people who had helped Fletcher during that tough first year. She adored the Hendersons, especially Lola. Hilda and Lola had forged a friendship while they were living in the German tent community. Both women loved to cook and had big hearts when it came to their families or someone in need. Lola wasn't much on reading but loved to hear Hilda describe whatever book she was reading. Whenever she and her husband came by, her first question once the two ladies got the greetings out of the way was, "What are you reading now? Tell me about it."

That was usually the men's signal to get away and enjoy each other's company. They'd head out to the garden, down to the creek, or out to the shed if John was working on something in there—anything to keep them from getting trapped in one of those long, drawn-out, boring conversations between their wives. Even working seemed more appealing to the two fellows than getting stuck in the parlor with their ladies when they were catching each other up. Their quick departure usually went unnoticed by the ladies, who were happy to have them out of their hair for a while.

Hilda and Lola discussed what they'd fix for dinner and gathered the vegetables they'd need. Lola had brought over an apple streusel to share and her homemade apple butter to go on the biscuits they'd bake later. Tonight, they settled on green beans, corn on the cob, stewed tomatoes, and sliced cucumbers. Mr. Henderson always liked a thick slice of sweet onion to go on his biscuit. He'd even gotten John to try it. John agreed that it might not sound good, but it certainly was right tasty. The women would roll their eyes. How on earth could the men eat raw onions like that?

While the two women snapped green beans and shucked corn, Hilda regaled her friend with the grand adventures or conflicts arising in the current book on her nightstand.

To hear them talk, you'd think they were discussing someone who lived down the road. Sometimes, John would overhear a snatch of their conversation and say, "That's awful.

Who was that again?" This would set the two women off in a fit of laughter and leave poor John scratching his head.

The Hendersons' son, Peter—Pete, for short—was courting a young lady who lived in town, Lola told her friend. She and Mr. Henderson had met her a time or two.

She was just a slip of a girl with golden hair and a shy way about her, but Pete seemed to like her. That was the important part.

"He works such long hours in the mine, I don't know how he even has time for romance, but love finds a way. Who knows, if all this courting keeps up, we might be hearing wedding bells before long," laughed Lola.

"Well, that would be nice. You need some grandchildren. I'm already four up on you." Hilda smiled as she teased her friend.

"Now don't go rushing things. She's the only girl he has ever paid much attention to. She eats like a bird too. I don't know if she doesn't like my cooking or is just trying to watch her figure," said Lola.

"Fletcher wasn't interested in any girl either until he met Rachel. Then there was no one else for him. He about drove us crazy going over to her house all the time. We just knew her parents were going to complain about it. I know for a fact that you're a good cook, so it must be her figure she's watching," said Hilda. "Sometimes girls don't care to eat much in front of their men friends."

"Her father works over at the college, tending the grounds, and her mother works too. Isn't that odd for her mother to be working outside the home? I don't know how a woman can keep a house and family going and not be at home. She said her mother helps out at that fancy little dress shop in town. She does alterations to the clothes for their clientele, very fancy-smantzy," said Lola with a flourish of her hands.

"I guess with them living in town, they don't have all the gardening chores that you and I do, Lola, so unless they have family in the area with a garden, it means they have to buy most of their food. I know it was very expensive for us when John and I first got here until we got a garden established," said Hilda.

"But speaking of dress shops and dresses, Hilda, have you noticed that the younger ladies at church are starting to wear their skirts shorter?" Lola said. "And when Pete's lady friend came to dinner last Sunday, her skirt was a good six to eight inches above her ankle!"

"I know, Lola. The times are changing, and you and I are going to have to change right along with them, but between you and me, I think the shorter skirts are a disgrace!" offered Hilda. "My daughters-in-law have been talking about the new fashions, so I'm sure their skirts will also get hiked up before long."

Lola chimed in, "You know with us living down here near the river that it's only a matter of time before the girls are going to want to wear those bathing suits they've come out with."

Hilda clucked her tongue and shook her head. "I declare, I blame it all on that Sears and Roebuck catalog. It is ruling—or should I say, ruining—our lives right now. The ideas it puts in folks' heads. I saw Rachel and Karen looking at the pantsuits for ladies. Imagine, going out in public or to church wearing something like that," Hilda said.

The ladies both shook their heads in disbelief and continued with their chore.

"No, I can't," said Lola. "Women need to dress like women and leave the pants to the men! I tell you, the best place for that catalog is in the outhouse." "I agree," said Hilda.

In their five or six years of living in Blacksburg, Virginia, the ladies had seen many changes. Neither of them had electricity at their houses. They'd heard that folks up on the main road, Prices Fork, who lived closer to town, were getting power. It was something to look forward to and something to fear at the same time. There'd be the expense, and they weren't sure how safe that electricity was. They'd leave that to the men to figure out.

The ladies moved on and discussed indoor plumbing, what little they had heard or seen of it anyway. Certain people and businesses in town had indoor plumbing. Lola and Hilda still had a well-worn path back to the johnny house.

Lola said, "I wonder why they call the toilet a johnny house? He must've been a really bad boy to get saddled with that. I wouldn't have the toilet inside my house. Now that's plain nasty having something like that in the house where you cook!"

Hilda said, "I guess you're right. I hadn't thought of it like that. But it certainly sounds like a convenience. I get tired of carrying the pot out every day. Joseph offered to do it for me one morning. Of course, he was in a hurry to get the job over with and ran it out there. He fell and flung the pot's contents hither and yon! I had to go out to the shed and get the lime to spread over it. I went ahead and threw lime in the hole while I was at it."

Lola laughed at her friend's chagrin. "They've got to learn sometime."

They discussed how more of their neighbors were getting motorized vehicles.

Lola said, "I saw one in the Sears and Roebuck catalog for nearly four hundred dollars, and it only carried two people. Just think how many cows, pigs, and chickens you could buy with that amount of money."

Hilda looked up. "It's foolishness, but it would be convenient. We'd need a larger one for our big family. Then there is the extra expense for the petrol to make it run. What if the fool thing broke down? Who would know how to fix it? Where would you get the parts you needed?"

They heard the big rumbling laughter of the returning men. There before them stood their husbands with their arms folded over their chests, laughing at their wives' conversation topic. The ladies had no idea how long the men had been standing there listening.

John said, "We leave you girls here on the porch getting vegetables ready to cook for our dinner and come back thirty minutes later and find you talking about horseless carriages!"

Mr. Henderson eagerly jumped into the conversation. "Now, honeypot, I'm pretty keen on one of those I saw in the catalog. Boy, it would be something to go squiring around in one of those contraptions." John nodded his agreement.

Hilda said, "Now, John Broce, don't you go getting any foolish ideas in your head! We can't even afford to build another house for our kids yet, and there are plenty of things we need here at the farm."

In his most soothing voice, John responded, "I know, dear, but if I've read the catalog correctly, we don't have to pay for it right away. They would deliver it and set up convenient monthly payments for us."

Mr. Henderson came to his buddy's defense. "Well, you two are probably like Lola and me. We've never been in debt in our lives, but this finance plan certainly makes it affordable to get the things you need today. Why, after we got the car paid off, you could get one of those fancy cookstoves or a new set of china the same way, Lola. What is wrong with that?"

Looking like young children on Christmas morning, the men peered expectantly at their brides. The women looked like they were about to explode.

"I certainly can't speak for the Henderson family, but we are not going in debt for one of those fool contraptions or anything else.

You never know what time will bring our way. We might not always have our health and the ability to make a living. Then what would happen?"

The men looked at each other. They thought they had come up on a honeycomb when they overheard the ladies talking about motorized vehicles, but instead it looks like they'd stepped into a thick nest of yellow jackets. For their own protection, the humble fellows decided it was best to move on.

"Well, Lola, we'd better get inside and get supper started before this crew gets back to the house. Is Pete coming over too?"

"Oh no, don't expect him. He'll be out courting this evening. He said something about taking his girl to the Lyric Theater to see a movie. You know, we should get those fellows of ours to take us there sometime. We could have dinner in town and then go to the show. Now wouldn't that be something?" she daydreamed aloud.

6

Clyde's Dilemma

Fletcher had taken Rachel by to meet Clyde at his little two-room abode. He lived on one side and operated his furniture business out of the other, larger room. He managed well in his wheelchair. He was developing a good reputation for the quality of his furniture. He had back orders and had recently hired a young man to help him with the extra work. The industrious hire was best at the measuring and cutting and preferred to leave the intricate detail work to Clyde. They made quite the team.

"Clyde, I've been meaning to get by here and introduce my wife, Rachel."

The two men shook hands and exchanged pleasantries. Rachel told him how much Peter and Karen loved the little cradle he had made for them. Clyde positively radiated with pride. Fletcher studied his old friend and was pleased with the progress Clyde had made, both with his business and his state of mind.

Their boys were getting bigger, and Rachel wanted to have twin beds made for them rather than have them sharing the full bed. They also hoped to get a small bookstand for their room if they could afford it. Fletcher and Clyde discussed measurements, and he promised to work up a design and price for them to consider. They would keep the full bed for Dotty when she was a little older.

Rachel walked outside and left the men inside talking. Fletcher asked Clyde how much longer it would be until his wife and children came here to be with him. Clyde's countenance seemed to darken slightly.

"Fletcher, I have had the money for their passage saved up for months now. My wife and I have written back and forth many times, but she hasn't committed to a date. I could be completely wrong about this"—Clyde's shoulders slumped—"but I don't think she wants to come."

Fletcher was taken aback. "Clyde, maybe you've misread her letters. Women can be so confusing sometimes. If you'd like, I can ask Rachel to read them and see what she thinks.

You know, it's possible that you are being overly sensitive because of your... uh"—Fletcher stumbled over his words— "your situation."

"It's all right. You can say my leg, Fletcher. I've come to terms with my limitations and my capabilities. It hasn't been easy, and there are days when that ghost foot itches. I'm not crazy, but I can't do a thing about it!"

"What? It itches? How is that possible? You're having some fun with me, aren't you, Clyde?"

"I am not, and that's not all. Sometimes it feels like it goes numb. I don't have much pain, or maybe I've gotten used to it."

"Well, anyway, Clyde, I'm serious about having Rachel look at your letters and give you a woman's take on it. Are you interested in that?"

"I don't see how it could hurt. Make her promise that if I get Clarisse to come over here, Rachel won't tell her about me letting her see the letters."

"I'm sure that won't be a problem. That girl can keep a secret. We'd better be getting on back home. Let me know when you get an estimate for us on that furniture."

Clyde said, "Hold up, Fletcher. Let me retrieve the handful of letters I've gotten since the accident. Please promise me she won't be leaving them lying around for anyone else to see." Clyde grabbed his crutches and went into his bedroom to get the letters.

Fletcher could see the trust in Clyde's eyes and the sense the hesitancy as the man handed them over. He studied the little stack of mail. The envelopes were worn from the enclosed letters being removed and replaced. Clyde must've read them countless times.

Rachel was waiting in the wagon. She was surprised when Fletcher handed her Clyde's letters. When he explained the situation, it made her sad for Clyde. He had been through so much with the grief over the loss of his leg and the inability to return to the mines with his friends and coworkers. Despite a difficult situation, he had managed to switch gears and seemed to be adjusting well.

Obviously, the heart and soul of his work was to continue to be the provider for his family. Was he right? Was his wife having second thoughts about joining him? What about their children? Didn't they deserve to grow up with their father's guidance?

"Fletcher, what makes you think I will be able to read between the lines and ferret out his wife's true intent? Clyde knows her better than we do. I think if he is getting that gut reaction, there may be something to it. You know, women aren't the only ones with intuition."

"I know, Rachel, but you have to remember Clyde's predicament with his leg. I think that colors how he sees things. He may not be thinking clearly if his fear is getting in the way. I would like to hear your opinion after you read the letters. I told Clyde he didn't have to worry about this going any further than you and me."

"Of course, I'll keep everything confidential. Oh, Fletcher, I hope he is wrong. What a blow that would be for him. He has overcome so much and has his heart set on a future with his family, as it should be. It will feel strange reading their intimate correspondence. Are you sure he has agreed to this?" Fletcher nodded.

That night, Rachel began to read the six or seven letters that spanned three years. The first thing she noticed was that there were more letters before Clyde's accident. Those letters were full of love, hope, and plans. The letters after the accident were fewer in number, more distant in tone, and generally less intimate. They seemed more like letters from an aunt or cousin than from a wife. Rachel certainly had no training in psychology, but she could read the letter with a woman's heart.

Fletcher had turned in early, but the letters troubled Rachel, and she couldn't sleep once she got to bed. What if she misinterpreted Clyde's wife's messages? She certainly wouldn't want him to make any life-changing decisions based on her comments. This was certainly tricky business Fletcher had pulled her into! Rachel decided she was probably overthinking the situation. She went to bed. Tomorrow would be another busy day in the Broce household, and she needed her rest.

When Rachel awoke the next morning, she smiled to herself. Her mind must've worked on the problem while she slept. She thought she had a solution to Clyde's worries. She could picture his wife feeling like she was caught between the devil and deep blue sea, with the devil being her fears about Clyde's physical prowess and his ability to support his family. The deep blue sea might represent the sheer distance between them.

It might seem foolish to her husband and Clyde, but Rachel thought she had a plan that might work. It had been heartbreaking to be separated those long months from Fletcher that last time when she was in New York and he and her boys were in Virginia. One thing that had been a source of endless comfort to her was the family pictures they'd had taken right before everyone parted. Looking at those pictures made her family seem less remote.

She saw Clyde as a hardworking man making the best of a tough situation. What if he erected a sign for his business and displayed his finely finished furniture, dressed himself up a bit, put on a radiant smile, and had his picture taken? His wife would be able to see him in the light of his present reality, a hardworking and successful man who had overcome obstacles and a very human man who was missing his wife and family.

Of course, she remembered how defeated Fletcher had said Clyde felt right after the accident. She could imagine that his attitude must've flowed over into his correspondence with his beloved. That would be natural because a couple shared their feelings and challenges with each other. If so, that may have scared his wife to death.

Her mind raced with other details, such as having Clyde work on being more positive in his letters to his wife, reminding her how much he loved and missed her and the children. Perhaps he could even begin to paint a picture for his wife about what her life here with him would be like. His Clarisse would want to know where they would live, who would help with the garden, where would the children go to school, etc. It was important to help her picture herself and family living here in America with her husband, who loved them all very much.

She couldn't wait for Fletcher to get home from work so she could discuss her ideas with him. They had agreed that they wouldn't talk with anyone else about Clyde's fears. Rachel would've loved to talk with Karen about the situation and get her take, but she wouldn't want to do anything that compromised their agreement. Clyde needed to know that he had a good friend like Fletcher, whom he could trust with his secret fears.

After supper, she and Fletcher sat on the big front porch and discussed her ideas. He respected how perceptive his wife was. He thought she had come up with the perfect plan to help his friend. Rachel even agreed to help Clyde draft the all-important letter to his wife that would accompany the photo. She could picture in her mind his wife's heart starting to melt when she looked into the eyes of the man she loved. She hoped Clarisse would share their pride in her husband's accomplishments. It wouldn't hurt to have Clyde boast—modestly, of course—about the number of orders he'd filled and the many new demands that he had pouring in.

Fletcher looked forward to sharing their plan with his friend. He was so proud of Rachel for putting so much thought and compassion into the project.

Fletcher thought it might be just the thing to get the reluctant Clarisse packing and beginning her journey to America to be with her husband. They would go see Clyde again the next day and see what he thought of their ideas.

On Friday evening, after supper, he and Rachel rode over to Clyde's and told him what they had come up with.

Many emotions seemed to play across Clyde's face as they discussed the plan. Finally, he smiled at them. "I can't tell you how much I appreciate you both helping me with this thing between Clarisse and me. Fletcher, it seems you always have to rescue me."

Fletcher laughed softly and said, "Hey, man, we were just hoping for a discount on that furniture we've ordered for the boy's room."

"I tell you what," Clyde said, "I'm making that furniture for you and not charging you a dime. How's that for a discount?"

"You know I was messing with you, Clyde. Rachel and I are going to pay for the things we need," said Fletcher.

"I won't take your money. I think your scheme may work. Will you help me find a photographer and buy a new suit? I wouldn't know where to start. I'm excited about a little good news I can share with Clarisse. A hotel in Christiansburg has commissioned me to make the bedroom furniture for all their rooms. It's a big job. They are giving me an advance. I'm going to need to hire at least one more, if not two more men to help me complete the order on time!"

"That's great, Clyde," Rachel told him. "I hope you have your wife and children here in no time. I know they are going to be so proud of their daddy!"

She and Fletcher rode home holding hands. It felt good to be able to help a friend when you got the chance. They left him with a big smile lighting up his face.

7

Clyde's Family

When Fletcher got home from work in the late summer of 1922, Rachel stood watching for him from the front porch. She ran out to meet him. Her excitement was too great to wait for him to reach her. "Fletcher, you're not going to believe this! When we went into town for supplies this morning, Clyde waved us over at his place. He was practically jumping up and down." She grinned from ear to ear.

"Rachel, slow down. Tell me what's going on," said Fletcher.

"The photograph and his upbeat letter worked! Clyde looked so dapper in his new suit and hat he got from the men's store in town. Really, how *could* his wife resist? The new wooden lettered sign he made and painted looks very sharp.

Clarisse and the children are coming! They'll be boarding the ship and expect to arrive in September. Her mother is coming with her," Rachel breathlessly informed him.

"Hey, that's great news, Rachel. I think that and all the many prayers might've had something to do with it. Clyde's probably about to burst from happiness," said Fletcher.

"By the way, you won't believe who his new apprentice is—that young fellow, Johnny Tilley, from the general store. Clyde says he is very smart and well-mannered too," said Rachel.

"Is that right? Johnny always has impressed me as an industrious young man. They should make a good team," said Fletcher.

"Oh, Fletcher, I can't wait to meet Clyde's family," said Rachel.

"I guess he will need to look for a bigger home for his family now. How old are the children?" asked Fletcher.

"His daughter is seven, and his son is four, close to our children's ages. But here's the best part, he doesn't have to find a home.

His current location has been good for business, so he is going to convert that structure into his home and add on more rooms. He will build a large work shed behind the house that is twice as big as what he has now."

"We can all pitch in and help him build it. We can work on weekends," said Fletcher. With the big hotel order, that will probably be the only time he can work on his house. Hopefully, we can finish the work before they get here, or at least before winter. I'll have to stop by and talk with him about it."

"Did he say how he plans to meet them once they arrive in America? We are so busy in the mines, it will be impossible for me to take any time off," said Fletcher.

"I've been thinking about that. Maybe Peter could accompany him and escort his family back. He could show them that nice boardinghouse where we stayed there in Manhattan. Why don't you talk with him about it, Fletcher? I'm worried about Clyde traveling alone for that great distance," said Rachel.

"If Peter is willing to go, it might be a good idea if Karen went too. Even though Clyde's wife knows about his condition, it might still be a shock seeing him. I think I met her once years ago, but don't feel like I know her very well," said Fletcher.

"We will have to stick close by them during the first little bit when they get here. You know, we can get them involved in the church. If she is crafty, we'll get her into the quilting club," said Rachel.

"Rachel, before you go planning their social calendar, please remember they haven't seen each other in nearly three years. I don't think they will need much interference from us well-meaning types." Fletcher laughed.

"Oh, Fletcher, you know what I mean." Rachel blushed.

"But seriously, those children were so young when he left for America. They are going to need to spend time getting to know each other as a family. Now, young lady, if you don't mind, I'd like to get some of this coal dust off of me and get ready for supper. I'm starved!"

As Fletcher walked back to the washhouse, he smiled to himself. He was glad he and Rachel were able to help his friend turn things around with his family. Other fellows had talked about reluctant families not wanting to come to America after the husband had come over. He and Rachel couldn't stand being apart from each other. He cherished that special bond they shared.

The young couples sat out on the porch after dinner. They discussed helping Clyde meet his family in New York and bring them to Virginia. Karen agreed that they should both go so that Clarisse, whom she had never met, would have a friendly woman to talk with if she needed to. They would take the toddling Andrew with them. They hoped to have the same photographer meet them at the boardinghouse and take a new picture of them with their son. That might be an interesting idea for Clyde and his family too.

Fletcher planned to talk with a few of the miners and see if they'd be willing to help with Clyde's house addition to accommodate his family. Depending on the number of volunteers, the weather, and the skill level of the help, they hoped to wrap up the job before Clyde's family arrived. They would need at least three bedrooms, a kitchen, and a sitting room. Peter's idea was to pop the roof off and add a half story for the kids' bedrooms. He'd seen a house plan like that in the Sears catalog. Hopefully, Clyde could supply the materials, and they could supply the labor. The house wouldn't be large, but it would suffice.

Karen suggested the ladies make curtains for the windows and help tidy up the place while they took Clyde to meet his family. Rachel thought that was a terrific idea. She was sure Hilda and Lola would want to help. They would talk with Clyde about the things he would need at the house, like pots and pans, dishes, glasses, etc. Rachel only remembered seeing a small potbellied stove with a kettle sitting on it, a coffeepot, one plate, one cup, a fork, a knife, and a spoon. If Clyde couldn't afford it, maybe he could get it on time from the Sears catalog.

Clyde was moved to tears at the overwhelming response from the miners to help with his house. It reminded him of a barn raising. Everyone worked together, laughed, and enjoyed themselves. Every man there knew that but for the grace of God, any one of them could find themselves in Clyde's predicament.

When the men finished, the wives came over to turn the place into a home, but only after giving it a thorough cleaning from top to bottom. Clyde had an account at the general store and authorized them to stock up on whatever supplies they thought his family would need.

Johnny and the other man working for him had built a serviceable shed so his furniture-making endeavor could continue and he could deliver by the deadline. They both appreciated the new energy and positive attitude Clyde exhibited as the time approached for him to go pick up his family.

It felt like they had been racing against the clock. When Clyde, Peter, Karen, and Andrew left the train terminal in downtown Blacksburg, almost everything was in place.

Clyde carried crutches and rode in his wheelchair. He was thankful that Peter had a strong back and could help him on and off the train. He wondered how his wife would react to his disability. While he managed well around his shop, there could be many new obstacles on the way to New York and back.

When they got to Pennsylvania, Clyde rented a horse and wagon to take them to lower Manhattan. They were able to get two rooms once more at the same boardinghouse. Karen and Andrew were exhausted. She begged to stay behind and let the men go down to the ferry dock to wait for the boat. Peter was concerned, but she assured him she was fine, just tired.

A crowd had gathered at the ferry landing. The large ships had been anchored offshore for nearly three hours. Clyde gave someone the name of the vessel Clarisse and the children were aboard. The ticket master confirmed that her ship was in port also. Peter patted him on the back.

"You know, man, it's a waiting game now. Let's find something to eat. All this traveling has made me hungry."

Clyde had been so nervous and excited about seeing his family, he hadn't eaten a thing all day. He suddenly realized how hungry he'd become. Maybe a sandwich or bowl of soup would take the edge off his anxiety. The men got their food and ate it right at the dock so Clyde could scan each face as the next ferry load of passengers arrived.

They noticed a couple of the large ships lifting anchor and departing. *Are Clarisse and the children at Ellis Island? Has she changed her mind at the last minute? Has something happened?* Clyde was beside himself with worry.

He noticed what looked like the last ferry chugging toward shore. This one was not as packed as the others had been. He still couldn't see Clarisse. He noticed a young dark-haired girl waving enthusiastically and casually waved back. She appeared to turn around and speak to someone behind her. Then Clyde saw her. With the sunset at her back, there was his Clarisse. She was holding their younger son on her hip, and his head rested on her shoulder like he was asleep. She shifted the child's weight and managed a wave. She flashed a lovely smile his way. Her tiny mother, Agnes, had a big smile on her face too. She waved at her only son-in-law. All four foot eleven of her was happy to be in America!

Clyde didn't notice that tears were streaming down his face. His family was here! Peter hugged the fellow around the shoulders. "There they are, young man!" he told Clyde.

Surely, it was Clyde's imagination, but the ferry seemed to be in slow motion. Each wave brought his family a bit closer. At last they were disembarking. Clarisse sat the young boy down and instructed his sister to hang on to his hand. Agnes put her arm around the children to give the young couple a moment.

Clarisse ran to Clyde. He speedily maneuvered his wheelchair forward. She covered his face with kisses and hugged him tightly around the neck. The children reached them but stood back a bit shyly, smiling at their mom and dad. Clyde opened his arms to them. Clarisse nodded her head that it was all right for them to come to their dad. They gave him a polite hug. The little boy's eyes were bright, and he was the spitting image of his father. Clyde had bought a doll for his daughter, Ada, and had made a little wooden ship for his son, Ambrose.

Clarisse explained that young Ambrose had a bad cold and was running a fever when they reached the port. It had taken them extra time during the health screenings. She'd feared they might hospitalize him, and she didn't have any way to get word to Clyde. She told him Ada had been a big help with her little brother. She was her mom's girl, always ready to help. Agnes gave her daughter's husband a hug and a kiss on the cheek. She found her eyes filled with tears. It was hard, very hard to see that strapping young man confined to a wheelchair.

Introductions were made to Peter. Clarisse thanked him for accompanying her husband. Many hours had passed for his family since they had eaten. Everyone was hungry. They returned to meet Karen and enjoyed a hearty boardinghouse meal.

Clyde told his family about their new home. His eyes shone with pride. "I think you're going to be impressed with all the work we've put into the place. Many of my mining brothers pitched in. We couldn't have done it without them. It wasn't set up for a family at all before. It was all messy from the construction when I last saw it, but the womenfolk were coming by to work their magic. They're all looking forward to meeting you and the children."

After a good night's rest, they met at breakfast the next morning. Karen had located the photographer, and both families had their pictures taken. They looked forward to receiving them in the mail shortly.

The long-awaited journey to Clyde's home with his family by his side was soon underway.

Clarisse and Agnes enjoyed the natural beauty of America. The train ride was a bit disconcerting at first, but Clarisse soon found herself more at ease. She and Clyde talked easily about his furniture business and the house he'd prepared for them all. It sounded so much nicer than their small three-room home in Germany. Agnes and Ada would be sharing a room, what a luxury. Their children were glued to the windows and busy pointing out scenery and wildlife to each other. Ambrose climbed up on his dad's lap and immediately asked him about his missing limb.

Alarmed, Clarisse hushed him and looked apologetically at Clyde. To her surprise, Clyde welcomed his son's questions and answered them as honestly as he could without overwhelming the boy's mind with too many details.

His daughter, Ada, listened carefully as he explained about the accident and surgery to her little brother. She couldn't understand how her daddy could still do his work. He explained that there were certain tasks that he needed assistance with. He told her about the nice young men who worked for him.

Ada came over and sat beside Clyde and said, "Now we can help you too. At least you won't have to cook and clean the house. Do you even know how to cook, Daddy?"

Clyde laughed. "Not really, dear. I'll probably gain twenty pounds now that your mother and gramma are here taking care of that job." He put his arm around her and pulled her to his side, maybe so they wouldn't see how his eyes watered. *It's going to be okay. There's probably not a happier man in the whole country right now*, he thought as he looked at his family.

Peter and Karen smiled at each other. They hadn't meant to be eavesdropping, but it couldn't be helped in such close quarters. It was good to see Clyde go from excited, but fearful to content.

Expectations

Peter held Andrew for most of the train ride to Roanoke. Karen said she'd slept well the night before but still didn't have any energy today. Peter recalled that she'd been tired the evening before too when he and Clyde went to the dock to pick up his family. She was sleeping. He studied her face and put his palm to her forehead. She didn't appear to have any fever. She was normally a healthy woman. Maybe it was a cold coming on. He put it out of his mind.

When they got home the next day, Fletcher's boys were waiting in the wagon with Papa. They'd come along to give them a ride to their new house. You might say they were the welcome wagon. The boys had missed their uncle Peter. He always played with them when he got a chance. When Uncle Peter and Papa were working around the farm, he explained things to the boys so they'd understand what was going on. He told them they'd make pretty good farmhands someday. Joseph especially was so gentle with the animals. Arwood was great with anything mechanical. He loved to take things apart and put them back together again. Sometimes, that got him into trouble.

They all told Clyde and his family good-bye when they dropped them off at their home. The boys were very quiet, but Peter could tell they were curious about Clyde's missing leg and his wheelchair and crutches. They had noticed him when they lived in the camp, but Mama said it wasn't polite to stare or ask folks about such things. Peter would mention their curiosity to Fletcher. It might be time to discuss Clyde's accident with them. He didn't feel like it was his place to say anything.

The boys told Clyde about the cow who was trying to have her calf while he was gone. "Papa said the calf was dead because it wasn't breathing," said Joseph.

Papa said, "The young cow was in terrible pain. I sent for Murphy, the farmer next door, to see if he could help me get the calf delivered. We tried and tried but couldn't help her. She looked wild eyed and just bellowed in pain."

Joseph chimed in, "Then all of a sudden, the crazy cow jumped up and went running across the field with the calf's head and a hoof hanging out of her. We laughed because we thought it looked funny."

Arwood said sheepishly and quietly, "Papa said it wasn't funny. He said she acted that way because she hurt so much." Joseph said, "We tried to help Papa catch her, but we couldn't stop her. That cow took off running as hard as she could go and smashed right through the fence."

Papa said, "It was dark. We looked for the cow for a while but couldn't find her last night. She'd gotten way down in the woods. Early this morning when we went looking again, we found her."

"Papa was sad because the calf died," said Joseph. "Mama said sometimes that just happens. She thinks there must've been something wrong with it." He stared quizzically at his uncle.

"Mama's right, boys. Nature takes care of problems like that. It doesn't seem fair, but that's the way life is sometimes," Peter told them. He knew Papa hated losing one of the new calves. They had been steadily building up their livestock base, and every new calf was a welcome addition. Peter thought sadly of the babies he and Karen had lost early on in their marriage. *Were they unhealthy?*

As the weeks dragged on and the weather turned cooler, Karen seemed to be dragging around. Peter was worried. She didn't have any cold symptoms. Mama and Rachel insisted that she see a doctor. Papa drove them into town. The three women were the only ones in the waiting room. Karen told them that she suspected she was pregnant. Mama gasped, her mouth opened, and she quickly shut it again without saying a word.

Rachel held her hand to comfort her sister-in-law.

"Don't worry, Karen. You may just need some vitamins." "But, Rachel, I haven't stopped having my time of the month, and they've been awful."

"Well, there you go, Karen. Maybe it's something else wrong that the doctor can quickly diagnose and get you back on your feet again."

Mama was studying the two of them closely but not saying anything. Karen and Rachel's eyes met. They wished she hadn't insisted on coming to town with them this time. Karen said, "Mama and Rachel, I'm sorry, but I want to see the doctor by myself. Please don't be mad at me. I'm so scared, but I want to face this myself first."

Soon, the nurse came for her. She had a chart in her hand and began to ask Karen questions as the door closed to the waiting room. Karen was back there with the doctor for quite a while. Rachel was getting nervous about the amount of time it was taking. She wished she could go through that door and check on her.

Finally, Karen emerged with an ashen look on her face. "I am pregnant, about three months. He couldn't hear a heartbeat with his stethoscope yet. He said it's too soon, but we probably will be able to listen to it in a couple of months. I told him about my past pregnancies. He wants me off my feet until the bleeding stops. At least, he didn't seem too panicky," she added weakly.

"Don't you worry about a thing, Karen," said Mama, "Rachel and I can help you with little Andrew."

They were a somber group riding home. Karen told Papa, "Peter and I are expecting another child. The doctor thinks it should arrive in March. Please don't say anything to anybody else until I get a chance to tell Peter myself."

Papa nodded. "That's good news, Karen. Andrew will have a little brother or sister soon." He couldn't help but notice how solemn the group of ladies were, a pregnant silence as it were. He offered up a silent prayer for both Karen and this new child's protection. The ride home seemed much longer today with hardly anyone talking. *That is very unusual when you got these three ladies together. What should be a joyous day for our family is marred by a lack of faith in the Good Lord above*, thought Papa.

Karen's bleeding issue soon resolved itself. While she remained weary and ate very little, she didn't have any morning sickness. Her abdomen had grown expansively, giving them all cause for optimism. Peter thought her lack of appetite was probably nerve related. Karen had always been the nervous type. They were guessing she might be about four to five and a half months along. It was the end of November, and Peter and Karen, along with baby Andrew, once again journeyed back to the doctor's office.

9

Double Trouble

Peter waited with Andrew in the outer room while Karen went back to be examined by the doctor. Peter had a good feeling about this pregnancy, but he could certainly understand Karen's fears. The midwife in Germany had warned her after she lost the first two children that it could be fatal for her to attempt another pregnancy.

His mind raced nervously. Surely, the doctor would be able to tell that she had not given birth to Andrew. He didn't know how they knew such things but suspected he would know. That might be awkward. They would have to ask him to respect their privacy. Didn't doctors have to take some type of oath to that affect?

Suddenly, he heard Karen shout, "No, no! It's not possible!"

He was on his feet, pacing with the sleeping Andrew in his arms. It wouldn't be proper for him to go racing back there, but—The door opened, and the nurse stuck her head out. "Mr. Broce?" Peter nodded slowly, not sure if he wanted to know more.

"Please come back here for a moment. The doctor would like to talk to you."

Peter took in a deep breath and slowly followed the nurse back. Karen was sitting on the table fully clothed with a startled look on her face. He went over and put his arm around her.

The doctor started, "Mr. Broce, I have to tell you, this is a first for me. When I listened for your baby's heartbeat, I heard something very odd—two heartbeats."

Peter said, "What are you saying? I don't understand."

Karen looked up at him. "Peter, he is trying to tell you that we are having two babies, twins!" Peter had to sit down. He was dumbfounded. "But how is that possible? Will Karen be okay? We were told that it would be dangerous for her to give birth again. Won't two babies make that twice as dangerous?"

"Calm down, young man. From what I can tell, Karen appears to be holding up just fine. Those were nice strong heartbeats I heard. I will need to see her every few weeks to monitor her progress. If I have any concerns whatsoever, she will have to stay in the hospital until the babies arrive." Peter must've still looked shell-shocked because the doctor teased him, "You haven't heard a word I've said since I told you your wife is having twins, have you?" The doctor laughed good-naturedly. Peter agreed.

"We have a fine midwife here in town, but given your wife's medical history, I want to be present when she goes into labor. It would be far too risky otherwise. I am putting her on bed rest. We don't want to take any chances now, do we? I'm concerned that your wife is not getting proper nutrition. She and I have discussed her eating habits."

The doctor watched the young couple leave his office. He hadn't wanted to alarm them, but they had a long road ahead. Getting his wife overly distraught would not help either of them. He planned to monitor her closely and also consult with a doctor friend of his in Roanoke. He prayed for a safe delivery and healthy babies for them. He wondered about the sex of the children. They all had exciting days ahead.

Time marched on. Karen's visits to the doctor were uneventful. The babies were growing, and Karen was healthy. The young mother was bored out of her mind having to stay in the bed all the time. She even had to eat her meals there. The trips to the doctor were a treat since they got her out of the house. Then there was the matter of how huge she'd become. The doctor told her not to worry because it was all baby. He took her vitals and was pleased with her progress.

Around her eighth month, Karen awoke to a wet bed. She feared her water had broken. She screamed for Rachel, who came running.

"Karen, what is it?"

Karen showed her the bed and the bloody sheets, not much, but it was too soon for any of that. She cried and rocked herself back and forth. "Oh, Rachel, I have been feeling so good. Now I'm so afraid something is terribly wrong. I want these babies so much." "Are you having any pain?" Karen shook her head no.

"I think that's probably a good sign. Let me go get Peter. We don't want to take any chances, honey. The doctor needs to examine you. We will pack a bag because he may want you to go to the hospital so he can keep a closer eye on things."

Peter took the steps two at a time getting to Karen. She looked good to him but very upset. "Come on, honey, it's going to be fine. You've made it eight months. Don't quit now." He rocked her in his arms while Rachel prepared the small overnight bag.

"You two go ahead. Mama has Andrew. We're all praying for you," Rachel said as she gave Karen a hug. When they left, she removed the sheets so she could scrub them. Hopefully, Karen would be back home tonight to sleep in her own bed. Rachel didn't believe that would be the case.

When they reached the doctor's office, Karen was immediately taken to the examining room. After his examination, the doctor had a very serious look on his face. He sat down at Karen's side and told her, "We've got an unfortunate development. Your placenta is beneath the babies, and the weight and movement of them is causing the bleeding you are experiencing. I am going to have to insist that you spend the rest of this pregnancy in the hospital." "Are the babies going to be all right?" Karen asked.

"The good news is they are far enough along that we can take them if we sense any distress. Your health will be at risk if the placenta ruptures. You'll have to stay in bed. You will have a bedpan and also have your baths in the bed. Understand, you could go into labor at any time. This is nonnegotiable," the doctor informed her.

"I will do whatever you think I need to. We want these babies to survive, and I want to live to see them too." Karen wept openly.

"There, there now," the nurse comforted her. "Let's get you to the hospital and give you the best possible chance to raise these healthy babes."

The door opened, and Peter came in with two other men with a stretcher. "We can't risk another horse-and-wagon ride right now. These gentlemen are putting you in their ambulance and taking you to the hospital. Will this be your first trip in a horseless carriage? I have to warn you, the vehicle is from the mortuary over in Christiansburg, but it is the safest way to transport you now," the doctor informed her.

"Karen, I'm riding with you. One of the men here in town is going to take the wagon and horses back to our house. I'm sure you'll have company tonight." Peter held her hand, hoping she wouldn't be frightened of riding in the vehicle.

The men placed Karen in the back of the vehicle and closed the door. Peter sat up front. Karen worried about whether they would be able to carry her into the hospital because she thought she was so enormous. The men laughed. "Ma'am, you are a lightweight. We'll be fine. Don't worry, dear, we won't drop you."

Karen was soon settled into her room. After lunch, she immediately fell asleep, exhausted from the busy morning and the mental stress. Peter sat beside her and watched her chest rise and fall with every breath. He prayed that she would survive. He loved her too much. He didn't want to imagine a life without her.

Rachel, Fletcher, and Mama came to visit that night. They made Peter come home with them to get his rest. Fletcher had to convince him that he needed to keep up his strength for Karen and the baby's sake. They hoped Karen would rest better if she wasn't worrying about him.

Two weeks later, Karen went into labor. Karen began to hemorrhage after the second child was born. The doctor and the surgeon he'd called in began to immediately work to save the young mother's life. She'd been given a tranquilizer and didn't feel a thing. The surgeon had to work quickly and carefully with his stitches to curtail the loss of blood.

When Karen awoke, she looked down at her considerably flatter stomach, and her eyes darted to and fro, trying desperately to figure out her surroundings. Where were her babies? Did they survive? She started to get up, and then her eyes found Peter sitting by the window. He looked half-asleep.

He has probably been awake the whole evening, she thought.

Her motion caught his attention, and he rushed to her side. "Karen, how are you doing? Do I need to get the doctor? You gave them all quite a scare—and me too," he confessed.

"Peter, the babies, where are they? Did they make it?" Karen asked somewhat groggily, frightened to hear his response.

"Oh yes, wait until you see them. They are perfect in every way. They are such itty-bitty little things, but the doc says they are healthy and have great lungs."

She was so relieved that tears streamed down her face.

Her eyes widened. "Peter, I don't even know what we had."

Peter signaled the nurse at the door and whispered something to her. He returned to Karen's bedside. "We have two sweet baby boys, Karen. The hospital staff asked what I wanted to name them. It occurred to me that we hadn't even picked out names. Remember, we were so scared that we didn't even want to guess whether we'd have boys or girls."

Suddenly, the door to her room opened, and in walked the nurse and her doctor, each carrying a tiny blue bundle.

They placed them on the bed facing Karen so she could examine them closely. The doctor counted their fingers and toes and said, "See, Mom, they're healthy baby boys with lusty lungs."

Karen studied the little red faces. They were such a miracle. How on earth did she and Peter end up with twins? "When can we go home?" she asked.

"Let's see how you are all doing in about a week," the doctor informed her. "In the meantime, you and your husband need to come up with names for the new additions to your family so we can update our medical records."

Peter and Karen discussed many names before settling on Kellen and Kolten. Karen nursed the babies later that morning and was shocked to find she had sufficient milk for them both. Both mother and babies continued to thrive in the coming week. Karen looked forward to letting Andrew meet his little brothers. She and Peter were truly blessed with their sweet little family.

Front Porch Chats

Rachel sat on the porch reading a letter from her father, Amos. She was feeling melancholy this evening. There had been many letters back and forth between father and daughter over the last few years. She hadn't been able to bring herself to tell him about the fateful ship ride to the States. It would break his heart to know that something so dastardly had happened to his little girl, so naturally, she never mentioned her pregnancy with Andrew. The secrets were mounting up.

It would soon be seven years since her mother had died. Rachel thought about her mother nearly every single day, especially when she was making dresses for her little girl. Dotty was now three years old. She recalled her father saying that Dotty reminded him of her mother, Katherine, with her delicate features. She had Rachel's pretty dark hair and Fletcher's curly locks and blue eyes. Of course, Arwood was born on the day she lost her mother. Joseph was so young when she died. He loved her, but the memory of that grandma had faded from his memory. That made Rachel sad.

Rachel was going to write another letter to her dad. Her father's existence was a lonely one, and it didn't have to be. This time, she had made up her mind to do something she'd promised herself she wouldn't do—beg him to come to America.

She knew he didn't have any real ties to Germany now. There had been no new romances. His life consisted of working, coming home, fixing a hodgepodge supper, and spending time at her mother's grave. He needed to be here watching his grandchildren growing up, and they needed their grandpa too. Most of all, *she* needed him here.

Fletcher came through the screen door onto the porch. "I should've known I'd find you out here." He came over and sat on the swing by his wife. He looked at her closely and couldn't miss the sad look on her face. He saw the letter from her father in her hand. "Rachel, what's wrong? Is your dad sick?"

"You know he would never tell me even if he was. He wouldn't want to worry me. It's not that. I'm just missing him so much lately. I'm having an inner struggle with myself tonight. I'm going to write and ask him to join us here in America." She looked hopefully at Fletcher.

Fletcher put his arm around her. "Ah, Rachel, don't go getting your hopes up. He is older and seems pretty set in his ways. I know it's hard not being able to see him."

"But, Fletcher, our children are growing up so fast. This fall, Arwood will be seven, Joseph nine, and our baby will be three. I don't think Joseph remembers my dad, and the youngest two didn't have enough time with him to get to know him."

"Do you think he will even consider coming?" Rachel shrugged her shoulders.

"Rachel, if he did, he'd want to be able to pull his weight. Remember how independent he is. I tell you what, let me check at the blacksmith shop and see if they could use someone with his experience. That might be just the thing to entice him, not that you and the children aren't enough to do that."

About that time, Karen and Peter came out on the porch with their little six-month-old twin boys and Andrew, who was about two and a half.

"Hi, you two," Peter said. "It's a warm evening, isn't it? We thought we come out here and cool off."

Fletcher started to get up and offer them the swing for the babies.

"Hey, you both sit right where you are," said Peter. "We'll be perfectly comfortable right here on the steps."

Peter noticed Rachel's somber face. "Is everything okay? We didn't mean to intrude."

Rachel said, "I'm homesick for my dad tonight."

Fletcher pulled her toward him, and she placed her head against his strong jaw.

Karen noticed the mail in Rachel's hand. "Any chance he'll come, Rachel?" she said as she bounced Kolten on her lap. Andrew loved his little brothers and always wanted to play with them. He was making funny faces at Kellen, who was sitting on Peter's knee. "Careful, Andrew, I don't want you to fall backwards."

"I don't know." Rachel smiled. "I'm shameless. I'm considering using the grandchildren to get him here."

"Well, if he is anything like Mama and Papa, that might work," said Peter. "They love having the house full of young ones."

Fletcher grinned. Amos used to love to come over and play with his grandsons, and now he could get to know his little granddaughter too. Would he make that trip alone? They both had said when they left Germany that they didn't think he would come if he didn't come when Rachel did.

Fletcher looked at his wife. He hoped she wasn't setting herself up for a big disappointment. He jumped to his feet. "Could anyone else use a cup of coffee or tea? I'm making it, so no complaints, you hear?" he teased, trying to lighten the mood.

Peter said, "I'll help you if Rachel wouldn't mind holding this little monster."

Kellen cackled with his toothless grin. His brother Kolten had a tooth about to break through the gums, and it made him a little cranky. Kellen was drooling, but so far, no teeth had appeared.

"Yes, I'll take him. Come on, Andrew, you climb up here too and keep Uncle Fletcher's seat warm."

Andrew loved Aunt Rachel. It didn't take much convincing to sit on the swing and snuggle with her.

After the men went inside, Dotty came running out onto the porch. She had been in the living room with Mama, listening to a story. She heard all the voices on the porch through the open window and came to investigate. Her sweet little pout came out when she saw her mommy holding the baby and hugging on Andrew. She was still adjusting to the babies. Sometimes she liked them just fine, but better when her mommy wasn't holding them.

The swing got a little more crowded as she climbed aboard. She wanted to sit on Mommy's lap so that put her between Rachel and Andrew. His temper flared, and he pulled on her arm. Dotty started crying, and that got Andrew crying too. Baby Kellen's little lip quivered.

"Oh my goodness, you two, stop that. I know you love each other," said Rachel. She petted the two older children and bounced Kellen. Soon, they were content. Dotty and Andrew were swinging their legs like they'd seen the older boys do. They were hoping to make the swing go faster.

As if on cue, Joseph and Arwood raced toward the porch from the backyard. "Mama is making hot chocolate for us," Arwood told them. They joined Karen on the front steps.

Joseph begged her to let him hold Kolten. Karen said, "Okay, but you have to sit down and hold on tight. He will try to jump out of your arms." She gently placed him in Joseph's arms. Joseph wanted to hold him close like a little baby, but Kolten wanted to sit up and see what was going on. Karen helped adjust his position. She stood up to stretch.

Arwood went over to his mother. "Can I have Kellen? Joseph's got Kolten, and it's not fair."

Rachel laughed and told him, "Yes, you can hold him, but you've got to go sit beside Joseph, and I'll bring him to you."

Arwood scrambled into position and stuck his tongue out at his brother.

"Now, Arwood, you stop that and apologize to your brother," Rachel told him. He did, and she placed Kellen in his lap. "You be careful with him and stay seated."

Andrew and Dotty jumped off the swing to go over and sit with the big kids. That's how quickly they lost interest in Rachel. Finally, the men emerged with the steaming mugs of coffee and tea. Mama brought out the hot chocolate. The boys relinquished the babies in exchange for hot chocolate, so that meant both of the men ended up with a baby.

"Mama, where's Papa?" asked Joseph.

"He's been out in the garden picking some more vegetables for your mom and aunt Karen to help me put up tomorrow. He's tired. I think he is going to get cleaned up and ready for bed. How about you two? You've got school tomorrow."

"Dad, can we stay out and catch lightning bugs before we go to bed?" asked Arwood.

"Sure, son, finish your hot chocolate first. When your momma calls you, I don't want any fuss, deal?"

"Deal!" they both shouted in unison and slurped down the last of the hot chocolate. They jumped to their feet, nearly knocking over the cups.

"Boys, aren't you forgetting something?" said their dad. They picked up their cups and took them into the kitchen, placing them in the sink. When they came back on the porch, they went over and gave Mama a hug and thanked her for the hot chocolate.

"I declare, they are the politest young boys. I think all of you are doing a good job raising your children. Those two remind me of you and Fletcher when you were young, Peter."

Rachel smiled. "I ran into Clarisse and her mother-in-law, Agnes, when I went into town the other day. Agnes thinks little Ada is sweet on our Joseph. She says Ada is always talking about Joseph this and Joseph that."

"I don't think Joseph is paying much attention to girls yet, is he?" asked Fletcher.

"Not really, all he and Arwood can talk about is when they get to go hunting with the men. They've enjoyed all the fishing trips this past summer. Yes, they are all boy. I don't think they give girls much thought yet," said Rachel.

"How are Clyde and Clarisse doing? They had a big adjustment to make. Do you think we'll be able to get them to come to church with us?" Mama asked.

Peter said, "I think everything is going fine with them. I'll talk to him about going with us the next time I take vegetables to town to sell. It would be nice to have them in church."

"Rachel, did I see a letter on the table from your daddy?" Mama asked her.

"Yes, every time I get a letter, it makes me more homesick for him. I wish he would change his mind and come be with us. We're the only family he's got, and his grandchildren are growing up not knowing him. They love you and Papa, of course, but I'd like for them to know their other grandpa too."

"Well, sure you do, and there's nothing wrong with that. Have you told him how you feel?" asked Mama.

"No, I wanted to respect his wishes, but he sounds so lonesome. It's not what he says but how he says it. I don't want him to be alone in Germany, grieving himself to death over Momma while we are all over here. He has always liked you and Papa. I know he'd be happy if he would just come." Rachel hung her head.

Fletcher saw the look in his mother's eyes and the set of her mouth. That was exactly how she looked when she planned to meddle.

Heaven help us all, he thought. This time, he was going to keep quiet and let her work her magic. From what he knew of his mother, they'd better be figuring out where Amos was going to sleep when he got here. He shook his head and smiled to himself.

11

Decade of Love

"What do you think of the ring design, Fletcher?" asked the jeweler as he handed him the beautifully handcrafted ring he had designed especially for Rachel and Fletcher's tenth wedding anniversary.

"It's incredible. I think she is going to love it. The best part is that she won't be expecting it," said Fletcher.

"There isn't a woman alive that wouldn't love it, Fletcher. It is exquisitely crafted in platinum with delicate filigree, a sparkling half-carat round European brilliant-cut diamond surrounded by glittering baguette diamonds. You aren't just purchasing an engagement ring. You are buying a timeless treasure, an heirloom for your family. Future ladies in your family will be proud to own this ring, and they will remember the very special love of a man for his wife." Fletcher's eyes glazed over. "Could you write that description down for me? It looks beautiful, and explaining it to her the way you just did is bound to make Rachel treasure it all the more. How much do I owe you?"

The jeweler cleared his throat and produced the sales ticket, sliding it across the counter to Fletcher. "Now we offer financing if you are not able to pay the entire sum today."

Fletcher gulped when he saw the price—seventy-five dollars! He had been saving a bit of his paycheck back each week since Rachel had first arrived in New York. "No, I can pay for it today. Our family doesn't care for time payments."

The jeweler said, "In that case, for a cash purchase, I can offer you a ten percent discount." He recalculated the total, collected Fletcher's payment, and placed the ring in a beautiful blue velvet hard jewelry box. Fletcher thought the container was so fancy that there would be no need to wrap the gift. He slipped the box in his pocket and left the store, his wallet a little lighter and his heart much fuller. He'd give it to Mama to hold for him until he was ready to give it to Rachel.

If Rachel happened to see the look on Fletcher's face, she would surely guess something was up. He couldn't hide how excited he was with the ring that had been made as an original design just for her. A fellow should never stop romancing his woman. He didn't want to live one day without making her aware of how much he loved her.

When he arrived home, Mama was sitting in the living room mending his and Peter's work clothes. "Where are the ladies?" Fletcher asked.

"They decided to take a walk in the woods with Joseph and Arwood as their guides. We might not get too many more mornings as nice as this one. They've packed a picnic.

I don't suspect they'll be gone long," said Mama.

"Why not?"

"Dotty and Andrew wanted to go too. They'll get tired and cranky soon. It's almost their naptime. If the little ones fall asleep, they'll be a heavy load for Rachel and Karen to carry back home. Kellen and Kolten are asleep. Karen got them down for their naps before she left."

Fletcher sat down at the end of the couch. "It's nice seeing Peter and Karen with a family of their own. They got lots of practice helping us with our children."

"Well, I hope they are done growing their family. Karen gave us quite a scare with the twins." Mama shifted her weight so she could look at Fletcher. "It seems like just yesterday that I was a younger woman in Germany chasing through the house after my two precious little boys."

"Actually, Peter was the cute one. I was the smart one," Fletcher needled his mother.

"You're both handsome and intelligent young men. I can't get over the fact that I'm the mother of thirty-three- and thirty-year-old sons! But beyond that, now at fifty-one years of age, I have six grandchildren. Where have the years gone?" said Mama.

"Speaking of years, Mama, I want to show you something I had made for Rachel." Fletcher reached into his pants pocket and extracted the beautiful midnight blue velvet jeweler's box. He handed it to his mother to examine.

She peered at him over the top of her glasses. He looked like he was about to pop from anticipation. How had she missed that air of excitement about him? She gingerly opened the box. Her breath caught at the beautiful ring inside. She didn't remove it. "Fletcher, this is beautiful. What is the occasion? Is it for Christmas?"

"No, Mom, it's to celebrate our tenth wedding anniversary. I couldn't ask for a better wife or mother to my children. I want her to know how much I appreciate her."

"Fletcher, I know you have your mine job, but isn't this a bit extravagant? I wouldn't want you to come to financial ruin. There will hopefully be many more anniversaries," his mother chided him.

"I hope so too, but I want to honor my wife in a very special way. She has been through and survived so much and never once stopped loving me or our children."

"I bet this set you back a pretty penny. I don't think it's wise, but you told me you're my smart son, so I guess I'll have to trust you on this one."

"I need yours and Karen's help. For our anniversary next Saturday, I'm taking Rachel to town for supper at the Café and then to see one of those silent movies at the Lyric Theater over there on Main Street near the fancy Preston Hotel."

"Do you need us to watch the children? Of course, we'll help you."

"Yes, thanks, Mom. I was hoping you would bake a cake and have coffee with us when we get back home. I want to give her the ring then."

"Of course I will. The children will love having a little party. Son, you are a hopeless romantic. I don't know where you got it, certainly not from your father. Maybe you could give him a suggestion or two every now and then?"

"I don't know, Mom. That might be a little awkward." Fletcher grinned uncomfortably.

Mama laughed. "Fletcher, I'm just joking with you. I wouldn't change a thing about your father. He is still the very same man I fell in love with those many years ago. Sure, he's quiet and doesn't always speak up when I think he should, but have you noticed that when he speaks, folks perk up and pay attention? He's a good man."

"Dad has always been there for us boys. The children all love him. He doesn't seem to get overly excited about anything, but he's right there when you need him. I still think he works too hard. Peter and I do what we can to help him. Oftentimes, he will already be headlong into a job before we know he's thinking about it."

"I hate to tell you this, but there's no changing him. Believe me, I've tried all these long years. I have learned to accept him for who he is," Mama said. "I'd better go put this little box away before everyone gets back here. I'm going to fix you men a sandwich for dinner. Inform them I'll have their food ready in a half hour."

The following week, the weather turned frigid and rainy, which kept the boys cooped up in the house. They were both cranky with each other this evening. Their dad sent them to their room and asked them to settle down before supper. Fletcher went out on the porch to survey the night sky. The wind had died down, and the stars sparkled as if winking. The air was still cool but not biting cold. Fletcher went inside.

The ladies had put their heads together and come up with a delicious supper menu including roast pork sandwiches, creamy potato soup, and homemade cookies. Everyone dived into the meal. The hot comforting food brightened the mood in the house. Fletcher invited the family to take a walk after supper. Peter and Karen didn't want to take the young children out in the night air, Papa was fighting a cold, and Mama and Karen wanted to get the kitchen squared away.

Rachel and the kids thought it was a great idea. They rushed to get their coats, hats, and gloves. Young Dotty had practically fallen asleep at the supper table. Fletcher carried her upstairs and tucked her in bed. They decided to walk down toward the river. He and Rachel walked hand in hand. She was enjoying breathing out and watching her breath steam the night air. They planned to walk about twenty minutes and then turn around and go back home.

Amazing how the brisk air refreshes the soul, thought Fletcher.

The boys ran ahead and talked of bears and wildcats in the surrounding mountains. Dad and Uncle Peter promised to take them hunting soon. They'd already been allowed to shoot at squirrels in the back field. Dad had taught them how to clean the rifle and load it with the black powder, but they wouldn't feel like real hunters until they got to shoot at deer and turkeys. Joseph was convinced that he was going to kill a bear on his first outing.

Fletcher stopped Rachel and kissed her under the bright moon. She looked lovingly into his eyes. "Well, what was that all about?" asked Rachel.

"Just another way to say I love you. Do you realize that tomorrow is our tenth-year anniversary? I've made some special plans for us to celebrate."

"Don't be so mysterious. What have you got planned? You know I might have to make arrangements…"

"Not this time. I've taken care of everything! You better be ready to leave around five." Fletcher loved the confusion on her face. His girl did not like surprises, but that didn't matter. She was going to get one or two tomorrow.

The boys ran back toward them. "Dad, we heard something down there," said Arwood. All their talk of big game had let their imaginations get away from them.

Fletcher smiled at Rachel, who looked alarmed. "Boys, look, you're scaring your mother."

"But, Dad, we did hear something," insisted Joseph.

"You know the most plentiful game in these woods is deer. They are more frightened of you then you are of them.

You're probably hearing them dashing away because of all the noise you boys are making. That's one of the first rules of hunting, to keep quiet so you don't scare off the animals."

Joseph and Arwood looked disappointed. Their shoulders slumped. They certainly had hoped for more adventure on this walk than their parents were anticipating. But just in case, they hung back and walked the rest of the way home with their parents.

When everyone came downstairs the next morning, Hilda was already up mixing the ingredients for a yellow coconut cake. "What's the occasion?" asked Papa.

Mama winked and said matter-of-factly, "Today makes ten years that Rachel has put up with our Fletcher."

Papa snorted. "How long have you put up with me?"

"Too long," Mama retorted. "Soon it will be thirty four years!"

Joseph's and Arwood's eyes got as big as saucers in amazement. "That's a long time, Papa!"

"Don't I know it, son. It has taken me many years to get your mama properly trained, but the old girl has come a long way."

He ducked as a dishrag sailed past his head.

The boys laughed. Their grandparents were always cracking them up with their joking around.

Rachel gave Mama a hug, thanking her for baking a cake for their anniversary. She and Karen got breakfast started while the older boys helped with the younger children. Kellen and Kolten, the twins, were crawling and getting into everything.

Dotty was playing teacher to the nearly three-year-old Andrew, and he was listening to her read him a storybook. She was very bossy in her tone with Andrew, but he didn't seem to mind.

The men were killing hogs today to put up the meat for winter. It would be a full day for all of the family. The hogs would be shot, their throats cut, and then they would be hung up in the tree until they bled out. Next, they would be gutted and placed in a metal barrel of scalding hot water so their hair would come off easily when scraped.

The older boys would observe and learn. Someday, the job would become their responsibility. A portion of the meat would be ground and seasoning added for sausage. The feet would be pickled and canned. The rest would become hams, pork roasts, pork chops, bacon, and such. Even the fat would be saved for cooking and soap making. Papa teased that the only thing they couldn't use was the curly tail.

After they got the men and boys fed, the women prepared breakfast for themselves and the other children. Rachel told them, "Fletcher has a surprise for me tonight. Do you girls know anything about it?"

The responses she got from them was, "How nice" and "Isn't that sweet of him." No amount of prompting got her any more information.

Rachel took extra care getting ready for her big night out with her husband. After her bath, she wound her stilldamp wavy hair up in a loose bun and pulled a couple of tendrils down on either side by her face. She recently made a new dress, which was more or less straight and fell to within six inches of her ankles. It was a deep rose hue. To go with the dress, she'd made a tailored black velvet jacket that buttoned snuggly at her waist. She topped off her outfit with black heels with a thin ankle strap, which she'd purchased from the shoe store in town. She admired herself in the full-length mirror Fletcher had given her last Christmas.

Rachel wished she could save up and buy one of the sharp-looking felt hats she'd seen in the Sears catalog. She hadn't even worn the new shorter dress to church yet. She and Karen had agreed to each make one but had been working up their nerve to wear it. Karen had made an outfit from the same pattern. Her dress was green and had an off-white jacket. They already knew what Mama thought of the fashion trend. Mama was never one to mince words and was quick to offer her opinion. They loved her dearly, but they couldn't dress like little old ladies now, could they?

Fletcher was having his bath. She'd asked him to wear his Sunday suit since she was dressing up. She was glad Papa had recently purchased one of the nice two-seater covered buggies with a horse hitch. Rachel had no idea how he'd talked Mama into getting one of those. Maybe it was the compromise for not getting the horseless carriage he was dying to have. Either way, it was certainly a more elegant way to travel than their old farm wagon.

When she started downstairs, Karen saw her descending. "Oh, Mama, look how stylish our Rachel looks in her new outfit. That girl can make anything. We saw an almost identical suit in the Sears catalog. Don't you just love her shoes?"

Mama studied her. "It's not my cup of tea, but I know you younger ladies like showing off your legs. At least it doesn't fit too snuggly like the dresses girls have been wearing to church. Those are disgraceful. The color looks very nice on you, dear."

The men teased Fletcher when he came downstairs in his suit, tie, and hat. Rachel had bought the hat for him from that same shoe store. Fletcher would have the last laugh because Rachel bought each of them an identical hat for Christmas. They were already wrapped and sitting in the top of her and Fletcher's closet.

Mama told them, "Don't forget I've fixed that coconut cake for your anniversary. We'll have dessert with coffee or tea when you two lovebirds return. Enjoy your evening."

When they got into the buggy, Rachel asked him, "Fletcher, where are you taking me now that we're so gussied up?"

"My dear, I thought we'd go to supper at the Café and then to a movie at that Lyric Theater. I hear they are showing a movie that everyone is talking about, *The Hunchback of Notre Dame*. I don't know how we will make any sense of it because there is no talking in the movie. They call them silent films. It will be something new for us to experience together."

"Fletcher, you are the most thoughtful husband," Rachel said as she leaned in and kissed his cheek. Her husband looked very distinguished in his suit. Rachel wasn't happy, however, that he was starting to grow a mustache, but it was the new thing. Papa and Peter were considering one too. "I've heard a few of the ladies in Mama's reading club talking about the book the movie is based on. The story takes place in Paris. It will be nice to see the grand city of Paris. Maybe the movie will show many of the landmarks. Fletcher, how exciting to go to a movie. I can't wait to tell the children about it."

They enjoyed a lovely meal of pork chops, slaw, and fried potatoes at the Café. They timed it perfectly to walk to the theater and secured their movie tickets. The inside of the theater was dimly lit, and if not for the ushers, they would never have been able to find their seats. The theater was filled to capacity to see the new show. They were awed by the new innovation that would allow them to see the movie. It lasted nearly two hours and had an intermission while the film reels were switched over.

Fletcher and Rachel were entranced by the characters and the dramatization. It was such a sad tale with many villains. Their hearts went out to the poor gypsy girl, Esmeralda, and Quasimodo, the hunchback. It was amazing how much a person's facial expression could convey.

When they left the theater, everyone was talking about the movie. Many people from the university were there. They overhead them talking about course material and their students. Maybe this movie would become famous. Many of the theater goers discussed it in very intellectual terms that were far over Rachel and Fletcher's heads, but it was interesting to hear. Fletcher told Rachel that he'd learned two things—that kindness prevailed in the end and that it's helpful to have a friend on your side.

They drove home slowly enjoying the beautiful starlit night. When they got home, although it was late, it seemed like every room in the house was lit. Fletcher smiled and helped his lady down from the buggy. Joseph had been watching for them. He came out and offered to put up the horse.

When they got inside, they found Mama had already sliced the cake and had the coffee brewed and the tea steeping. She and Karen served everyone. Rachel thought the evening had been perfect. She couldn't ask for any more exciting way to ring in their tenth year together.

Mama slipped the little blue velvet box into Fletcher's hand. He promptly dropped it into his pocket. Fletcher clinked the coffee cup with his fork to get everyone's attention. He went to stand in front of Rachel. "I have one last trick up my sleeve tonight," he said as he produced the jeweler's box.

"Fletcher, my evening has been perfect, and you don't have to do anything else. It was special spending it together."

"Rachel, you are the most wonderful thing that has ever happened to me. Every breath that is in me loves you. I want to give you a very special gift to commemorate our tenth year of marriage."

He handed her the blue velvet box and watched her eyes light up when she saw the magnificent ring inside.

He read the description the jeweler handwrote for him and told her, "Just as you are one of a kind, so is this ring. It was designed specifically for you. No one else will ever have one identical to this ring."

Rachel was speechless. The ring sparkled in the light. Fletcher removed her black onyx engagement ring and slipped the new ring on her finger. It was a perfect fit. He leaned over and kissed his bride of ten years. "I'm hoping you'll tough it out with me for at least another ten years."

"Oh yes, I think this is good enough for at least twenty-five more years!" Rachel teased. "I certainly could never have guessed that you had this wonderful evening planned. I actually have a little surprise that I planned to share with you tonight. We're expecting another baby! How's that for a grand finale?"

"Oh, Rachel, it's perfect!" Fletcher spun her around in a circle and kissed her again. The older boys groaned, but everyone else clapped and told them how happy they were for them.

Amos

In late January 1924, Rachel asked Joseph to walk out to the road and see if they had any mail. As he strode across the living room, she was shocked at how tall her young son had gotten. He must've grown a couple inches in the last three months. That didn't sound like much, but his pants were getting too short. She'd have to see if there was enough material left in the hem to lower them a bit. If not, she'd put them up for Arwood.

Rachel hadn't heard from her dad since that letter she'd sent to him back in September asking him if he would reconsider coming to America. That was nearly four months ago. She told herself she wasn't getting her hopes up, but a girl can still dream, can't she? No one had spoken anymore of the matter, as if they had dismissed it as a possibility.

When Joseph got back inside, his cheeks were rosy from the brisk air. "All we got was a new Sears catalog, and there's a letter from Germany addressed to Mama and Papa. Momma, can Arwood and I go play in the woods? It's starting to snow."

"Yes, son. Make sure you button up your coat this time and put your cap on."

Joseph scrambled up the steps to get his brother and look for his stocking cap. Arwood was playing with Dotty. He was a guest at a four-year-old's tea party, him and an old bear who'd seen better days.

"Come on, Arwood, let's go up in the woods and see if we can kill a bird or squirrel with our bows and arrows."

Arwood looked happy to get a reprieve from playing with his little sister. "Sorry, Dotty, I'll come to another one of your tea parties real soon."

Dotty was standing midpout with her little teapot, poised to pour. She stamped her food and started to cry. "You have to stay for the party," she pleaded with Arwood's departing back.

"Can't," said Arwood. "Brother and I are going to try to kill a few squirrels. Mama can cook them for breakfast if we shoot any."

Dotty put on her sweater and gloves and had her hat on sideways. She couldn't find but one of her shoes, but that didn't deter her. She marched down the stairs and announced to Momma that she was going with her brothers to kill squirrels.

"Oh, Dotty, you can't go out there, it'll be too cold. Look at how you're dressed. You'll freeze your pudding off."

"No, I promise I won't freeze my pudding, Momma. Where's my shoe?" Dotty insisted while looking under the couch to see if her shoe was there.

"Dotty, come over here. You and I will sit here by the fireplace where it's nice and warm. We'll watch the snow coming down. Won't that be fun?"

"No, I'm going with Joseph and Arwood!" Dotty screamed at her Momma and headed toward the big front door.

Rachel ran after her little rebel. "Dotty, now that's enough. You are being very rude. I said no."

Dotty's face turned red, and down her cheeks rolled hot tears.

"Now you go sit on the couch and stop acting like that. I'm surprised at you," her Momma told her. Neither of them heard Andrew come down the steps. He'd been taking his afternoon nap. He was rubbing his eyes.

"Look, you woke up your cousin."

Dotty turned to see him approaching. Suddenly, her brothers were forgotten. She went over and took Andrew by the hand. "Come on, Andrew, you need some tea."

As they climbed the stairs, Andrew asked her why she had her hat on. Dotty told him, "I was going to take a walk in the woods, but since you woke up, I have to make you a cup of tea."

Rachel smiled. That little one was a charmer as long as she got her way or had someone, namely Andrew, to boss around.

She picked up the catalog to browse through and noticed the letter on the table where Joseph had tossed it. Yes, it clearly said "John and Hilda Broce" in neat squaredoff letters. Her heart skipped a beat. It was her father's handwriting; she'd know it anywhere. But why had he addressed a letter to them? Where was Mama? She'd been sewing earlier. Maybe she was taking a nap. Well, soon Rachel would find out what was going on! She hoped it wasn't something with his health. That would be just like him to not want to worry her. Should she ask? What should she do? Pretend she hadn't noticed the letter?

Rachel went into the kitchen to start supper. She thought this weather called for something hearty.

She decided on a bean soup. She added more wood to the cookstove to get it hotter. Maybe Mama would fix corn bread when she came down. She added a little water to the beans, grabbed a lid, and put them on the stove to boil. They'd take at least a couple of hours to get soft. After gathering the ingredients, she began to chop the onions. She would fry them with a little bacon grease to give the soup a good flavor. Rachel chopped the parsley and thyme, got out the salt and pepper and a little flour for thickening. She would add the spices once the beans were nearly done and let them simmer until supper was ready. She'd gotten the recipe from one of the ladies at church. It was always a hit with her family.

Karen came downstairs with the twins, who were now ten months old. They were getting huge. She had one on each hip like saddlebags. Rachel laughed when she saw her. "No wonder you got your figure back so soon, Karen. You certainly get your exercise with those two. How was Andrew? Dotty hardly gave him a chance to wake up before she whisked him away to her little tea party. He didn't seem to mind, though."

"Dotty's got him lying on the bed with a pencil stuck in his mouth. She was nursing him back to health when I went by the bedroom." Karen smiled.

Rachel rolled her eyes. "That child has got so much imagination. Poor Andrew, good thing he's so easygoing!"

"What have you got cooking? You know, it's my turn to cook, not that I'm complaining, mind you," Karen asked.

"I thought bean soup and corn bread would be good on this freezing day," said Rachel.

"Sounds good to me. I hadn't given much thought to what to fix. You're right, these little butterballs keep me busy. We have a little bologna left if you want me to make sandwiches."

"Why don't we make some and put them on a platter? The men may want something more substantial. I'd still like to have corn bread if Mama will make it. Hers is better than mine. I've watched her make it dozens of times, but mine still doesn't turn out as good," said Rachel.

Mama came out of her bedroom. She was pulling her apron over her dress and smoothing her hair. She had a brisk step and quickly crossed the room. "Karen, let me have one of those little sweethearts. Is it time for you to nurse them?" she asked.

"No, they're not complaining, so I'm going to hold off a bit."

"Something certainly smells delicious, but not this baby—he smells ripe!" said Mama, making a face.

"Oh my, I changed them both. Kellen was wet, but I guess he wasn't finished with his business. Here, Mama, you take Kolten so his brother and I can take a little trip back upstairs. What a stinkpot!"

"Were your ears burning? I just told Karen I was hoping you'd make the corn bread when the beans get ready. Karen suggested we fix bologna sandwiches too," said Rachel.

"Sure, I'll make the corn bread. Sandwiches are fine. What they don't eat, we'll put up for dinner tomorrow. I think we're out of cheese and getting low on mustard too. I'll get John to pick up some when he goes into town tomorrow. I think that Andrew might be part mouse, Karen. I've caught him hiding hunks of cheese," said Mama.

The girls laughed. They now had twelve people living in one house. Rachel's abdomen was getting bigger every day, so soon they would have a baker's dozen.

Karen teased her as she came down the stairs, "Rachel, are you sure you're not having twins too? It might run in the family, you know."

"Karen, you nearly gave that poor doctor a heart attack worrying about your twins. He has only heard one heartbeat, so don't worry about me having twins."

"Still, wouldn't it be fun, both of us with a set of twins to grow up together?" Karen laughed.

"Bite your tongue, Karen! I can imagine all the extra laundry, no sleep, and if I had twins, mine would probably be screamers. There'd be no peace in this house!" moaned Rachel.

"Rachel, do you like the midwife in town?" Mama asked as she danced around the living room with Kolten. He giggled with glee.

Rachel picked up Kellen and walked over to look out the window with him. His breath steamed the cold glass. With a look of wonder in his eyes, he reached out his little fingers to draw on the fogged windowpane.

"Yes, she is much younger than Mrs. Meyer, but she is very personable, and it seems she has gotten a lot of experience since she is the only midwife in town," said Rachel.

Rachel let him play for a while and then put him back on the blanket on the floor so he could explore. She couldn't stand to wait another minute to find out what was in the letter and if it was from her father. She went over to Mama and handed her the letter that had arrived earlier that day.

"Here, Mama, you've got mail. Let me have Baby Kolten. I'm going to put him on the blanket too so he can play with Kellen," said Rachel.

The baby boys reminded her of windup toys. As soon as she sat them down, they gently fell over on their sides and proceeded to crawl all around—in opposite directions, of course.

Mama promptly dropped the letter in her apron pocket, to Rachel's dismay. "I was hoping for a letter from my father. I thought it looked like his handwriting on the envelope. When I looked at it closer, I noticed the mail was addressed to you and Papa, so I must've been wrong."

Mama took the letter from her apron pocket and appeared to study it closely. Rachel watched Mama's face intently, but she didn't reveal a thing. She waited impatiently for Mama to open the letter. "Who is the letter from, Mama?

"Oh, don't worry, dear. It's from an old friend Papa and I have been anxious to hear from. He and I'll read it later. For now, I think I'll get in the kitchen and whip up a batch of oatmeal cookies for the boys. They love it when I put raisins in them, but that's another thing for Papa's store list. The secret to a good oatmeal raisin cookie is to add a little salt, but you'd be surprised how many cooks don't add it."

Rachel was downcast. Was the letter from her father? She'd have to gently prod Mama again tomorrow for a clue.

The older two boys came bursting into the house, chasing each other and tracking icy snow melt all over the floor. In their excitement, they'd left the door wide open. Before Rachel could correct them or reach the door to shut it, right behind them came the rest of the men of the family—Papa, Fletcher, and Peter. They'd been hunting and although freezing, were proud of the turkey, rabbit, and deer they'd gotten that day. They'd put them in the shed to work on the next morning.

Joseph shouted, "Momma, Uncle Peter let me shoot at a deer. I missed him. Hunting is harder than it looks. We didn't see any more deer, but Daddy did. I saw a big hollow log. I told Arwood he could crawl through it because he was small. Good thing he didn't because when we got down there, it had a whole family of skunks inside."

Everyone laughed at the boys' near-disastrous encounter. "We got out of there fast," said Arwood. "I like skunks. They look like furry cats. I wish we could have one for a pet."

"Oh no, don't you even think about bringing a skunk to this house. When you men get cleaned up, we'll have a bowl of Rachel's bean soup. I'm making some corn bread and cookies," said Mama as she winked at the boys.

February and March weather made them all long for spring and the sight of anything green. The new baby was growing, and Rachel wondered whether this one would be a boy or a girl. She didn't have strong feelings either way.

She was much larger than normal with this child. She hoped whatever it was that she wouldn't have problems with delivery because apparently, she was having a big baby. So far, her pregnancy had been trouble free, but already at seven months, she felt like she was waddling like a duck.

She hadn't been eating any more than usual.

Fletcher teased her about having a whale. The last time he'd teased, she'd burst into tears. She was very selfconscious about her weight. The midwife didn't seem overly concerned and assured her everything looked like it was proceeding fine.

In April, everyone was busy outside working in the yard or garden, getting things ready for a busy growing season. The ground had been so wet, it delayed the job for a while, but at last, they'd had a clear week. The slightly moist soil was soft and perfect for plowing now.

Rachel was inside the house by herself except for the sleeping babies she was tending for Karen and Peter. She was feeling fat and miserable, her ankles were swollen and her face puffy. Truly, she was relieved not to have morning sickness with this pregnancy, but she didn't ever recall experiencing all these strange sensations all at once. She went into the kitchen to make herself a cup of tea.

Then something unusual happened, something that had never occurred before at their house—there was a knock at the front door. Rachel looked out the kitchen window, but she couldn't see a wagon or anyone on the porch. Thinking it was one of the children playing a game, she ignored it.

The knock came again, but somehow it seemed more insistent. This got her attention, and she crossed the room to the front door. Papa had gone into town earlier that morning to pick up the things they needed. Maybe he had his arms full. She pulled open the door, and to her surprise, there stood Amos, her father!

"Oh my god, it's you, Daddy! I had no idea! What are you doing here?" Rachel blurted out as happy tears cruised down her cheeks.

Amos set down his bags and gave his daughter a big hug. He kissed her wet cheeks and pushed her hair back so he could look at his daughter, his only child. "Rachel, it's so good to see you.

I thought I would leave this earth without ever setting eyes on you again." Amos's own eyes teared up as he studied her face.

When Rachel looked over his shoulder, there stood her whole family on the porch, beaming their joy at her reunion with her father. They all knew how down she'd been and how she'd longed to see him. She didn't know how they'd pulled this off without her knowledge, but at this moment, she didn't care. *My daddy is here! My daddy is in America!*

"Rachel, won't you invite a weary old man inside?" her father implored.

"Yes, yes," she said, stepping back and giving him an impromptu curtsy. "You are so welcome here, kind sir!"

Her family flooded into the living room. Everyone gave Amos embraces, pats on the back. The children were a little shy around him. Joseph remembered his grandfather once he saw his face again.

Fletcher carried his bags upstairs. He and Peter had their work cut out for them today getting everyone rearranged. They wanted Amos to have his own room. Dotty was moving downstairs into Mama and Papa's bedroom. Later today, one of Clyde's helpers was delivering another twin bed that would be used for Dotty. Amos would have her old full-size bed. Dotty's reaction might be difficult, but they would not have her acting like a spoiled brat. Families needed to accommodate each other whenever possible.

Fletcher and the boys had already discussed moving Andrew in with them. The twin babies, Kellen and Kolten, were going to Karen and Peter's room. When their new baby arrived, he'd be in their bedroom. *He? Where had that come from?* They had boys and a girl, so Fletcher hadn't given an inordinate amount of thought as to which one this would be. Had Rachel? *Probably not,* he thought. *Poor thing, she was so miserable.*

Fletcher smiled to himself, remembering that look on his mother's face last fall. He fully expected Amos's arrival, whether anyone else did or not. It was no surprise to him. If women could be president, his mother would be a good candidate. She got things done, even the seemingly impossible!

13

A Sign

Rachel couldn't wait to get out on the front porch and enjoy the beautiful spring day. Her thoughtful father had brought her a book to read. It was written by a lady named Emily Post, and it was called *Etiquette*. Someone had told him it would be a very suitable book to give his daughter. She looked forward to reading it. Maybe it would be helpful to teach her children to always use good manners, Rachel thought.

She opened the book by Emily Post and begin to scan through. It seemed to cover every imaginable topic from which side of the curb a proper man should walk on, to how to correctly make introductions, to how a woman should dress. Yes, she was going to enjoy reading this book.
It was so thoughtful of her dad to get it for her.

Rachel couldn't be happier having her father here with them all. He folded right into their family life. He had gotten a job with the blacksmith. Fletcher had been right. Having a job made him feel like he was contributing to the family. The older children were warming up to him. Dotty adored her new grandpa. She did her best to monopolize his attentions. He'd already attended many a tea party. Rachel smiled, thinking of his big smile and wink at her when determined Dotty would whisk him away.

She and her father had many nice conversations sitting on this front porch. She remembered asking him if he had any regrets about leaving Germany. His eyes had saddened, and he dropped his head. He seemed to steady himself before he replied.

"Rachel, I have something to tell you. Before I left our homeland, I went to your mother's graveside and had a long conversation with her." He glanced over at his daughter, gauging her reaction. "I don't want you to think your old man has gone plum crackers now, but I had to explain to your mom why I wouldn't be able to come visit her grave and talk to her anymore."

Rachel felt tears welling up in her eyes. "Oh, Daddy!"

"There, there now. I don't want you to feel sorry for me. I think I've managed about as well as can be expected. I said my piece to your mom about how I thought it might be time for me to make a change or two." He patted his daughter's hand. "I told her our girl needed me. I mentioned that I wasn't sure what good an old man like me would be but that I felt a calling to come here."

Rachel's tears flowed freely. He had always been such a dear. This decision hadn't been made lightly, she knew.

"It was late in the day. The air was chilly as I knelt there by her grave. The sky had been cloudy all day and looked like it might rain. Now before you start to fret, you'll probably be happy to know that I was the only one doing any talking at your mother's grave. Still, I seemed to sense her presence when I was there, and it comforted me."

"You will always miss Mom, won't you, Dad?"

"Yes, I believe I always will. You don't ever forget your first love. While I was kneeling there, I prayed that somehow I would get a sign that coming to America was the right decision. I know it sounds like something a foolish old man might wish for. A sign, indeed. Then it happened."

"There was a brightening of the sky, and from out of the blue, a single turtledove flew down and sat on the tombstone behind your mother's. She began to sing her sad, mournful tune. She looked straight at me and didn't seem a bit frightened. I kept real still. I'm not even sure I breathed. Then she flew up to the limb of the big tree beside your mother's grave. She kept her eyes on me. She sang the sweetest song I'd ever heard and then flew off. I took that as a sign that Katherine was giving me permission to leave."

She knew that probably a day didn't go by that her dad didn't miss her mom. He kept busy with his work, helping the men around the house, hunting and playing with the grandchildren. He seemed much more relaxed, but occasionally he'd get a distant look in his eyes. Rachel knew that his mind had journeyed back to that little graveside far, far away, and most likely, he still had conversations with his bride.

At their last talk on the porch, Amos told her, "Rachel, my dear, I love being here with you and the children. I'm thankful that Fletcher turned out to be the man I thought he would become. It does my heart good to know that you are so loved. I think that young man loves you almost as much as I loved your mother."

Rachel rubbed her huge belly. *Only a couple more weeks till my due date*, she thought. "Dad, we've had a wonderful life together so far. He is a good man and an excellent father to our children. They respect him and know they'd better mind him, and they deeply love him," Rachel told him.

14

More to Love!

Rachel sat swinging with her feet barely touching the floor of the porch. Dotty and the other children were running around the yard. The boys were trying to talk their dad into taking them fishing. Karen and Mama were weeding the garden. Peter and Papa were building an addition on the barn. Her dad was at work. Such a pleasant day! The gentle rocking motion made her eyelids grow heavier and heavier. Soon, Rachel drifted off to sleep.

She was suddenly jolted wide awake by a sharp contraction. She'd had the normal warning signs that her time was getting close—the tiredness and inability to sleep comfortably—but this morning, she had felt energetic. She'd sorted through the children's clothes, pulled many garments out to pack away, made mental notes about new items the children would need, did a little mending, and carried a handful to the washroom out back.

This was it.

The sudden burst of energy should've prepared her. She tried to stand but immediately felt another contraction ten minutes after the first one. When it passed, she stood and felt hot fluid running down her leg.

Oh no, not today. I'm not ready yet. I wanted to clean the kids' rooms, pick up material at the store, plan a few sewing projects. She was supposed to still have a little more time!

"Fletcher," she yelled, "the baby's coming!"

He was at her side in a flash. "Are you sure, Rach? Isn't it too soon?"

Rachel grinned, but it looked more like a grimace as another contraction started up. "I guess this baby doesn't think so."

Fletcher looked out at the two women standing in the garden looking his way.

Mama called out, "Is everything all right, Fletch?"

"No—well, yes, but the baby's coming! Rachel's in labor. I need to go get the midwife."

Karen shouted, "Fletcher, you stay with Rachel. I'll send Peter to get her."

Mama reached the porch and was out of breath. "Rachel, honey, how are you doing?" She touched her shoulder. Her hands were sweaty from the cotton gloves she'd been weeding in. She noticed the beads of perspiration on Rachel's brow.

"I'm okay, but I'm in a lot of pain. How come you never get used to this whole labor —oh me!" She tried her best to make herself relax as the next contraction spiraled inside her. "I didn't even have the luxury of false labor this time," she said breathlessly, "just this sudden onset."

Mama noticed the mixture of blood and fluid that had pooled on the porch. She didn't like the looks of that much blood so soon, but of course, this was not her area of expertise.

"Fletcher, Rachel cannot go up those steps. Take her in mine and your dad's room. I'll put old blankets on the bed. She'll have the baby in there. Go upstairs and get one of her nightgowns. I'll help her change."

Out of the corner of her eye, she saw Peter hitching the horse to the carriage. Karen was walking quickly back toward the porch. The children were all standing at the bottom of the steps, looking worried but not saying a word. "Now you kids go on and play. Behave yourselves. Sometimes having a baby takes hours or even all day. It just depends. Uncle Peter is going for the midwife to help your mother. I'm going to fix dinner in a little while. I'll call you when it's ready," Mama told them.

"Mama, I'm the oldest. What can I do? I want to help," said Joseph.

Mama tousled his hair. "There's nothing you can do right now unless you and your brother want to help finish weeding the garden. I declare there will still be weeds to worry about when you've got nothing else to worry about," Mama told him.

"We'll do it. Come on, Arwood, it won't take us long to do that, then we'll throw the ball again," said Joseph. The boys raced toward the garden to see who could get there first. Joseph was the tallest and had the longest legs, but Arwood was fast. Everything was a competition with the brothers.

Karen went in to help with Rachel. Mama was helping her get out of her clothes. "Karen, Fletcher is always an emotional mess when Rachel goes into labor. He has brought down her nicest gown, this little pink satin number. I didn't want to say anything, but this is not what we need right now." Mama laughed. "In fact"—she winked at Rachel—"it might just be the start of all this trouble."

"Oh, Mama!" Rachel attempted a smile but got hammered at that moment by another crushing contraction.

"Hurry, Karen, go get us something more practical to put on Rachel," said Mama.

"I'll be right back, Rachel. If I don't see anything, I'll bring you one of mine. They're all practical, unfortunately." The ladies all enjoyed a big laugh.

Hilda made a mental note to tell Peter to get Karen a nice peignoir set this Christmas to surprise her. Girls their age needed impractical things like that. She knew the Sears catalog carried them. *I'm too old to worry about such frivolities. Of course, calling the bedclothes that fancy name made them pricier too.*

Karen returned with one of Rachel's old gowns. It had been worn soft and thin from repeated washings. "Rachel, let me help you with this."

"I feel like I'm in a recurring dream here," said Karen. "Haven't you and I been through all this before, sometime long ago and in a distant land?"

"Yes, Karen, I believe we have. At least this time I won't have to tell you what to do now you are 'experienced,' as Mrs. Meyer would say," said Rachel as another contraction swept over her. "Karen, don't these pains seem awfully close together?"

"Yes, they do, Rachel, but you've had several children, I guess your body has gotten more efficient at this birthing thing," Karen soothed her and wiped her brow with the cool well water Mama had brought in.

"I don't know about that," said Rachel. "Every one of my children's births were as completely different as my children. My back is killing me with this one."

"Let me help you turn on your side, and I will rub it for you. We'll see if that helps, probably can't hurt," said Karen as she gently helped Rachel shift her weight to her side.

Mama had gone out to clean up the front porch and wipe up the fluid drops from the hardwood floors. She stopped in her chore long enough to offer up a prayer for Rachel and this impatient new grandchild about to make its appearance at their house. John came in and noticed her kneeling in the middle of the living room. "Are you okay, Hilda?" he said as he quickly crossed the wooden floors. "I'm all right, John, just cleaning up the floor. I thought while I was on my knees, I'd ask our Heavenly Father to take care of our girl and this new baby," said Hilda.

"Yes, I've been praying the same thing. She's a little earlier than they thought, isn't she? I remember Karen's twins came early, and she ended up in the hospital. Do you think Rachel is going to be okay?" he asked again, still uncertain.

"I'd feel better if that midwife would get here. How long has Peter been gone?" asked Hilda.

"Hilda, it hasn't even been an hour yet. He probably had to find her. Where is Fletcher?" asked John.

"I chased him out while we got Rachel situated in our room. I saw him walking out the driveway when I came out to clean the porch. I guess he is watching for Peter and the midwife to get here. He's worried about Rachel," said Hilda.

"Well, that's understandable, I guess," said John as he walked over to the window to peer outside.

They both looked up as they heard their bedroom door open. Karen looked pale as a ghost.

"What is it, Karen? How is Rachel doing?"

"She's in a great deal of pain, more so than I've ever seen her go through in childbirth. She nearly fainted from the last couple of labor pains. I think we'd better get everything ready in case I have to deliver this one too," Karen said, feeling none too sure of herself. "Papa, I think you better go into town and bring the doctor back here. I can't be counted on if anything goes wrong. My experience is very limited."

Papa grabbed his hat. "I'm going to get Fletcher to ride in with me. Hopefully, we'll pass Peter and the midwife on the way."

Mama noticed that Karen was shaking like a leaf. She put her arms around her to comfort her. "Now relax, Karen. You're going to do fine. Papa and I've asked the good Lord to protect Rachel and this new baby." She took Karen by her hands, which were damp with anxiety. "Now we're going to ask Him to strengthen you for this task. He has you here at this very moment for a reason. Just trust Him, Karen."

The two women prayed together as tears streamed down both their faces. Karen wiped her eyes and steeled herself to go back to help Rachel. She did feel more peaceful, somehow calmer.

Good, she thought, *I don't want to alarm Rachel.*

Rachel was soaking wet from the exertion of labor. "Karen, thank God you're back. I was afraid you'd thrown in the towel," said Rachel. "Do you think everything is going the way it should?" She searched Karen's face.

Karen took Rachel's hand. "Of course, you know I don't have any medical training, only what you and Mrs. Meyer taught me. I think I remember most of it. I stepped out to ask Papa to take Fletcher and go get the doctor too, just in case, especially since this is all happening a bit sooner than you thought it should. If we don't need him, we'll give him dinner and take him back to town."

The door opened again, and Mama rushed in. "Karen, here comes Peter with the midwife. You run on out and meet them and let her know how things are going with our Rachel." She smiled reassuringly at Rachel. "Don't worry, dear, I'll stay and keep you company."

Mama took Rachel's hand as the next pain took hold. Rachel squeezed Mama's hand hard. Even though she was certain it cut off the circulation momentarily, Mama kept the same sweet smile on her face and continued to speak soothing words to her laboring daughter-in-law.

The midwife knocked gently on the door and let herself inside. She was towel drying her just-washed hands. Karen came in with her. She introduced herself to Rachel as Miss Carroll. She enlisted Mama to gather supplies for her and prepare the water to sterilize her equipment. Relieved that the woman was here, Mama hurried out to do what she could to help.

Miss Carroll quickly approached Rachel. She took her vitals and asked her a few general questions about her labor so far. She told Rachel that she was going to need to examine her to see how far her labor had progressed. She was well aware that sometimes the amount of pain the mother endured didn't always equal readiness for delivery.

Getting right to work, she quickly assessed the situation. Rachel was almost fully dilated. She didn't like what she saw. The child appeared to be breech, buttocks first and facing its mother's right thigh. On a positive note, the infant didn't appear to be oversized as they had all worried.

In fact, the baby appeared to be on the smallish side. Still the midwife worried about the umbilical cord becoming constricted with the baby in this position. The problem was that if that happened, it could affect the oxygen supply.

"Rachel, this is going to be a bit more challenging than we anticipated. I have good news, though. The baby is smaller than we expected. Your child is upside down. We normally prefer to deliver the head first, not the bottom. Also, you have a narrow birth canal. We're going to have to work around these obstacles."

Rachel endured yet another contraction. "I feel like I need to push now!"

"I don't want you pushing yet, Rachel. Concentrate on something difficult. For me, counting backwards from one thousand is hard. I don't know why, but it is. Try that, but don't panic on me. We'll get you through this. Now excuse me while we get everything ready. Karen, please come with me."

Both women left the room.

"Karen, it is very important that we get the doctor here right away. He may need to perform an emergency Caesarean section surgery. We cannot transport her to the hospital at this point. It's possible he will have to use forceps to turn the baby. I have that equipment but admit I'm reluctant to use them in Rachel's situation. The baby is not in distress yet, but I am concerned about its oxygen supply."

"Oh my god," wailed Karen. "Give me your equipment.

I'll sterilize and pray hard."

"We should all be praying. It is very important that we don't upset Rachel. Our primary job is to keep her as calm as possible," said Miss Carroll.

Mama immediately sensed that something was amiss when she saw Karen and the midwife talking quietly in the kitchen. She'd just come in from standing on the front porch, watching for John, Fletcher, and the doctor as if her watching would make them appear any faster.

Karen tearfully explained to Mama what was going on. Mama looked shocked. Karen feared Mama might faint. "Here, you sit down. All we can do is pray and keep Rachel as calm as we can until the doctor arrives. Miss Carroll has a plan in case things start happening faster than anticipated."

To all three women's relief, the front door opened, and in stepped the good doctor. He immediately took control of the situation. He pulled Miss Carroll aside and asked for a summary update as he scrubbed up. He asked her to accompany him to the patient's room. He gave Karen his scalpel and other instruments to sterilize. He asked her to place a clean towel on a platter and use another clean towel to deposit the instruments onto the platter. When they were ready, she was to immediately bring them to him. No one else was to enter the room. Karen was to leave as soon as she brought the instruments in. She hurried to carry out his instructions to the letter. She was relieved and praising God that the doctor was there with them.

The doctor went in and spoke gently to Rachel and patted her on the arm. His experience told him that the mother was near the end of her endurance. "Young lady, I understand you need a little help with this baby? You've done great. I'm going to check your vitals again before we get started. You hang in there."

Talking to Miss Carroll, he said, "BP is slightly elevated, but given the situation, it's expected."

"Rachel, I'm going to give you a little painkiller now to help ease your discomfort. It won't harm your baby. We're going to get busy and try to take care of this little person and you. I'm going to examine you now. Miss Carroll has agreed to assist me. Any questions?"

Rachel shook her head no. She felt very weak. The doctor filled the needle and gave her an injection. He asked Rachel to tell him what she was going to name the baby. She appeared to be collecting her thoughts. She opened her mouth to speak, but then her face relaxed as the medicine took hold.

He began his examination and agreed with the midwife's assessment. "Great, the umbilical cord doesn't appear pinched. I think we can carefully turn the baby with the forceps. Like you, I'm glad to see that the child is small. This mother has had multiple healthy births. That will make our job a little easier."

Karen came in bringing the instruments as requested. She looked at her laboring friend, touched her shoulder, and then quickly left the room.

It took much more effort than anticipated, but at last the baby turned. The doctor listened with his stethoscope.

Everything seemed normal, but there was almost an echo with the heartbeat. Together, they delivered a petite baby girl with damp reddish-blonde hair. She looked like a little princess. He clamped off the umbilical cord and handed the baby to the midwife to clean up.

The doctor was preparing to stitch the mother when he felt something—another baby's head! "Oh man, what is it with these Broce women? We have undisclosed twins. Luckily, this one is in the right position. Turning the first baby might have gotten this one turned around too. Amazing!"

Five minutes later, another strawberry-blonde female infant made her appearance. Rachel's medication was wearing off, but she thought she was seeing double. She focused on the doctor, only one of him, just one Miss Carroll, but two reddish blonde little babies. She blinked and tried to focus again. The doctor noticed Rachel's reaction and laughed out loud.

Outside the door, in the living room, the crowd gathered there included Fletcher, Karen, Peter, Amos, Mama, and Papa. They all heard the doctor's laughter ring out. The tension in the room evaporated. Karen spoke first, "Fletcher, it must be okay. The doctor should be out in a minute to tell us what you and Rachel had."

Fletcher had never been a nail-biter, but he had worn all his nails down to the nub from the stress of the situation. He was on his feet, his eyes glued to the bedroom door. Mama went over and rubbed his back. "Relax, son, the good Lord took care of them for us. I'm going to put on a pot of coffee. Karen, can you ask the kids to get cleaned up and come on in. Tell them they have to be quiet."

About thirty minutes later, the bedroom door opened. Everyone held their breath. The doctor stepped out. His eyes danced merrily and somewhat mischievously. "Fletcher, could you join us for a minute?"

Fletcher practically ran into the room. He couldn't wait to see Rachel and their new baby. His nerves were raw from worry. When he stepped into the room, the doctor quietly closed the door. He couldn't wait to see this dad's expression when he got the news.

Fletcher didn't disappoint the doctor. He looked at his wife and had to do a double take.

There are two babies! What on earth is going on around here? Another set of twins? But we didn't know we were having twins!

Rachel smiled at her husband's funny face.

The poor man is in shock, she thought. "Fletcher, darling, come over here and meet your new daughters. I know, I was as surprised as you are."

Fletcher stuttered, "But, but...how did this happen?"

Everyone laughed at his befuddlement. The doctor patted him on the back. "You, my good man, are doubly blessed today. Miss Carroll and I are going to step out of the room and give you a moment. Don't worry, we aren't making any announcements. We'll leave that up to you two. We'll let your family know that everyone is fine. I'll need to know their names, so you might talk that over if you can't think of anything else to talk about."

When they left the room, Fletcher went over to Rachel and kissed her gently. She looked exhausted but happy. He was glad to see that. "I had to have stitches this time, Fletcher. The doctor doesn't want me trying to carry them both at once for about a month. Isn't that funny since I've carried them for almost nine months?" Rachel smiled weakly at him.

Both babies were sleeping peacefully so he couldn't see their eyes yet.

"What color are their eyes, Rachel? Can I hold them?"

"They look hazel like Joseph's, but the doctor said the color could change. Isn't that funny? Oh, Fletcher, aren't they beautiful and so dainty?" Rachel asked him.

"They are so small. They look smaller than Kellen and Kolten did when they were born, but then they're girls. I guess that's to be expected."

"What do you think of the names Ruth and Ruby, Fletcher?"

"I like those names. Do you think they will look alike when they grow up?"

"I don't know. They are identical now. I'm sure each will develop her own personality traits. I hope we can tell them apart."

Rachel giggled, still feeling a little fuzzy headed from the medicine.

Fletcher kissed Rachel again. "Don't worry, we'll figure it out as we go, just like Karen and Peter had to. Let's unwrap them and take a good look at our little daughters to see if we can find any distinguishing features." They admired the tiny sleeping forms that seemed perfect in every way. They noticed that one of the infants had a faint red birthmark on her side. That helped them decide on her name.

"I can't wait to see our other children's reaction. Let's bring them in first. Is that rude? I want them to be a part of this special moment with us. Why don't we let them make the announcement to everyone else?" said Rachel.

"That's a perfect plan. Here, I'm going to lay them down beside you again while I go get the children. Dotty is the only one I'm worried about. She is our little green-eyed monster with blue eyes," said Fletcher, smiling.

Fletcher stepped out into the living room and surveyed the much-relaxed faces seated there having their coffee and chatting easily. "Sorry, folks, but Rachel wants our children to come in first."

Joseph and Arwood lined up in front of their dad. Dotty ran past him and into the room with her mommy. Fletcher quickly ushered the boys inside before Dotty let the cat out of the bag.

"Mommy, why do you have two babies? Is one of them Karen's or Miss Carroll's?" four-year-old Dotty wanted to know.

Rachel and Fletcher's laughed. "No, sweetie, they are both our babies and your new sisters."

"Just like Kolten and Kellen," Joseph complained. "Why does our family keep having two babies? I don't know anyone else that has two babies."

"The doctor told your mother and me that our family is doubly blessed. I think he's right," said Fletcher.

"They're really cute for girls. I'm just glad we were only blessed one time with Dotty. She is too bossy," moaned Arwood.

Dotty stuck her tongue out at him, crossed her arms, and pouted her pretty little lips. "I don't like you, Arwood!" she said and stamped her foot for emphasis.

Fletcher bent down to her level. "Now, Dotty, that wasn't very kind of you, or you, Arwood. I want you to apologize to each other."

They grudgingly obeyed their father while their older brother, Joseph, rolled his eyes.

Rachel and Fletcher smiled at each other. Rachel told them, "Your father and I've decided to name your little sisters Ruth and Ruby."

"Which one is Ruby?" asked Arwood.

"This one on the left is Ruby. She has a tiny little birthmark on the right side of her tummy. See, it looks like a little red stone. The funny thing is, we picked the names out before we discovered the little marking," Rachel told them.

"I think they're ugly," said the petulant Dotty. "Why are they so red and wrinkly?"

"That will go away soon," her mother assured her. Dotty didn't look at all impressed. Rachel had to laugh at her crabby little girl. "Come over here and give Mommy a hug, all you kids. We love every one of you. We're so happy to share these newest members of our family with you."

The children hugged their mom and dad. Joseph and Arwood gently kissed their new little sisters. Dotty made a face and backed away from them.

Fletcher told the children, "Now your mother and I need your help. We want you to announce your sisters to the rest of the family. Here's the plan. Dotty, you go first. When we open the door, you run out and announce that Mommy and Daddy have two babies. Next, Arwood, you go out and tell everyone that both the babies are girls and look just alike. Then finally,

Joseph, you go and tell them the babies' names. You can tell them how we know which one is Ruby if you want to. Ready, set, go!"

Dotty was out the door in a flash with her announcement, and the others followed in rapid succession. Fletcher followed the children, carrying the two babies with an enormous smile on his face. Everyone gathered around and congratulated them. He explained that the doctor wanted Rachel on bed rest for a couple of days due to her stitches. Mama and Papa could sleep in Fletcher and Rachel's room until they could move her upstairs.

Amos came forward to look at the new babies. "They are beautiful, Fletcher. Is it okay to go back and see Rachel?

I've been so worried about my girl."

"Certainly, everyone can go in and see her. Might be best if you went a couple at a time so it doesn't overwhelm her," Fletcher told them. "She's had quite an ordeal today. She is very weak and tired."

Everyone understood. They, too, were tired from the stress of waiting and worrying. What wonderful news they'd received in the form of two special and healthy little newborns and a recovering mother.

Lightning Strikes Twice

Amos enjoyed going to church with his daughter and her expansive family. He surveyed the three pews the family occupied. On the front pew sat John, Hilda, Joseph, Arwood, and Andrew. The next pew contained Peter, Karen, Kolten, and Kellen. Fletcher, Rachel, and the twins Ruby and Ruth, five-year-old Dotty, and he were seated in the third pew. Directly behind them was Fletcher's friend Clyde, his wife Clarisse, their children Ada and Ambrose, and Clarisse's mother Agnes.

Amos was learning more faces and names as he went along. Over the course of six months, he knew most of the church folk at least by their first name. There were older couples, young couples, teens, and lots of children. He and Clarisse's mother, Agnes, were among the oldest of the unmarried congregants.

He happened to sit directly in front of Agnes. He thought she sang like an angel. His voice was passable, but he often sang low so he could hear her sing the beautiful old hymns that were universal in their appeal. To be such a small church, about fifty in attendance, they were blessed to have a number of talented singers. He didn't count himself in that number.

Hilda had been practicing with Fletcher, Peter, and himself to perform special music this morning. She played the piano at home and tried her best to keep them all in tune. They would be singing, "Every Hour for Jesus." Hilda made them practice the song over and over until they could sing without the hymnal. She didn't want them looking down all the time. If they were looking out at the congregation, she told them, their voices would project better.

He didn't know how he had gotten talked into singing with this quartet. Suffice it to say, Hilda could be very persuasive. Amos was nervous this morning. He'd never sung in public before. Fortunately, the other men had nice, strong voices. He would try his best to harmonize. Fletcher was their lead singer. The sweet refrain drifted through his mind.

Every hour for the Lord,
Every hour for the Lord let us spend;
Every hour for Jesus till He comes again,
When the labor of life shall end.

Soon they reached the part of the program where it was their turn to sing. Hilda announced them as the Long Shop Singers. Everyone clapped.

Prematurely, Amos thought, *This is our debut performance. Ha, it might be our last one too.*

The men's quartet rose from their seats and went to the front of the church. Hilda began to play the opening notes on the piano.

Hilda said that if you got nervous, pick a person or spot to look at and don't pay any attention to the rest of the crowd. Amos looked around at all the faces. His eyes met Agnes's. She flashed him a bright smile and did a silent clapping motion with her hands to the beat of the music. Well, he'd just look at Agnes, he decided. A few minutes later, they had finished the song. Once it got started, Amos's nerves settled, and by the end, he was actually enjoying himself. The congregation clapped again, and there were even a few whistles. When Amos returned to his seat, Agnes patted him on the shoulder and nodded her approval.

After the service, as they were exiting the building, she told him how much she enjoyed their singing. Amos said modestly, "At least we didn't embarrass ourselves too much."

"That was a lovely hymn. I'm not familiar with the song, but it was very catchy and had a good message too." Agnes smiled at him. "If I find myself humming it all week, I'll blame you."

"Don't worry, if Hilda has her way, she'll have us working on another song for next month. You are the one who should be up front singing. You have a beautiful voice."

Agnes blushed and told Amos, "I don't have any formal training. I'm a simple farm lady, but I do enjoy singing. My life has had many ups and downs. Singing has always helped me forget my troubles."

"Well then, maybe I should try it more often if it's an elixir for troubles," said Amos.

Over the next several months, their casual conversations continued, and their friendship grew. Amos thought Agnes was an interesting lady. He wanted to get to know her better, but it was difficult to do so without arousing the curiosity of his family. He pondered how he could spend a little time with her without everyone reading too much into their friendship. He'd never had a woman "friend." His interest was not what he would call *romantic*, just curious. This was uncharted territory for him.

He found himself looking forward to seeing Agnes on Sunday mornings and chatting a bit about their week and upcoming activities. Maybe his daughter, Rachel, would be a good one to talk to about this new *friendship*.

When Amos got up for breakfast the next morning, Rachel was in the kitchen making coffee and preparing to scramble eggs. They had the kitchen to themselves. "What are you doing up so early, child?"

"I got up to fix Fletcher's breakfast and lunch pail, then couldn't go back to sleep. The babies woke up. It's hard to believe the girls are five months old now. They have the sweetest dispositions. I nursed them and put them back down for a nap. After all that, I'm wide awake, and the sun is starting to come up."

"It's a nice October morning. We won't get too many of these. Let's grab a cup of coffee and have our breakfast together on the front porch. You take your coffee and go on out. I'll take care of breakfast this morning to give you a break." Her dad smiled at her.

A while later, he opened the front screen door with his elbow. He carried out two scrambled egg sandwiches and joined her on the swing. The sun was rising in the east. It was a little cool for Rachel, and she had pulled a lap quilt around her shoulders. "Thanks, Dad, this is nice."

"I'm glad we've got a little quiet time to ourselves. That's hard to come by in this busy house. It's hard for me sometimes to imagine my only child in this role, with so many children and living with so many other people. How do you do it?"

"Oh, Dad, I love being surrounded by so much family. We laugh and cry with each other, are there for each other, work and play together. I can hardly imagine my life any other way. Maybe growing up as an only child is what makes this all the more special to me."

"Yes, I guess our existence must've been lonely for you growing up," her father admitted. "It had to be hard on a child having so much responsibility at such an early age. I know I counted on you, probably too much."

"Dad, please understand I wasn't unhappy, and I'm not complaining. That's all I ever knew. We made so many precious memories together, but it is definitely a different dynamic being part of a big family. Of course it has its challenges too, especially the lack of privacy, at times."

"Rachel, I appreciate everyone's hospitality and friendship here, but I wonder if I wouldn't be happier in my own little place. Do you think John and Hilda would take it the wrong way if I were to move out?"

"I can see where all our activity could take some getting used to. I want you to be happy." She patted his weathered hand. "I'll speak to them if you'd like."

"Please do. Make sure they understand I'm used to a quieter pace. I've been looking for a small two- to three room house to rent. There's a little place between here and town that has become available. The old gentleman who used to live there died. I thought I might go see it. Would you like to come with me?"

"Yes, I'd love to. Just let me know when you want to go so I can make arrangements for someone to look after the children. Can you believe Fletcher and I have five children now?"

"Yes, I can. You've always had a nurturing spirit. I'm thankful God has blessed you with so many young lives to care for. He knows they're in good hands. Let's plan for Wednesday evening. It's fine for Fletcher to come too if he'd like."

"It may just be me. He's putting in such long hours at the mine now. He's exhausted when he gets home. Fletcher feels like he needs to help with the chores around here too. He makes good money now, nearly three dollars a day."

"Yes, he has always been a good provider and never been afraid of putting in a full day's work either." Amos paused and looked at her. "Rachel, there's one more kind of sensitive thing I'd like to talk with you about. I need you to keep this confidential, if you will."

Rachel lowered her coffee cup and gave her father her full attention. "What is it, Dad? I won't speak of it to anyone else. Is everything okay?"

Amos cleared his throat before proceeding. "Rachel, I think I may have *feelings* for Agnes. I don't know how to describe those feelings. They aren't the same as the feelings I had for your mother, but I am interested in her. She cheers my old soul, and I like being around her. I don't know if our friendship will ever amount to anything, but I want to find out." He let out a big sigh. "There, I got it out."

Rachel watched her dad's face carefully. She was speechless. She certainly didn't see that coming. Maybe he was just lonely?

"I've shocked you, haven't I? Rachel, I'm nearly sixty-five years old now. I loved your mother with my whole being. She has been gone for eight years. I've missed her so much that my heart has physically ached. I never expected to be interested in another woman in my lifetime. I haven't spoken to Agnes other than in a social way. She might not be interested in a rough old fellow like me. Who knows?"

Tears were streaming down Rachel's face. She knew how hard this conversation had to be for her father. He looked wracked with guilt…and hope? It would be good if he could find a nice lady to spend the rest of his years with. She didn't know Agnes very well, but she seemed pleasant enough.

Rachel gave her dad a hug. "Dad, I think you should talk to Agnes and get to know her better. Maybe she is part of the reason the Lord brought you to America. She shares our heritage and our faith. It would be wonderful for you to have someone closer to your own age to share things with."

"I suspect she is about eight to ten years younger than me. I plan to take it slow and just see where it goes. To tell you the truth, it is right scary for me to think about courting at my age."

"Dad, you're such a gentleman. How could any woman not appreciate your attention? I'm happy for you. I've often worried about you leading such a lonely life." Rachel hugged her father.

He'd lost track of time while they were talking. Amos had to hustle to get to work on time.

They looked at the little frame house that Wednesday evening. Rachel thought it was perfect for her dad. It was neat as a pin and had been freshly painted. It was also only about a mile down the road from his new heartthrob, Agnes.

He gave the man the first month's rent of eight dollars to hold it for him.

With Rachel's help, they let the family know that he would be moving to his own place over the weekend. Everyone was happy for him and wished him all the best. He smiled gratefully at his daughter for helping make this transition a smooth one.

In the spring of 1925, Amos went over to Clyde's house and asked him if he might have a word with him in private. Clyde looked puzzled, but he and Amos started toward his workshop.

A small commotion in the farmyard caught Amos's attention. He couldn't believe it. There was the dainty little Agnes wringing a chicken's neck. Amos was taken aback. He had never seen a woman do such a thing, and it sickened him.

"What did you want to talk about, Amos? Do you need furniture for your new place? I can send one of the men by to take measurements if you'd like," said Clyde.

Amos didn't answer. He was still watching Agnes taking the chicken toward the house. "Would you like to stay for dinner? As you can see, we're having chicken," Clyde added with a smile.

"No, that's okay. Thank you. I have a little pot of soup simmering, nothing fancy. I've never seen a woman wring a chicken's neck before. I used to chop their heads off. That was a bloody mess with the bird's headless body running all over the yard. You know that's where the expression 'running around like a chicken with its head cut off' came from, right?" asked Amos, still peering toward the house.

"Amos, I'm not able to do as much to help the family around our little farm because of my condition. Everyone has to pitch in and do their part. Killing the chicken that way is easier for the women. It's not anything new. Are you all right? You paled a little there."

Amos pulled himself together and looked directly at Clyde. "Son, if your mother-in-law will have me, I'd like to ask her to marry me. I'd be honored to have your blessing before I ask her."

Clyde looked at the kindly old gentleman waiting patiently in front of him for a response. He appreciated the honor-bound tradition of asking for a woman's hand. He was tempted to tease Amos about the chicken neckwringing incident but knew that would be inappropriate given the solemnity of the occasion.

He propelled his wheelchair around to face Amos. He extended his arm to shake Amos's hand. "We'd be honored to have you become a part of our family. Good luck, man. We will miss our cook if she says yes, but you will get a real jewel of a lady."

Agnes said yes, and Amos slipped a dainty new engagement ring on her finger. He gently kissed her lips for the very first time.

They set a June wedding date and agreed to be married in the church they attended together. Amos picked her up in his two-seat horse and buggy the next day, and they went down to Long Shop to officially break the news to his daughter and her family.

To Amos's surprise, no one else was shocked at their announcement. They'd all watched the little romance budding since the early days when the couple had met. Hilda had predicted wedding bells to John nearly a year before. John hadn't paid her any mind because well, she was always predicting things.

Come to think of it, most of them came true too, thought John.

16

Polecat Poultice

In the winter of 1925, it seemed like everyone in the house had a cold, was getting a cold, or getting over a cold. Both Karen and Rachel were coughing their heads off, and even Papa was starting to sniffle. The boys had recovered from their colds. At the grocery store, Hilda talked to a dear older lady who told her about an old mountain remedy that her mother had used successfully to cure the common cold. Hilda thought it sounded a little bizarre, but at this rate, she was willing to try anything. The lady called it a polecat poultice. She laughed when Hilda looked confused.

When Hilda asked what a polecat was, everyone within hearing range laughed. She didn't know what was so funny and was a bit taken aback at being laughed at. Finally, someone pulled her aside and said, "Honey, it ain't nothing but a plain, long, old skunk, what we call the garden variety. People around here call it a polecat."

"But does that poultice work to cure a cold, or is it just a joke?" Hilda seriously wanted to know.

"I've never made or used it, but I've heard about it all my life. I know there are people who swear by it. I guess it might work if you can stand the smell." She chuckled. "I think I'd rather let the cold run its course than put up with that stink. Can you imagine?" The kind lady laughed and shook her head.

The recipe seemed simple enough. Different people had chimed in about how their family used "the cure." Many said they put a few drops of the pure skunk oil onto a teaspoon with sugar and took it orally. They admitted it tasted terrible. Others described using the oil more like a poultice or a chest rub. For that, the extracted oil was mixed with lard and a little kerosene or turpentine. Then it was simply a matter of keeping the sick person's room as warm as possible and adding the rub to their chest. Usually, after a couple of days, the cold was better.

Hilda thought, *Well, what can it hurt? If it works, it would be worth the trouble and the smell!*

The first order of business was to get a skunk. Her oldest grandson had started hunting with the men. Since the men were all working late tonight, she'd get Joseph to try to kill one for her after dinner. She chuckled to herself. Her family would think she'd lost her mind. Maybe she had, but she was desperate! She didn't want the younger children getting sick too.

Of course, her grandson knew exactly where to find a skunk. While hunting in the woods behind their house, he'd seen skunks coming out of a big hollow log. He thought that might be their home. She warned him and his brother to be careful not to get sprayed. Joseph and Arwood thought this would be a grand adventure. She gave them an old sack to carry the creature home in. They returned with their prey a couple of hours later. Mama had been worried about them being in the woods so long.

Of course, the animal stunk. *What a job!* She dreaded getting this thing skinned and disemboweled. Then she had to cook it.

Oh, mercy me, thought Hilda as she sat on the back stoop working on the animal. Even in the open air, the odor was horrible. She put the black-and-white fur and entrails in the sack and had the boys carry it off into the woods and bury it. She put the fatty layer, which was beneath the fur, and the rest of the meat in her metal pot and took it inside to cook. She had to raise the kitchen windows so she wouldn't pass out from the stench.

She certainly hoped those ladies hadn't been pulling her leg about this remedy. This was a lot of trouble for a gag. Mama waited for the boys to get back. She had them wash up and go to bed. She decided the easiest way to get the grease from the creature would be to boil it and let it cool. The fat should rise to the top after it cooled, and she could skim it off. She put it on to boil and threw in a little garlic in to help with the smell. She went into the other room and folded the clothes she had carried in from the clothesline.

When she got back to the kitchen, the *meat* looked done. Hilda removed the bones and threw them in the trash. She wasn't sure about letting the dogs have the bones. She put the lid on the pot and put the meat in her ice chest to cool. It had been a long day, so she decided to turn in. John thought he might be coming down with a cold too. He had gone to bed right after supper to try to get his rest because he wanted to go hunting with his sons before daylight in the morning. Hilda had sworn the grandsons to secrecy about their mission. She hadn't told her husband anything about her big scheme to cure them all.

Early the next morning, when Hilda woke up, she went down to the kitchen. The men had left the house hours before. She had meant to pack a lunch for them, but it completely slipped her mind with all the excitement over the polecat poultice preparation. *Oh well, they'll make out this time*, she thought. The boys had wanted to go too. The men had told them they had to stay home this time to help with the farm chores. Papa promised to take them next time.

When Hilda got to the stove to start breakfast, she nearly dropped the basket of eggs in her hands. What was going on? There was that pot she'd put in the icebox last night sitting on the sink! The meat was all gone, but at least the broth was still there. *Oh well, the men must've thrown the meat out to the dogs*, she thought.

She skimmed the fatty oil from the top of the water and placed it in a canning jar. She added the turpentine and lard as instructed until it had a salve consistency. It still reeked of skunk. *The turpentine helps the smell a little, very little*, thought Hilda. She decided they would give it a trial run tonight and see if it worked, as advertised. She still couldn't help but feel a little foolish.

Hilda kept busy with her housework and cooking. She had an enjoyable day talking with her grandsons and playing with her granddaughters. It was nice and warm in the house, thanks to the fireplace in the living room and the big cookstove in the kitchen. About midafternoon, the men returned. Peter had shot a deer, and they were going to work on it. They were all cold and hungry. She heated up the soup and gave them each a hunk of bread along with hot coffee.

John came into the room and sat down at the table with his boys. "Hilda, what kind of meat was that you left in the icebox for us? We made sandwiches and put mustard on it. It was some kind of good, but had a funny smell. In fact, so did the whole house, for whatever reason. We figured there must've been a skunk out on the front porch this morning."

Hilda dropped Fletcher's bowl of soup to the floor with a loud crash. She feared she might faint. They hurried to her side.

"Mom, are you all right? What's wrong?"

She quickly recovered and then started laughing hysterically. She tried to tell them what was funny, but every time she opened her mouth, only laughter came out. She pointed at them and at the pot sitting in the kitchen sink. She'd scrubbed it a dozen times today to chase away the skunk's scent. Finally, she managed to get the whole story out. The three men sitting at her kitchen table looked a little green around the gills at first, and then they too joined her laughing at the thought of their delicious *skunk* sandwich.

That night, John, Rachel and Karen received their polecat poultice. In a matter of days, they all felt better and were completely over their colds. Of course, the whole house smelled terrible for about a week.

17

Hilda's Christmas Surprise!

What on earth is keeping Papa? He and Peter left for town over three hours ago, Mama fretted. It was a sunny but blustery December day. She and the grandchildren had made plans to go look for their Christmas tree later this afternoon. Of course, that meant she needed Papa or Peter to help them get it home. She knew Papa had work to do at the farm. She needed Peter back home to finish his chores so one of them was available. Papa would probably be too tired. Well, there was always Peter.

Lord knows they had plenty of pretty cedar trees to choose from. She preferred the little pine trees to the cedar, but everyone loved the woodsy cedar aroma wafting through the house. With its sharp, needlelike branches, it was hard to decorate without pricking yourself.

It was hard to believe that 1925 was almost over and they were thinking about Christmas, already. Papa's farm was flourishing. The men had smoked two big hogs that year. She had plenty of sausage canned. She had pickled pig's feet in the big crock in the corner of the kitchen. Rachel and Karen thought they stunk, but she and John loved them. *What is wrong with those young ladies anyway, not liking pickled pig's feet?*

The henhouse was producing more eggs than they could possibly eat, even with her big clan. Hilda had a steady little cottage business selling her eggs to neighbors and the grocery store in town. Neighbors also sought out her sweet clover butter and jars of fresh milk. Yes, John and his sons had almost worked themselves to death building up this farm and were being richly rewarded for their efforts. Peter wanted to learn beekeeping. A friend from church was going to work with him on that this spring. Soon, they'd have honey to sell too. Maybe she could get Fletcher and Peter to help build a little covered shed up at the top of the drive to sell her goods. If it was nice enough, she could have her quilts, aprons, and bonnets up there to sell too.

This was the first year their oldest grandsons had helped the men cut trees and haul the timber out of the woods. They had to learn if they were going to be able to take care of a family of their own someday. Of course, that was the farthest thing from those boys' minds. It was a thrill for them to get to go with Papa, their dad, and Uncle Peter. The men counted on the mules for that work. A good amount of the wood was taken to the mill and cut to build additional barns and sheds. Most of it they chopped for firewood for the family's use or sold by the wagonload to neighbors. The boys were taught to plant more trees when trees were harvested. That was a sound farming principal, and you didn't need any agricultural college education to know that.

John was proud of his team of mules. They had one stud jack and two jennets. He'd named them Jack, Sugar, and Peaches. Hilda was always calling them donkeys. John patiently explained to his wife that a mule was the result of the union of a male donkey and a female horse. His herd had multiplied and were mighty useful for plowing the fields or pulling farm wagons.

The harnesses were expensive, but what could you do? You had to have them. She'd always heard the expression "stubborn as a mule," but John could whisper in their ear, and they seemed to do his will. She watched how he babied them. Even a beast knew when it was loved. She saw how he nurtured and talked so kindly to them. *Well, no good will come from being jealous of a mule.* Hilda laughed to herself. The farmer next door to them had a fine pair of oxen that John admired, but he said the mules helped him get his fields plowed faster

Karen, Rachel and Mama were making quite a reputation for themselves with their cookies, pies, and cakes of every description. She had a couple of coconut and egg custard pies cooling on the table right now. She thought that would be a nice surprise for the family. The most popular pies they sold seemed to be lemon and chocolate chess, egg custard, coconut, apple, and pumpkin.

She liked to make berry pies, but often those vines seemed to be in the snakiest areas on their land. She hated to ask the boys or their mothers to pick them for fear they would get snakebitten. It wasn't worth the risk when her other pies were so well received. Of course, a side benefit was that the house always smelled wonderful. If one didn't look just the way she wanted it to for her to sell, her family was more than happy to help devour it. You couldn't afford to waste good food.

Mama made a mean coconut layer cake. Karen's specialty was her three-layer German chocolate cake. Rachel made what local folks referred to as sad cakes. They were sometimes called applesauce cakes. The finely chopped apples made the cake extra moist, and Rachel usually added chopped walnuts or pecans. Those pesky squirrels often got the pecans before they could harvest them. Just this year, a friend had shared a lovely recipe for a carrot cake that used finely grated carrots. Mama didn't think it sounded all that good, but it was amazingly tasty and popular. They normally put a butter cream icing on the carrot cake even though the recipe called for cream cheese.

Karen had gotten a little fancy on them and would decorate the carrot cake with a little bunch of icing carrots in the center. Peter had given her a cake decorating set last Christmas, and she seemed to have a natural talent for decorating. She did custom cakes for birthdays or anniversaries. She was doing quite well with orders. Those were simpler cakes, usually a sheet cake with either chocolate, yellow, or white cake. Mama's favorite was lemon with a tart lemon icing. That was what Karen had made for Mama's birthday this year. It had been a small cake because only the three women liked that one. She'd made a chocolate cake with chocolate icing for everyone else.

Rachel and Karen had taken the younger children and gone to help hang the greens at the church for the Advent service this Sunday. All the ladies took either soup or finger sandwiches so they could feed the volunteers. Rachel had prepared a short devotional for the ladies. Karen had offered to work with the children on a Christmas play, so after dinner, they would be rehearsing. It had taken a fair amount of coaxing to get Joseph and Arwood to participate. They thought they were too old for that stuff, but Karen assured them she counted on them for the harder parts. She knew just how to butter them up.

Hilda had been practicing with the men's group. They had a couple of nice Christmas songs under their belts for the first two Sundays. This first Sunday, they'd be singing "I Heard the Bells on Christmas Day." Next Sunday, they'd be performing "Hark the Herald Angels Sing." Agnes was going to do a solo the third week, and Hilda was playing for her. She had such a fine voice that it wouldn't take much rehearsing, except for the nerves part. She was singing "Away in a Manger."

Playing the songs on the piano, Hilda softly sang the beautiful words. She had an acceptable voice but not anything like the other gifted singers in the family. Her heart swelled thinking how much everyone was going to enjoy the music during this special time of the year. The old songs always touched her heart. She didn't hear the men return.

They heard Mama on the piano. They softly opened the front door and stood there enjoying the Christmas music and the sweet expression on Mama's face. They rarely got to hear her sing, so it was a real treat for them. The house smelled heavenly from the pies she'd baked earlier.

Mama was startled to see them standing in the living room. She'd been wrapped up in her music. "Where have you been for so long?" Mama quizzed them. "I was getting worried. I thought I might have to hitch up the buggy with those old mules and come looking for you."

"I would pay good money to see that," quipped Papa. "But if you must know, we were working on a Christmas surprise for you, my dear."

"You'd better not be buying no blame motorized vehicle because we all know that would just be a backdoor way of getting *you* a vehicle," wailed Mama

In a most dramatic fashion, John clutched his heart. "Why, Hilda, I'm shocked at you thinking such a thing." He winked at Peter, who couldn't stop grinning.

"You two are such a hoot sometimes." Peter laughed.

"Are the women and kids back yet? I'm starved." "Fortunately for you both, I have cooked you some dinner. It's just beans and corn bread with slaw," Mama told them as she rose from the piano and crossed to the kitchen to serve their food.

"Now, John, I hope you haven't gone out and spent a passel of money on me for Christmas. There's not a thing I need but another laundry tub right now. Well, maybe I could use more fabric and thread to make more quilts," she stated, watching his face. *No, that's not it*, she thought as she read his face.

"Oh no, dear, it's big, really big, probably going to arrive on the train just any day," her husband teased her.

"John Broce, you'd better not have gotten me any oxen!" his wife protested.

"I wish I'd thought of that. Now that would've been something." John smiled, stroking his new mustache. It tended to be a bit wispy and surprisingly dark when the rest of his hair was more salt than pepper. "Now, Hilda, I don't want you to frustrate yourself trying to guess because this is something you would never figure out in a hundred years."

He may as well be whistling in the wind because Hilda's mind was already turning over the possibilities. She'd try to worm a few more hints out of him when his guard was down. Too bad that man didn't talk in his sleep.

By the time everyone had gotten back to the house that afternoon, the sky was losing daylight. The Christmas tree would have to wait until tomorrow.

John had already arranged for Rachel to make a very special stocking for Hilda for that Christmas. Karen was going to embroider it with a little house surrounded by flowers with two big shade trees in front. Unfortunately, the house materials would not arrive in time for Christmas, so he was going to do the next best thing—tear that page out of the Sears Modern Homes catalog, and that was what was going in the stocking for his sweet wife.

Won't she be surprised? He grinned to himself, picturing her face on Christmas morning.

He'd put half of the money down on it and was financing the rest on time! It was a very affordable monthly payment for them. If he managed to save enough, why, they would pay it off early. He was right proud of himself for coming up with this great gift idea. It was getting too crowded in their big house. It should be just right for his sons and their families for a while longer yet.

It would be nice to come home at the end of the day to their own quiet little house like old times. He dearly loved his grandchildren, every one of them, but he missed meals with only the two of them. The house was noisy. He sometimes had a hard time getting to sleep early in the evening. He and Hilda both were up with the chickens. He looked forward to having his breakfast with her and their simple suppers together. Neither of them were spring chickens anymore, and it was high time they settled back into a calmer routine.

The man in town told him the house would come with all the materials, which were marked for easy construction. They expected it to arrive early March. The timing wasn't great since they'd have the garden to get out, but then again, when did they ever have nothing going on? It might take them awhile, but he and his sons were looking forward to seeing it come together. He hoped they'd all still be civil once they finally got it built. It would be a big project for them. He figured they only needed two bedrooms. The bedroom in the front of the house could be her music room or quilting room, whatever she wanted to call it. It was a small house with no upstairs, but it had a good-sized living room and kitchen. It would have a covered front porch so she and Lola could sit out there and continue to solve all the world's problems. That meant they'd leave the old fellows be for a bit.

Hilda always teased him about loving the farm animals, but she was the same way about the chickens. They'd have to build her a new chicken coop behind their new house. That way, Hilda could watch her chickens while she was cooking or washing dishes. He lit his pipe. He was right proud of himself for coming up with this grand surprise for his sweetheart.

Christmas rolled around right on schedule. It had been a busy month with church activities, caroling, lots of good eating, spending time with family and friends, and of course, the daily routine of running a farm. The ladies' pin money had allowed them to spoil the grandchildren with several nice gifts this year. The older boys got their first rifles and immediately headed for the woods. Hilda had ordered John a fancy new suit for church and a fine felt hat to match. His sons and their wives had bought him a new pair of boots and dress shoes to go with his suit.

Hilda had been a sputtering mess when she pulled the picture of the house and the house plans out of that stocking. Yes, indeed, that had been something to see. She had a hundred questions, which he'd anticipated. When she asked about the cost, he'd reminded her that it wasn't polite to question price when receiving a gift. He thought she was going to explode, but all in all, he thought she took it well.

When the shock wore off a little, she and the girls started studying the floor plan. He told her to get her coat and scarf on, and they walked out to the spot he'd chosen to build their new home. With his arms outstretched, he described which way the house would sit, told her about his plans to build her a bigger chicken coop and about the extra room she'd have for her piano or whatever she wanted to use it for. She loved the two big oaks that would flank the house on either side.

Hilda and husband stood in the brisk air picturing their new house. She shivered. John put his arms around her and held her close. They were a long way from their homeland, but that didn't matter at all. They were home! He studied her happy face, noticed the new lines and the fine silver that had all but taken over her once dark hair. He could still see the young girl he'd fallen in love with those many years before. She'd been the best helpmate he could've asked for. He loved being able to do something nice for her that she didn't see coming.

18

Building a Sears House

In 1926, spring was long awaited and slow in arriving.
Hilda sat at the kitchen table enjoying the quietness of the house by herself with her second cup of coffee. It was Saturday morning, and she'd already given John his breakfast. It was only five o'clock, but he'd been anxious to get the animals fed. Joseph and Arwood were always eager to help their grandfather, but he'd told her to let them sleep.

John had big plans for today. The lumber, nails, windows, doors, and roofing material for their new home had arrived at the train station earlier in the week. He'd hired a couple of men from town to pick it up and deliver it to him. It was all going to be stowed in the barn for the time being.

When it arrived, he hadn't quite anticipated how much material it took to build even a small home. And this wasn't all of it. Sears, Roebuck & Company would ship the rest in another two months or so. John and his sons had built barns and farm buildings, but he was beginning to feel completely overwhelmed by the task of building his own house. Other German friends assured him they would lend a hand. Like himself, they had good intentions, but they also had farms and outside work that kept them busy.

John rubbed his bristly, unshaven face with his rough farm hands. He told Hilda she might not get her home until Christmas. Unexpectedly, bright tears had filled her eyes. She'd been dreaming that their new home would be ready by the end of summer so they could get settled in before cold weather set in again.

As quickly as the tears appeared, Hilda, embarrassed, wiped them away and apologized. "Oh, John, I'm sorry. I got so anxious for our new house, I forgot how much work it takes to make it a reality. I know you have your hands full with this farm and the garden that has to be put out," said Hilda.

"Hilda, I know how excited you've been about us having our own place again. There's nothing worse than feeling like I'm disappointing you," John comforted her.

"Now, John, don't you worry. I'm a foolish old woman with no earthly idea how long building a house takes," said Hilda, feeling ashamed of her emotional outburst.

"I hope I haven't bitten off more than I can chew," John said. "I think I'll go into town after a while and see if I can find some men to help us. I want to do as much as Peter, Fletcher, and I can to keep our costs down. The fellows over at the sawmill can probably recommend someone to frame it and get it under roof for us. If we can get that much out of the way, I think we can finish it."

"Of course, dear, I know it looks like a huge undertaking, but it's going to be much smaller than the barn," Hilda reminded him.

Her comment got a big chuckle out of John. He looked over at Hilda and realized that she was being serious. He rose from the table and planted a big kiss on her plump cheek. "The difference, Hilda, is we don't have to live in the barn. I'm certainly hope we can build your new home to a higher standard than the barn."

"Well, don't you discount what fine workers our sons and grandsons are, John," Hilda reminded him.

"I'm not, but there are just so many hours in the day. Fletcher is worn out when he gets home from the mines. That's hard, dirty work, and he still pulls his weight around the farm too. Peter does most of the heavy lifting around here. I depend on him. Once we get the fields plowed and the crops planted, Peter will be able to help with the house a little more. The boys can fill in with the farmwork. It won't be long before school is out. Then they'll be able to help us more," said John.

Hilda hated to add to his burden but interjected, "John, do you think we could get some of that pretty river rock to use on the foundation? To me, it looks like the sky, the water and the rich earth all rolled into one."

"That's a great idea, Hilda. We can use the big wagon and mules to haul the rock back here," said John.

"Now, that sounds like a good job for Joseph and Arwood," said Hilda. "They love any excuse to go down to the river."

"There's plenty of rock here on our land too. Don't you remember how much stone we cleaned out of the fields when we settled here? We put most of it back near the edge of the woods," said John as he headed out the door to start his morning chores.

As Hilda finished up her coffee, she began to dream about the chicken coop she'd have at the new house. As she washed up their breakfast dishes, she visualized it all taking shape in her mind.

By the time she finished daydreaming, the house full of people began to wake up. Hilda mentally thought about the ages of the assorted brood that lived together in this house. Peter was thirty-five; Karen, thirty-four; Andrew, five; their twin boys, Kellen and Kolten, were three. Fletcher was thirty-two; Rachel, twenty-nine; Joseph, eleven; Arwood, nine; Dotty, six; and the twin girls, Ruth and Ruby, would be two in May. John would be fifty-six, and she would be fifty-three.

It seemed like once your own children grew up and began having children of their own, the years just flew by. She dearly loved every one of them but longed for a little quiet solitude. Soon, this big old house would be humming with the not-so-quiet roar of voices, laughter, children squabbling or crying, singing, pots and pans clattering, and so on.

As the busy spring and summer months sped by, Hilda and John's little cottage began to take shape. They'd talked about whether or not to wire the house, but that seemed like such a distant prospect, they couldn't see the point in it. It would probably be decades before electricity reached them. She and John might not even be around when it did. That would save them a little money.

A true luxury was having a new kitchen sink, bathroom sink, and tub. They'd still have to carry the water and heat it, but with the new well they'd had dug, it would be much closer to the house. Hilda had to put her foot down once again when the men started talking about putting a toilet in the house. "Absolutely not while I'm alive," she told them. She didn't notice John roll his eyes. There wasn't much persuading his old girl to change her mind.

A new outdoor johnny house was built. Peter carved out a little moon on the door to dress it up for his mother. He and Fletcher surprised her with a pretty white picket fence they built in the front yard.

The last thing was to add the new chicken coop. Fletcher thought his mother might be as happy about that as she was about the new house. She supervised the construction. Hilda couldn't wait to bring her laying hens over to their new place. She got good money in town for the eggs. She wanted to put a little sign out by the road advertising her fresh eggs for sale.

While having supper with the family the night before the big move to a house of their own, Hilda expressed her dread of having to move all her chickens to their new roost.

Fletcher said, "Mama, don't worry. You have plenty of good helpers here, isn't that right, kids?" They all nodded their agreement.

Peter said, "Mama, we thought we'd move the piano first and get that situated exactly where you want it, then start in on the rest of your things. We should have you all settled by the end of the day tomorrow."

True to their word, everyone was up early the next morning getting their chores knocked out so they could help move Mama and Papa. Rachel and Karen were in the kitchen quietly preparing them an evening meal so the older couple could celebrate the first night in their new home without worrying about cooking. Fletcher and Peter had given them a small kitchen table and chair set that they'd had Clyde build for them as a surprise.

Once they got her furniture, pots and pans, dishes, clothes, and other personal effects moved, the men and boys took a little break to have dinner on the front porch. They were hot and tired from their labor. The heat had been brutal. The cold lemonade Rachel served them hit the spot. When they finished eating, they stood and stretched and got ready to transport the chickens.

Hilda had been looking forward to seeing how her chickens liked their new henhouse. She loved those silly birds. It might be her imagination, she thought, but they all seemed to have their own personalities.

As the men finished the job, they noticed Rachel running toward them. She looked frantic. "I can't find Dotty," she exclaimed, catching her breath. "Is she here with you?"

"No, I haven't seen her since dinnertime. I saw her slip off the porch and go around back of the house, but I assumed she was playing. She is a six-year-old child," said Fletcher.

"That's been nearly an hour ago," wailed Rachel. "It's not like her to wander off. I'm scared she's gotten hurt or something."

John and the rest of the family joined in the search, calling out Dotty's name. Hilda stayed at the house in case she came there. She was nowhere to be found. They sent Arwood and Joseph into the woods to look for her. Suddenly, Rachel heard Dotty's little singsong voice emerging from the tall cornfield. Her face was sweaty and dirty, her hair tousled, but other than that, she looked all right. Dotty was half carrying, half dragging a big feed sack.

Rachel ran over to her child, hugging her close to her. "Dotty, what were you doing out there in the cornfield? Did you get lost in there? We have been worried to death that something had happened to you."

Pushing her sweaty hair out of her face, Dotty looked quizzically at her mother. "I was helping Mama." She proudly hoisted the big feed sack she had dragged through the cornfield. She sat it down, and everyone laughed as Mama's prize hen exited the sack looking slightly bedraggled but no worse for her journey. Mama gave her little granddaughter a big hug and thanked her for helping move the chickens.

19

Puppy Love

Winter officially arrived with a blast of polar air in December of 1926. It brought snow squalls, two feet of fresh snow on top of the eight inches already on the ground.

When Joseph got home from school on Friday, he was nursing a black eye. He also had bruised pride and a feeling of bewilderment. He looked a sight, but Arwood was proud of his tough-looking brother. Rachel was shocked to see his face. She'd rushed him inside and got ice to put on it while she waited patiently for an explanation.

Rachel said, "Joseph, I won't have you getting into fights at school. I expect you to mind your teacher the same way you do me. Now tell me what happened."

"Mom, my friend Sara Cox was outside the schoolhouse crying after school. I asked her what was wrong. She put her head on my shoulder and kept on crying. I just reached around her and patted her on the back."

"What did she tell you?"

"She was crying so hard, all I could understand was that her boyfriend, James, had teased her about how funny her hair looked. She had a big ribbon on top of her head. It looked like she hadn't even brushed her hair. I noticed it too, but I didn't say anything about it."

"Who is James, and how did you get a black eye, son?"

"His dad is Paul Conner. We met them at the German camp when we first moved here. I can't remember his mom's name. We called her Mrs. Conner. James is the same age as me. He thought I was hugging his girlfriend. He came over and socked me in the eye."

"That was very ugly of him. Did you hit him too?" asked Rachel.

"No, because I guess I *was* hugging his girlfriend, but I didn't mean anything by it. I was trying to make her feel better. You know, like you and Mama and Aunt Karen hug us when we're upset about something."

"Then something else bad happened. Well, really two things—Sara got mad at James for hitting me, and then she kissed my hurt eye. Oh, Mom, it was awful. Now Sara thinks I like her." Joseph looked mortified.

Rachel had to fight to control a smile. How sweet and innocent her oldest son was. She could imagine it all happening, just the way Joseph described it and him at a complete loss trying to understand the resulting chain of events. "Well, do you like her, Joseph?"

"Sure, Mom, but not like a *girlfriend!* It was yucky having her kiss my eye," moaned Joseph. "Now this other girl that I do like is mad at me too because she saw Sara kiss me. What a big stinking mess!"

Rachel's ears perked up at the mention of a girl her son *liked*. He had never mentioned any girls to them. Raising a twelve-year-old son just got interesting, though she could tell his life was a little too dramatic for him right now.

"I didn't know you liked a girl. What's her name?" his mother asked.

"You've met her, Mom. It's Ada. Her dad is Clyde. He makes furniture. I don't know if it's okay to like her now because my grandpa married her grandma Agnes. Doesn't that mean we're cousins or something? One of my friends said you can't like your cousin because that's just crazy."

"Oh, Joseph." Rachel tousled his hair. "You're growing up way too fast. I think it's okay if you like Ada because you are only related by your grandparents' marriage, not by blood."

"Huh? Well, it doesn't matter because now she is mad at me. I was going to buy her some candy for Christmas. I've earned fifteen cents helping Papa," said Joseph.

"You can still do that and just explain to Ada that it was all a big misunderstanding," said his mother.

"Girls are a lot of trouble, aren't they, Mom? Not you, even though you're a girl too," said Joseph, still looking confused.

"It'll get easier as you get older," said Rachel.

When Fletcher got home, she told him what happened so he wouldn't be shocked like she'd been when she saw their gentle Joseph's shiner. His response was not what she expected.

"I need to teach him how to fight so he can defend himself," said Fletcher.

"Fletcher Broce, this was a simple misunderstanding among kids," his wife told him.

"Still, it's time I worked with him a little, and Arwood too. I don't expect them to start fights, but they need to know how to defend themselves if the occasion arises. Relax, Rachel, this is something men do. My dad did the same thing with Peter and me when we got to be about Joseph's and Arwood's age."

Rachel shook her head, not sure what to make of all this physical training. She heard one of the twins crying and went to check on her.

It was such a cold night. Rachel knew the men and boys had to go back out before supper. They had been busy all fall getting their wood supply ready because Papa, rightly so, predicted this would be a rough winter. Fletcher and Peter had loaded the wagon with firewood for Amos and Agnes. Joseph and Arwood were going with them to help unload and stack the wood.

The women had gotten together a list of items to pick up in town for their family's Christmas meal *if* they could make it to town. Their roads were dangerously icy. They didn't know how bad the main roads would be. Rachel asked Fletcher to stop by Clyde's and see if Clarisse needed them to pick up anything for them from town while they were going. She noticed that Joseph ran upstairs to get his money when he heard her ask his dad to stop at Ada's house.

My little romantic son, sighed Rachel. *So it begins.*

Mama fried potatoes and thick sliced bologna for supper. Her meal also included sauerkraut. As she fixed the corn bread, Mama kept looking out the window to see if she saw the men coming back. Rachel had started getting worried about them too. *What is keeping them? Hopefully, they haven't had an accident.* It was still blowing snow, and the wind was whistling. Fortunately, it was nice and warm in their house.

She looked at her daughters playing in the living room with their cousins. Dotty was six, Ruby and Ruth were two. Andrew was five, and Karen's twin boys were three going on four come March. What beautiful children they all were. She thought them every bit as attractive as the children in the Sears Christmas catalog. With Christmas coming soon, they'd all been on their best behavior too, since Santa was coming to see them soon.

It was nearly dark when the men returned. Rachel slipped her coat around her and went out on the front porch to wait for them. The night air had a bite, but at least the wind had finally died down.

She gave the boys a hug, and they ran inside. Fletcher put his arm around her and asked her what she was doing outside in this cold. "Just waiting on you all to get back and imagining the worse," said Rachel.

"It took a little longer than we thought," said Fletcher. "The roads were passable, but when we stopped at Clyde's, we had to shovel a path in the front and back for them. You know Clyde isn't able to manage that. When we got to your dad and Agnes's house, we had to do the same thing again."

"How are Dad and Agnes and Clyde's family doing? Did you invite them all to Christmas Eve dinner this Friday?" asked Rachel.

"I certainly did. Clarisse is baking dinner rolls, lots of them, she said. Her mother is baking an egg custard and coconut pie to bring," Fletcher informed her.

"Were you able to find all the supplies we had on our grocery list?" asked Rachel.

"Oh, sure. When we got to the grocery store, Joseph was buying candy to give to Ada as her Christmas gift. Arwood was complaining that he wanted candy too. I think Joseph ended up splitting it between his girlfriend and his brother."

"I'm glad you're all back home safely. Hope you're hungry. Mama has fixed enough food for an army. This cold weather's got her in a cooking mood," Rachel told him.

They stood on the porch and looked through the shiny picture window at the big fir Christmas tree decorated with Rachel's mom's ornaments and strands of berry and popcorn garland. Fletcher kissed Rachel and wished her a merry Christmas.

20

Karen's Discontent

February 1927 produced more snow, ice, and freezing rain. The first three weeks in March brought no better weather. Everyone in the house had a short fuse. The brutal weather made work on the farm especially hard. The adults were fatigued. The children argued and fought with each other. There was many a trip behind the woodshed to correct some wayward behavior. Getting to town was tricky, so often the family went without basic things they wanted. That was followed by complaining.

For some reason, Karen especially struggled with all the mayhem. Everyone noticed that she appeared to be withdrawing within herself. Her husband was perplexed about the changes in his wife. When he finished the morning chores, he went by his parents' house hoping to talk to his mother and see what advice she had for him. He found his mother napping in her rocking chair. His dad was at the barn. He tried to slip quietly out the kitchen door again, but his heavy footsteps woke his mother.

"Peter! I'm sorry, I didn't hear you come in. I've been up since around four thirty this morning. I'm coming down with a cold and didn't sleep well last night. Once I got over here in the rocker near the stove and got warm, I fell right to sleep. Mercy me," said Mama.

"It's okay, Mom. I just came by to talk with you about something. It can wait," said Peter.

Suddenly, Mama's radar was on high alert. Her oldest son never consulted her on anything. If he was here, something was up. "Nonsense, Peter. I'm glad you woke me up. I've got plenty of work to do today. I should be working on learning some new hymns to play at church next month," Mama said as she crossed the room.

She touched his arm and looked up into her tall son's face. She couldn't miss the furrowed forehead or the worry in his eyes. "What's wrong, Peter?" she inquired.

"Probably nothing, but I'm worried about Karen," he said.

"Son, take your coat off. Your clothes are soaking wet. Hang it on the chair by the stove so it can dry out a little," she told him as she pulled out her coffee tin and began measuring out the coffee. "I've got a couple of biscuits leftover from breakfast this morning. I'm going to warm those. We'll butter them up and put some of my good strawberry jam on them. How's that?"

"Mom, I don't want you to go to any trouble," said Peter.

"Are you kidding? This is a treat for me. I don't get much time to be alone with my handsome son," said Mama as she sat the coffeepot on the kitchen stove so it would percolate.

"Karen's walking around like she is in a trance. She's not acting happy or sad, necessarily, but she's not her normal bubbly self," said Peter.

"Peter, it's probably this dismal weather. It's starting to get to all of us," said Mama as she got down her jam and slid the butter dish toward him.

"I think it's more than that with her. She doesn't seem interested in anything, not even the children. I mean she is taking care of us all, but she doesn't act like she's engaging with us," said Peter. "I can't explain it exactly."

"How old is Karen now?" asked Mama. "Women go through a lot of changes in their lifetime."

"She'll be thirty-five this July," said Peter.

"That may be the problem. She is on the cusp of becoming middle-aged. Women start worrying about getting older. They need more affirmation from their husbands that they still find them attractive. Sometimes, they even consider having more children to try to hang on to their youth while they still can," said Mama.

"Well, in our case, it would be too dangerous for Karen to have more children. Do you think that's it? Our children are driving us crazy right now. Seems like all they want to do is squabble. I've warmed all of their backsides more than once in the last month," said Peter.

"Hmmm…Peter, you know what? I think its Fletcher's fault!" exclaimed Mama.

"What are you talking about, Fletcher's fault?" asked Peter.

"Well, you know what a romantic your brother is. He is always showering Rachel with love and attention. Karen might be noticing that and comparing your relationship to theirs," said Mama.

"Do you think that could be it?" asked Peter.

"Maybe. Now you are your Father's son. He has never been overly romantic. I remember a time when you boys were young that I seemed to notice all the thoughtful things my friends' husbands did for them. I didn't feel like I was loved as much as my friends were," said Mama.

"Mom, that's silly. Dad has always had eyes only for you. Everyone can see how much he adores you," said Peter.

"Yes, back then, everyone else could see that, but I couldn't. I was the only one that counted." Mama laughed. "Of course, it was hogwash, but I was too blind to see it. I remember it felt very real to me. Yes, your lady might just need extra love and affection right now, son. Give it a try."

Peter agreed to try. Mama stood at her kitchen window watching Peter making his way through the snow-covered hayfield toward his house. *I had better get Fletcher to give him some pointers*, she thought. *Oh, John, you just don't know how lucky you are to have a girl like me who doesn't need constant propping up!*

That night, when the house was finally still, Peter reached for his wife. She pulled the covers around her and turned over with her back to him.

"Peter, I'm tired. You need your rest too," Karen told him as she blew out the lantern.

Peter couldn't sleep. He stayed awake there in the dark wondering how he was going to manage to be more romantic. It was ludicrous.

Can't Karen see that I love her as much as I always have? Why, I've never looked at another woman. Could there be some other man that she was interested in? God, I hope not!

He eventually wore himself out and drifted off to an uneasy, restless sleep. Peter awoke the next morning with a new resolve. He'd ask his romantic fool brother to tell him specifically what to do because he didn't even know where to begin.

That night after supper, he asked Fletcher to walk out to the barn with him for a minute. When they got out there, Fletcher asked his brother, "What's going on, Peter?"

"Have you noticed that Karen is acting funny? Mama says she thinks Karen needs more romancing," Peter told his brother.

"Well, I'm sorry, brother, I can't help you. I've got one wife. That's all I can handle," said Fletcher, laughing. Then he noticed Peter's serious face. "You know I'm just joking around? Tell me what's wrong, Peter."

Peter talked about his wife's and his relationship. He told Fletcher that he'd even considered whether she might be interested in another man.

"Peter, stop right there. We're talking about Karen. You two have been in love since childhood. Has she ever seemed interested in anyone else?" asked Fletcher.

"Not that I know of," said Peter, "but maybe a fellow can't tell if there's someone else."

"I disagree, Peter. I think if the woman you love loved someone else, it would be like having a ghost hanging around. You might not be able to see that other person, but you couldn't help but sense their presence," said Fletcher.

"What do you think I need to do to make her happy again? Mama said it might just be the weather getting her down," said Peter.

"Women can be moody at times. Sometimes, you just need to keep your head down, keep a low profile until the mood passes," said Fletcher. "Honestly, brother, I think you need to pretend you're dating again. I try to think like that when I'm romancing Rachel. You know, do little things like telling her 'I love you,' telling her she's beautiful, telling her you're proud of her—all that. I don't hear you doing that very often. I figured you did it in private, but if you're not doing that, that's where you start!"

Peter was absorbing his smart brother's advice. They'd always been able to talk. Fletcher was better at human nature stuff. It all made perfect sense to him now that Fletcher had spelled it out so plainly. He didn't do any of that. He thought she knew he felt that way. He thought back about all the times Fletcher even publicly spoke of how much he loved his wife.

"I'll give it a try. You would really think she knew all that. I'm home all the time trying my best to take care of her and all our family. I work hard," a confused Peter said.

"It takes all that and more," said Fletcher. "I'll send you a bill for my professional consultation."

"Fletcher, this is just between you and me. I'd rather you not even talk to Rachel about it. You know how tight those women are," said Peter.

"Of course, Peter. Just remember, I'll be watching and listening so I can coach you better next time we talk," said Fletcher as he hugged his brother. "Now get in there and start all that sweet-talking!"

Peter put the brotherly advice into practice. Slowly, he felt Karen starting to blossom again. Soon, they were back to giggling like kids over funny things that were always happening all around them. They held hands, took walks, talked about the children, and made plans together to steal away for a weekend just the two of them.

That opportunity came up a few months later. Another couple invited them to go with them to dinner at the ritzy Hotel Roanoke. The couple was planning on making a weekend of it and invited Peter and Karen to join them. They had a car, so that was a real treat for Peter and Karen too. She and Rachel excitedly planned her wardrobe for the weekend.

Peter enlisted Rachel's help to buy her a special nightgown set. Rachel picked black lace to complement Karen's blonde features. The weekend was a big success. Peter bought Karen a diamond engagement ring and asked her to be his forever. She agreed.

He never could quite figure out whether it was the weather or his new romancing skills that brought her back to him. Maybe both, he concluded.

21

Fire!

In late December 1927, Joseph stuck his head in the front door and called out to his mother, "Mom, Dad wants Arwood and me to take some firewood over to Grandpa Amos. We're going to eat with him and Grandma Agnes. Don't fix any supper for us."

Rachel came out of the kitchen drying her hands on her apron. "Joseph, it's nearly suppertime now. Maybe you should wait till tomorrow morning."

"Can't, Mom. We're going hunting with Uncle Peter and Dad tomorrow morning while it's still dark. Dad said he noticed last time he was over there that their woodpile was getting thin. We don't want them to run out."

Rachel ran her hand through her tall son's curly hair and gave him a hug. "Thanks for taking care of your grandpa and Agnes. If I know Grandpa, he's probably worrying if he has enough wood too. "

"If we have time, I want to go by and talk to Ada for a minute," said Joseph shyly.

"Aha, now I see why you're so enthusiastic about this job. Don't stay too long," Rachel teased her son. She put on her coat and walked him out. The old farm wagon was loaded with cut firewood. Fletcher was so good about helping her dad and Agnes.

It was a nice winter evening, cold, but at least it wasn't snowing, she thought.

Her sons were all business, turning the wagon around and getting on their way. She imagined they felt pretty important being trusted to make this short run by themselves. She wondered if the friendship between Joseph and Ada would ever develop into something more, maybe a young romance. You could never tell about such matters of the heart. They were only thirteen. She watched her sons until they were out of sight before going back into the house.

Joseph and Arwood continued up the road a piece. They passed another wagon heading the opposite way. The older man in the wagon nodded at them. They nodded back. That was the neighborly thing to do. When the fellow got out of sight, Joseph, as promised, let Arwood take the reins. He wasn't normally allowed to drive a wagon. He'd begged Joseph to let him try his hand. Joseph agreed provided Arwood promised not to tag along with him and Ada when they got to her house. Arwood quickly promised. He didn't want to hang out with those lovebirds anyway!

Joseph was hoping Ada's parents would let him and Ada take a walk together. He was trying to work up his nerve to kiss her. He was nervous about how that would work out.

Shoot, everyone knows she's my girl, he thought. At school, his teacher said public display of affection was strictly prohibited. Sometimes, they held hands at recess. They tried to make sure the teacher didn't catch them. That might be okay, but he was pretty sure kissing wasn't allowed. It wasn't the kind of thing he wanted to discuss with his mother.

They reached the intersection of McCoy and Prices Fork Road and made a left-hand turn to head toward Grandpa Amos's house. Joseph thought he could smell something burning. The wind was blowing in their direction, and there was definitely a strong, smoky smell. It wasn't the same smell as you noticed with folks burning wood in their stoves or fireplaces. It was much stronger. Dusk had set in. Joseph strained to see where the smoke was coming from.

As they got a bit further down the road, dense smoke filled the air and made them cough as it burned their throats. Their eyes watered. The wind seemed to be blowing the smoke right into their faces. Joseph told Arwood to give him the reins, just in case the horses acted up. As they proceeded down the road, they spotted a huge blaze off the right side of the road.

"Oh no!" moaned Joseph. "I think that's Ada's house!"

He pushed the horses as fast as he dared. The wagon was loaded with wood, and he certainly didn't want to dump it out in the road and have to pick it all up. As they got closer, he saw that it was actually Ada's dad's furniture factory that was ablaze. The sprawling structure was behind their house and sheds. A number of neighbors had seen the same thing he had and were running across the field to help put out the fire.

Joseph wished his dad was with them. He wasn't sure what he and Arwood could do to help, but he knew they needed to try anyway. The men were grabbing any container they could find and filling them up at the stream behind the burning building. They threw the water on the building, trying to douse the flames.

"Come on, Arwood. We've got to see what we can do to help," said Joseph. Arwood looked scared. Joseph pulled the wagon up by the fence and tied the horses there. They ran toward the men at the creek. When Joseph looked back toward Ada's house, he saw her dad sitting in his wheelchair in the middle of the field. He was watching helplessly as his building went up in smoke. Joseph could see tears streaking shamelessly down Clyde's dirt-smudged face. It looked like he'd tried to get out there to help only to have his chair topple over dumping him on the ground. He was covered in mud. Ada's mother was muddy too. She must've run out to help her husband back into his chair. Ada and her mother were standing behind Clyde watching and holding each other. He learned later that Ada had repeatedly rung the big wrought-iron dinner bell trying to attract the attention of the neighbors to enlist their aid.

Everyone worked tirelessly but seemed to make little impact. Suddenly, they heard the clang of the shiny new fire truck as the town's volunteer fire department arrived. They had chemicals to put on the flames. Everyone cheered and stood back so they could get to the scene. No one left; they stayed to help in any way they could.

Joseph was surprised to look back and see their dad, Papa, and uncle Peter coming across the field toward Clyde. He and Arwood started running in their direction. "Dad, Dad," they shouted.

When they reached them, Joseph said breathlessly. "Dad, I know we were supposed to go straight to Grandpa Amos's but we had to try to help!"

Fletcher hugged the boys. "You did the right thing. Looks like they're getting the fire under control. Why don't take the wagon on over to Grandpa Amos's and get it unloaded. It's late now, so when you get done, just head on home."

Papa noticed the boys were soaking wet—and cold, he suspected. He told them, "There's some blankets in our wagon. Take them with you to wrap up in when you get through at Amos's." He hugged his grandsons and sent them on their way.

Fletcher and Peter reached Clyde's side. "Clyde, we came as soon as we heard. Looks like we're too late to do much good."

Clyde's eyes were riveted on the devastation. Fletcher knelt down so he was eye level with his old friend. "Man, I'm so sorry this happened," said Fletcher.

Clyde looked at Fletcher and nodded at Peter and Papa. "Not since the mining accident have I felt so utterly helpless and hopeless. It's like I've taken two steps forward and three backwards tonight."

"Clyde, the important thing is that you and your family are safe. It won't be easy, but you can rebuild," said Fletcher.

Peter looked at Clyde's muddy appearance and the wheelchair with the mud caked on the side. It was obvious what had happened. His heart went out to the man. He had endured so much. "Clyde, let's get you inside before you catch your death of cold out here. Dad and I'll get your chair cleaned up for you, right as rain. Maybe that good wife of yours can put on some coffee for these men who've been out here working so hard."

Fletcher said, "Rachel and Karen are making sandwiches and warming up some of our home-canned tomato soup to bring over. They're bringing coffee too."

Clyde looked at Fletcher. "It's all gone, Fletcher. Everything I've worked so hard to build. Why is God punishing me again?"

"I know everything seems bleak right now, Clyde. Let's wait until the light of day, then we'll see what can be salvaged," said Fletcher.

Clyde dropped his chin to his chest, and his shoulders trembled as the sobs racked his body. Peter saw Clarisse and Ada coming toward Clyde. He met them. "Let's give him a moment to collect himself," he said as he walked the mother and daughter back toward the house.

Ada clung to her mother, who was also sobbing. When they reached the house, she encouraged her mother to take a seat at the kitchen table. Ada put another log in the cookstove and stirred the hot coals left over from supper. Then she started the coffee. She'd never actually made coffee, but had seen her mother do it a hundred times. Her mother's crying wrenched at Ada's heart.

Through sobs, Clarisse said in despair, "Your father has worked so hard. This is so unfair!"

About a half hour passed as she sat and sipped the strong coffee her daughter had made. She quickly wiped her eyes when she heard the men helping Clyde up the steps. Ada handed them her father's crutches. Her father shuffled off to get himself washed up and changed into cleaner clothes.

Papa got a pan of water and a rag and went back outside to clean the mud from Clyde's wheelchair.

Rachel and Karen arrived and busied themselves in the kitchen. They soon had hot soup and sandwiches for all the firefighters. The men crowded into the house to warm their bones and for a bite to eat. As they were served, they headed back outside so the others could get into the kitchen. Several of them were planning to stay awhile and make sure the smoldering coals didn't surge again. They were all cold and tired.

The men thanked Karen and Rachel for the food. The soup was put into coffee cups so the men could sip it and not fuss with spoons. Clarisse and Ada took them coffee and thanked all of them for their efforts to save the family's furniture factory.

A couple of hours later, everyone had left. As Ada tidied up the kitchen, she watched her parents sitting together on the couch. They were holding hands. She gave them a hug and went upstairs to her bedroom. She was surprised to see her nine-year-old brother, Ambrose, still awake and sitting on his bed.

"How are Mom and Dad doing? Ada, it's really bad, isn't it?"

Ada sat on the bed beside her little brother and gave him a hug. He had a bad cold and had been running a fever. He wanted to go outside and help, but his mother made him stay in bed. He'd helplessly watched all the disaster from his bedroom window.

"I wish Mom had let me help," Ambrose said. "She said I could help by staying in here and getting well."

"She's right, Ambrose. I think the factory is destroyed. Mom and Dad are sad and worried. They are still downstairs sitting on the couch. Everyone else finally left. I left them alone so they could talk," said Ada.

Ambrose nodded. Ada noticed the tears streaming down his face. "Don't worry, they'll figure things out. Are you hungry? Joseph's mom and aunt brought over some cheese sandwiches and tomato soup. I can go fix you some," said Ada.

"I'm not hungry, sis, but I am thirsty," said Ambrose.

Ada felt his forehead. It was still warm. "Let me go get you a drink. Then I'll tuck you into bed so you can get your rest."

When Ada quietly slipped downstairs and back into the kitchen to get Ambrose's water, she looked in on her parents. Exhausted, they'd both fallen asleep on the couch. She put a blanket on them and blew out the lantern.

The next morning was Saturday. After an early breakfast, Fletcher and Peter left for Clyde's house. When they got there, Clarisse told them that Clyde was already outside at the burnt building. She's tried to talk him out of going out there because it couldn't be safe. She let the men out the backdoor. They crossed the field to catch up with Clyde.

Fletcher called out to him. Clyde looked around. "Fletcher, Peter, I didn't expect to see you two this early in the day," said Clyde.

"How are you doing this morning, Clyde?" asked Fletcher.

Clyde looked up at them with a somewhat sheepish expression on his face. "You're not going to believe this, but I've been out here considering how blessed I am," said Clyde.

Fletcher and Peter exchanged a puzzled look. "How so, Clyde?" Fletcher asked.

"First, let me say I'm embarrassed for railing at God last night. He has given me a fresh prospective this morning. I'm blessed to have so many friends who came to my assistance in my hour of need," said Clyde.

"They were glad to help, Clyde," said Peter.

"Not only that, but two weeks ago, we delivered all the Christmas furniture orders. Also, last week, we delivered the new furniture to the bank in town. I've been paid for all those orders, too," said Clyde.

"That's great. Then your losses were minimized," said Fletcher.

"It gets better. We'd decided to wait till after the first of the year to get in the new supply of lumber. I can see the Lord's hand at work in this situation. I gave the crew a few days off and paid them a small cash bonus to thank them for helping me meet our deadlines. A couple of the men had been working late into the evening. I'm thankful they weren't here last night," said Clyde.

"Clyde, I hope you don't mind me asking, but did you have fire insurance on the building?" asked Peter.

"Yes, I did. A young fellow came by here back in the summer selling insurance. He was quite persuasive so I decided to take a policy," said Clyde. "He said we could make payments each month, but I'd just had a big sale, so I paid it up for a year. I put the policy in our safe deposit box at the bank for safekeeping. When they open Monday, I need to go by there and get it out so I can read it closely."

"I hope it will cover your machinery too," said Peter.

"Me too," said Clyde. "The fire chief said he will be back today to try and determine what caused the fire."

"I'm happy for your new outlook, Clyde," said Fletcher. "Sometimes, things don't look so bad in the light of day. You may be able to build something even better than what you had. I hope you aren't planning to go inside that burnt-up building. You should probably let the fire chief be the first in there so you don't risk doing anything that might go against your insurance policy."

"You're probably right," said Clyde as he wheeled around and headed back toward his house.

Later that day, when the fire chief completed his investigation, he found that the rear window at Clyde's office had been broken out. It appeared that his desk had been rifled through. All the drawers were standing open like someone had been looking for something. A locked file cabinet had been jimmied open and the contents dumped on the floor. The documents were lost now, just charred ashes remained.

Clyde was shocked that someone would break into his building to rob him right there in his backyard without him being aware of it. He had no idea who would do such a thing.

"They probably came through that back field there. Maybe a neighbor saw someone," said the chief. "It could've been someone who overheard you talking about your Christmas sales. I know the bank is pleased with the furniture you made for them. I heard them telling some customers what a good job you did."

Clyde shook his head. It bewildered him to think of someone trying to steal from him. He obviously didn't live extravagantly. He was just getting by like the next guy.

"The sheriff's office will be investigating the arson and the robbery attempt. I wouldn't expect too much, though, since the would-be robber apparently didn't get anything. I'll type up my report for you to send to your insurance company. I'll walk back to the house with you so I can get their contact information. Hopefully, you'll be able to rebuild soon. I'm sorry, man," said the chief.

Three months later, in March of 1928, Clyde received his five-hundred-dollar check from the insurance company. After much consideration, he'd decided to buy a building on the north side of town. It had a good-size front room area that he could use to display his furniture. He would use the large warehouse space in the back as his production area.

By the end of the year, Clyde's business was flourishing. Custom furniture orders had grown significantly. He employed six men in the factory and had added an upholstery service to his enterprise. To keep up, he'd hired an outgoing salesman to manage the showroom. Clyde was able to spend his time designing furniture and doing quotes for custom work, which was his favorite part of the business. One of the first things he did, after he settled his books that year, was to make a three-hundred-dollar donation to the volunteer fire department as a token of his appreciation for their efforts to save his old factory the previous year.

Lola's Lament

Mama paced on her small front porch and watched for her dear friend Lola. It seemed like lately, Lola gave her one excuse after another for why she couldn't come over or do something with her. They used to spend so much time together and always enjoyed each other's company. Now they hardly ever saw each other. When they did, Lola seemed distracted. John and Lola's husband always got along so well too. You could count on those two men to hightail it to the barn or out to one of the sheds when they got together. *Probably to get away from us women.* Mama chuckled to herself.

Where is she? They needed to get down to the church to help make the apple butter. Mama's grandchildren had picked five bushels of apples. She'd had John pick up some cinnamon and sugar from town. Everyone was counting on her and Lola to supervise the apple butter making.

That's what happens when you get older, got to teach the younger folks and keep the old traditions alive.

It was early November, 1929, and the air had turned cool. Mama was just turning to go inside to warm her hands when she heard the clop-clop of horses at the top of the hill. *Now's that strange.* Lola was driving the wagon herself. Her husband wasn't with her. John had been looking forward to seeing him. He'd specifically told her to send Tom on out to the barn when he got there.

Lola pulled the wagon in front of the house. "I'm sorry I'm late, Hilda. Something last minute came up."

Hilda looked closely at her old friend. "For heaven's sake, Lola, what happened to your face? How'd you get that black eye?"

Lola dropped her head and her voice. "It's nothing, Hilda. I was clumsy and took a spill off the back porch last weekend. It's almost healed. I started once not to even come. I know I look a fright."

"I understand. I've had some near spills myself. We're not as young as we used to be. Both of us need to slow down, but tell me, how do we do that?" said Hilda. "John and Joseph carried the apples to the church yesterday. Don't worry, other folks are bringing some too. Them that don't have apples are bringing sugar, cinnamon, or jars."

Hilda climbed up onto the seat beside her friend.

"Where's Tom? John was hoping he'd come along with you." "He's not feeling well. I asked him to come, but he said no."

"Lola, did you bring the recipe?"

Lola patted her ample bosom. "Got it right here."

"You know those younger ladies make fun of us for carrying our money tied up in a hankie in our brassieres, don't you? Shoot, they don't understand, we put all sorts of things in there for safekeeping!" Hilda laughed and smacked her friend on the arm.

Lola winced in pain.

Hilda quickly apologized. "I guess I don't know my own strength. Did you hurt your arm too when you fell?"

"No, I mean yes, that's it." Lola smiled weakly and unconvincingly.

Hilda suspected something was amiss but decided to talk with her friend about it later. Everyone would be at the church waiting for the silver saints to arrive. They had a long day before them. The two ladies made small talk as they continued toward the church. They had a lot to catch up on.

They arrived at the church and smiled as a big cheer went up from all the workers assembled there. The hot fire made blue smoke. The men readied the big kettle, placing it over the flames. The women had already gotten out the long stirring sticks. They had been washed thoroughly. Lola went over to the table where the ladies were finishing up peeling apples. They'd been there yesterday afternoon peeling too. She instructed them on what size to cut them up. She then hurried into the church basement to help Hilda take inventory of the supplies they had on hand.

Hilda told her, "We have about eight heaping bushels of apples, different types. So after they're all peeled, cored, and cut up, I figure we'll actually have around six bushels, twenty quarts per bushel, give or take a few, for any apples that have gone bad. We're going to need more jars and probably more sugar too. Do you think we have enough spice? We have cinnamon, allspice, and cloves. I like to add some brown sugar. It looks like we have enough of that."

"I think so. Do you think these jars have been freshly washed? I always like to scald them right before I use them for canning. Some of them look a mite dusty to me," said Lola.

"Just remember, Lola, we don't have to do it all. Just let those workers outside know what needs to be done, and they'll help. That's why they're here."

As the day wore on, the scent of apple butter sweetened the air. It was left up to Lola to determine when it reached the desired consistency. Hilda put some of the ladies on cleanup duty. The apple peels and cores were divided between the families present. The ladies would take the discarded apple, boil it down, strain it, and make delicious apple jelly. Nothing went to waste.

About eight hours after they started the whole process, the apple butter had passed Lola's readiness test. She looked for the wonderful dark brown color and sweet spicy taste. To judge the proper density, she considered it done when you could stand the big wooden spoon up in it without it falling over. Then the production line went into high gear to get it all canned. Some of the ladies had brought soup and sandwiches to feed the exhausted workers. They were satisfied with the nearly 125 jars they'd made.

The church would begin selling the apple butter right away. The church workers already had taken a number of orders in advance. Their good apple butter was always a bestseller. It provided much-needed funds for the church to support its activities.

Lola and Hilda slowly climbed back up into the wagon to make their journey home.

"Oh, my aching body," Hilda complained.

"Mine too. I don't know why I let you talk me into this little project every year," Lola protested.

"Yes, you do. It's because you love me as much as I love you. We always enjoy our time together. When we get to the house, I insist you come inside and let me fix you a real cup of coffee. I've been reading a book called *To the Lighthouse* by Virginia Woolf. It's about a family living in a summerhouse near the shore in Scotland. It takes place just after World War I in Scotland. I'll tell you about the Ramsays and their eight children. I'm about halfway through it now."

"I'd love to hear about them, but we better pick another day. I'll take you up on that cup of coffee, but then I'll need to scoot on home and check on Tom."

"But, Lola, dear, I never know when I'll see you again. You haven't been mad at me, have you? I've been trying to recall our last visit. I don't remember saying or doing anything out of the way. If I did, I certainly apologize. I have missed you, my friend," Hilda told Lola.

Tears slid down Lola's cheeks. She pushed her glasses up so she could dab at her eyes. "Oh no, it's not that. I promised myself I wouldn't say anything, but it's Tom. I think he is losing his mind. He can't remember things. Sometimes, he talks out of his head. I'm worried to death about him."

Hilda put her arm around her friend's shoulders. "I'm so sorry, Lola. I had no idea. I haven't been much of friend. I should've come looking for you."

Lola sniffled. "The worst of it is that he has started striking me. My Tom would never do anything like that. I miss my old Tom. I don't know what to do. I feel like I'm at my wit's end. I keep hoping he'll wake up and be his old self again, but I think that's a fool's dream."

"I'll have John come by tomorrow to check on him. He won't say anything about our conversation. I have to tell you, I'm very worried about him hitting you. Have you told your son, Pete?"

"No. He's married and got troubles of his own with that spoiled brat wife of his. He'd love to start a family, but she doesn't seem interested. I'm afraid that marriage will end up in a divorce. She is snippy to Tom and me. It gets Tom all stirred up, so I'd just as soon Pete keep her at home. We'll figure it out."

"I think your first step needs to be to get him to go to a doctor for a thorough physical examination. Maybe there's some medication that will help. He has always been a gentle-natured man," Hilda told her friend.

"I'm embarrassed to tell you this, but I've started sleeping with the bedroom door locked. He practically attacks me if I don't. That's every night. You know what I mean, right?" Lola said, looking at Hilda. "I know I have wifely responsibilities, but this is too much. I'm not sleeping well at all."

Hilda felt hot, angry tears streaming down her own face. "Oh my goodness, Lola. I know he's sick, but we have to get you some help. You can always come to us."

"I've said too much. I'm sorry to bring this burden to you Hilda. Don't worry, I'll manage somehow."

The two women rode on in silence for a while, something very uncommon for them. When they reached Hilda's house, Lola told her, "It's late. I'd better get home now. Don't worry about what I told you, I'll figure it out."

"No, *we'll* figure it out. John will be by tomorrow morning, and will convince Tom to ride into town with him. From there, they'll go by the doctor's office. I'll be praying for you both and for your safety. Promise me you'll talk to Pete soon. He needs to know about his father's condition too. He may be able to reason with him."

The two women hugged and said their good-byes. When Hilda got inside, it was nearly eight o'clock in the evening. John was asleep in his rocking chair. Hilda went over and gently nudged him. His eyes flew open. He cleared his throat and stood up slowly. "I must've dozed off waiting for you to get home."

"You've had your supper, haven't you?"

"Oh sure, Rachel sent me over a bowl of beans and corn bread and a piece of ham. She's getting better at her corn bread, but it still isn't as good as yours. How did you all do today with your apple butter making?"

"Good, really good. We had some mighty hard workers this year." Hilda sniffled and grabbed a hanky to blow her nose. John knew she'd been crying.

John came over and put his arms around her. "Here, here. What's wrong, Hildie?"

She leaned her head into his chest and told him about Lola and Tom's situation.

John shook his head. "I don't know what to say. It's hard to believe what you just told me. We haven't seen them in a couple of months. How could he change so much in that time? I've noticed Tom's been quieter, but then he's never been a big talker. I didn't think anything of it. How could I miss something like that?"

"Lola's ashamed of their problem. John, I wish you could've seen her face. Her black eye is almost healed, but you can see the yellow-and-brown bruising pattern. Her arm was sore to the touch. She pulled away."

John squeezed her shoulder. "Don't you worry. We'll get to the bottom of this. If he's as bad off as she says, the doctor might suggest he be removed from their home. They've got that asylum over in Radford. I think it's called

St. Albans. He might end up in there. I hate to hear about my old buddy Tom having this problem."

"I don't know whether they can afford to have him stay there. They've never made any real money to speak of. Let's see what the doctor says. I want to ride with you to their house tomorrow morning. I can stay and visit some more with Lola."

Troubled heads hit the pillow that night. Though weary to the bone, mind, and heart, sleep was elusive. Hilda was up at dawn making coffee and fixing John's breakfast while he took care of the livestock. She gathered fresh eggs. She'd fix a basket of eggs for Lola. They had part of a pecan pie left. She'd carry that too. If only her piddly offerings could fix the problem in the Henderson household.

When John and Tom returned from the visit to the doctor later that morning, Lola and Hilda were waiting. They'd fixed the men some dinner, and everyone tried to pretend everything was normal. Tom was quiet. He went over to his favorite chair and pulled it closer to the window so he could peer out.

John handed Lola a prescription and gave her the doctor's instruction. From the best he could tell, the doctor was prescribing a mild tranquilizer for Tom. He'd given him the first dose in his office. Tom had become belligerent with the doctor during the examination. They'd ruled out any physical ailment.

John quietly explained that the doctor suspected Tom was suffering from dementia. He wouldn't get any better and would probably get worse. The medicine would help, but unless she could get someone to help her with Tom, more than likely he would have to be institutionalized.

Lola looked mournfully at her two friends. It sounded like a death sentence for her husband and all without warning. Things had just gradually gotten worse over a very short period of time. Her heart ached with the confirmation of what she'd already suspicioned.

"Please sit down and have some dinner with us, John. I can't tell you how much I appreciate your help today," said Lola as she placed the prescription bottle in her apron pocket.

She walked over and spoke quietly to her husband. He shuffled to his feet and came to the table. He didn't participate in any of the mealtime conversation. He ate very little of his food. He stared absently into space, and soup drooled down his chin. Lola wiped his mouth and then wiped her tears.

Lola walked her friends out and thanked them again for coming over. John told her, "Now, Lola, you give him that medicine. That should keep him calmer until they can figure out what to do with him. Let us know if you need our help. I'm going to start stopping in to check on you when I go into town, if that's all right."

Lola nodded her consent. Hilda hugged her precious friend and wished they could do more. She and John held hands driving home. Life was so unpredictable and fragile. It made them feel fragile too. Hilda thought, *A person never knows what they're going to have to go through in their lifetime.*

Within six months, Tom's condition deteriorated significantly. He was removed from his home and made a ward of the state of Virginia with a comfortable bed and trained hospital staff to care for him at the St. Albans Asylum. He didn't know Lola at all and had become completely withdrawn. Her Tom was lost in his own mind. She visited him each week and tried to make him some of his favorite foods. He stared blankly at her and refused whatever she'd prepared for him. A year later, he died. For Lola, her grief had begun nearly two years prior to his actual death. She chose to remember the wonderful man she'd married and cherished her memories of their life together. She never remarried.

Mothers Know

"Fletcher," Rachel called out from the garden, "where are you?"

"Rachel, I'm over here at the barn," Fletcher shouted.

"Yes, stay right there. I'm coming over. There's something I want to talk with you about," Rachel called as she made her way toward the sound of his voice in the barn. She looked up at him up in the hayloft. The men had cut plenty of hay that summer, and Fletcher was busy taking the heavy bales up for storage. Joseph and Arwood had been helping him all morning. He'd given them the afternoon off so they could go fishing.

Fletcher was working alone. His shirt was off, and his strong muscles glistened with sweat. This summer, they'd celebrated his forty-first birthday. The hard work he did in the mines, plus his farm responsibilities, helped him maintain his youthful physique.

It seemed like just yesterday that they'd met for the first time. Now here they were, the parents of five children. Joseph and Arwood could hardly be considered children. They were nineteen and seventeen, with their next birthdays coming up in another month. Dotty had turned fourteen back in May, and the twin girls, Ruth and Ruby, were now ten years old! Today, Rachel had Dotty on her heart.

Fletcher looked down and saw Rachel standing there with the water bucket and long metal dipper, smiling up at him. Her brow was damp from perspiration, and she had a tired smile on her face.

"Thanks, my lady, I could use a drink. I'm burning up! I've been watching those clouds, and I'm afraid we've got a storm brewing. Hope the boys get back before it breaks loose," Fletcher said. His parched throat welcomed the refreshing water. He'd been working double time trying to get as much hay put up as he could before the rain started. He sat down on a couple of hay bales. Rachel rubbed his back.

"Rachel, if you don't stop that, I'll never get any more work done today. That feels so good," Fletcher said as the leaned into her touch. He took her hands and pulled her around to face him. "What's wrong? Something is, I know. I can see it in your face."

"Well, it's probably nothing, just a mother's intuition, but every time I turn around, Dotty has taken off again, and I don't know where she is. She's always so mysterious when I ask her where she's been. She's old enough to be pulling her weight around here, but I can never find her." Rachel moaned.

"I noticed she stayed home from church last Sunday. Said she wasn't feeling well, and then on the way home, we saw her walking down the road towards the house," Fletcher said.

"Yes, and she was quick to say she just took a little walk," Rachel said, looking at Fletcher.

"She's a good girl but a mite too independent to suit me," said Fletcher. "So out with it, Rachel. What do you think is going on?"

"Dotty is a beautiful young lady. She is tall so it makes her look older than her age. She got all that height from you, Fletcher. I suspect she has a boyfriend. So if that's the case, why doesn't she bring him around to meet us?" said Rachel.

"Why don't you sit her down and talk to her about your suspicions?" Fletcher asked. "She is certainly too young to be dating. Has she even expressed an interest in anyone that you know of?"

"No, she's so contrary, I didn't think she'd ever find a boyfriend." Rachel laughed.

Fletcher smiled. "I'm sure you're getting yourself worked up over nothing, pretty lady." He gave her a quick peck on the cheek. "Now I have to get back to this hay. We'll talk later."

Rachel walked back toward the house reflecting on her young daughter's life. These last couple of years had been rough. With the Depression going on, they'd all had to tighten their belts. Rachel had cried when she had to use feed sacks to make dresses for her daughters. They were growing so fast, and there was no extra money to buy fabric in town. The twins were younger and didn't seem to mind, but Dotty had been so disappointed.

She was so much taller than Rachel, so there was no passing down her own clothes to her daughter. Rachel used her dressmaking skills to make the clothes they wore as attractive as possible, but they couldn't afford fancy buttons or lace, so perhaps they were a bit plain looking to a young lady.

Her friends certainly didn't have anything that looked any better, so it wasn't that. They were all wearing "chop sacks" clothes made from feed and flour sacks. The mills had started putting pretty patterns on them once they realized the women were using them to make clothes. Even the mill names faded after a few washes, which was very considerate. The poor families in America couldn't afford to waste anything right now.

She'd quizzed Joseph and Arwood about their sister's whereabouts a time or two. She was convinced they knew more than they were telling. Arwood was on the verge of blurting something out but seemed to be silenced by a look Joseph gave him. She was worrying herself to death and was determined to get to the bottom of the matter. Her daughter was too young to be running off by herself. There always seemed to be more and more strangers coming around looking for work or a handout. It just wasn't safe!

She would discuss this with Karen and Mama. Maybe she was overreacting. That evening, as the three women were canning vegetables, Rachel brought up the subject of her oldest daughter. "Have either of you heard Dotty mention a certain boy, as in boyfriend?" she inquired.

"I've never heard Dotty talk of having a boyfriend. She has made it known that she thinks most boys her age are silly gooses," laughed Mama. "Why do you ask, Rachel?"

"Haven't you noticed how she simply disappears at times?" asked Rachel.

"I think she's just a dreamer," said Karen. "You know, she has always had a lot of imagination. She's probably wandering around with her head up in the clouds."

"It worries Fletcher and me when she runs off and we don't know where she is. Actually, it worries me more than it does Fletcher," Rachel admitted.

Karen watched her closely. "Rachel, have you tried to sit her down and discuss your concerns?"

"I have, and she is always evasive. Of course, that worries me all the more," said Rachel.

"What does your mother's heart tell you?" asked Mama. "Always pay attention to your mother's heart. God gave us that for a good reason."

"I agree, Mama. That's the problem. It's telling me that her secrecy means that she is going somewhere or doing something that she shouldn't be doing," Rachel told them.

"Then that's all the more reason to get to the bottom of this. Don't let it be a mystery any longer. Just tell her you are her mother, she is a child, and demand answers!" said Mama.

Rachel's eyes filled with tears. "I think I'm afraid of the answers."

Karen came around the table and gave her sister-in-law a comforting hug. "Rachel, you're never going to feel better until you know. I'm glad I have boys. You, my dear, have two more girls to worry about," Karen teased her.

"Will you both pray for me, that I will have the strength to be the mother my daughter needs me to be right now in her life? I need to make sure that she understands that I love her but have a responsibility as her mother."

Mama stretched out her hand and took Rachel's hand in hers. "Sweetheart, you have always been an excellent mother to your children. As they grow up, they may make decisions you're not comfortable with. That is not a reflection on you and Fletcher or the way you raised them. God gave all of us a free will, an independent spirit. That spirit allows us to make choices. No matter how much we might want to, we cannot live our children's lives for them."

Holding hands, the three women bowed their heads in silent prayer.

24

Child Bride

It was nearly dusk. Rachel sat quietly in a chair near the corner of the porch railing waiting for her daughter to arrive home. Dotty was startled when she reached the top step and heard her mother call out her name. She nearly jumped out of her skin.

"Dotty, I think it's time we had a little mother-daughter talk. Where have you been? I want an honest answer this time."

"I don't think you will approve, Mom," Dotty said as she sat down on the porch and pulled her knees up to her chest. Hot tears streamed down her face. She looked pitifully up at her mother. "I'm in love, but the man I love is older than me. He loves me too, but he says I'm too young for him." "The man?" Rachel asked weakly. "Don't you mean the boy?"

"No, Mom, he is twice my age," Dotty said, watching her mother's face carefully. "It doesn't matter because he said he can't wait around for me to grow up."

"Dotty, has he, has he…taken advantage of you?" Rachel felt like an eternity passed while she waited for her daughter's reply.

"Mother, No!" Dotty said, looking downcast. "I have practically thrown myself at him, but he doesn't even know I'm alive."

Rachel sat down beside her daughter and put her arms around her. "Dotty, he's right. He is too old for you. Why, he's older than your brothers. He is a man, and you are only a child."

Dotty jumped to her feet. "I'm not a child! I love this man with all my heart. I will die if I can't be with him. I love him like you love Daddy—with all my heart."

"Honey, I know it feels that way now, but you don't know anything about love," Rachel tried to comfort her daughter.

"You're wrong, Mom. What I feel is very real. I know he loves me. It's just the difference in our ages that makes him hesitate to express himself."

"I don't like all this secrecy about this man. Maybe he's already married! Are you sure that he hasn't…touched you?" asked Rachel.

"Mom, it's not like that. He isn't married. He is terribly shy. He tells me I'm beautiful and that when I grow up, I'll meet someone closer to my own age. I don't want to find anyone else. My heart wants him, Mom. I didn't talk with you about this because I knew how you and Daddy would react."

Rachel tried to compose herself. Her heart broke for her daughter. Dotty was confused and couldn't possibly understand what love was all about, not at her young age. "Dotty, why don't you invite this young man to come meet us? We can all have a little picnic together. That might be easier than meeting our whole big family at once. How's that sound?"

"Oh, Mom, I don't think he'll come. Do you think Daddy will beat him up for talking to me? It's not his fault I fell in love with him. I just did. He works at the mill. I met him when Mama and I went there one time. As soon as our eyes met, I knew he was the man for me."

"Oh, Dotty, I don't know what to say. You've got to stop running off without telling us where you're going. It is worrying us to death. Where are you meeting him?" asked her mother.

"I go by the mill when it's time for him to get off. We simply walk around and talk. He is a good man. He takes care of his mother. His father died. He has two younger brothers. They all help at their family farm like we do here. I don't even know where his house is. He says they don't have much and that he doesn't have anything to offer me as a husband."

"Honey, you need to slow down. Let us meet him. We trust your judgment. You need to trust ours too. Your father and I want to make sure his intentions are honorable, that's all. Don't say anything to your daddy. Let me talk to him first. This might be somewhat of a shock for him."

"You're not mad at me?" Dotty looked pleadingly at her mother.

"No, I'm not, Dotty. I wish you would've confided in me. Maybe we could have our picnic at the mill? Talk to your young man and ask which day might work best."

Rachel put her arm around her daughter's shoulders. The late summer evenings were starting to cool off. Dotty wiped her tears as they walked inside together. She went into the kitchen and made a sandwich and got a glass of water.

"Mom, I'm going upstairs. Good night, everyone," Dotty told her family. They were playing cards in the living room. Her younger sisters were playing with the paper dolls Mama and Papa had given them a couple of Christmases ago.

Once the rest of their family went to bed, Rachel put on a pot of coffee. She sat down at the kitchen table to discuss the situation with Fletcher. He was tired, sunburned, and could hardly keep his eyes open. His day would start before dawn the next morning. When Rachel began to tell him about Dotty's infatuation, Fletcher was suddenly wide awake. She watched a storm of emotions cloud his face. She thought he was remarkably controlled as she recounted what Dotty had told her, but now he looked like he might explode at any minute.

When she finished, he jumped to his feet and began pacing. "Rachel, do you believe her? Do you think there has been any monkey business?" Fletcher asked her.

"I believe her. She is still innocent. He sounds like a nice young man. Maybe he has shown her all this attention because he didn't want to hurt her feelings. This whole thing is probably very one-sided," Rachel soothed her husband.

"Rachel, I hope you're right because I will certainly knock this man on his rear if I find out he has taken advantage of our daughter in any way!" Fletcher warned.

"I know. I felt outraged too when Dotty first started to explain what was going on. I'm glad she was honest with me. I want to honor that honesty by meeting this young man. I want the two of you men to have a civil conversation. I know you will be on your best behavior, won't you, Fletcher? You know this guy will probably be scared to death meeting us, and especially you, the father."

It was all arranged. On Tuesday evening, they were finally going to meet Dotty's young man. Rachel made thin ham sandwiches with a little mustard and carried a bowl of potato salad to share. Karen made a batch of sugar cookies. The morning after Dotty's revelation, Rachel and Karen had gone for a walk out through the cleared hayfields. Rachel cried as she told her Dotty's news. "I'm doing my best to keep Fletcher calmed down. I'm choosing to believe my daughter's assurances that this young man has always acted decently towards her."

"It's okay to be upset, Rachel. This is still a shock for both of you," Karen spoke in a soothing manner.

"I guess my heart is breaking for the little girl I still see her as. How could she go from hating boys to being in love with *a man*?" Rachel's anguished voice demanded. "Perhaps it comes from the fact that when I was carrying her, Fletcher and I were apart, and I missed him so. Do you think that somehow *marked* her?"

"No, I don't, Rachel," Karen told her. "I don't hold much with all that superstition. That sounds like something Mama would come up with, not you."

"I know her young man must be as nervous as a cat with a long tail at a barn dance. I don't know how he will get any work done today worrying about this picnic we have planned," said Rachel.

"Trust me, it will be no picnic for him." Karen laughed. "He will be fully aware of why you and Fletcher are there. Rachel, have you thought this through? What if he is in love with Dotty and wants to marry her?"

"Fletcher and I've talked about that. It's not an easy matter to consider. We would like to get to know him, to know exactly what kind of fellow he is. We'd want to know how he plans to support her. Times are hard now, and Dotty says his family doesn't have much to go on," said Rachel.

"Well, honey, at least he has a job. It sounds like he has had to be the man of the house for a long time. Losing his father and having to be responsible for his mother and younger brothers has matured him. I believe those circumstances has made him sensitive to protecting Dotty," Karen told Rachel.

"When Fletcher gets cleaned up, we will go down and have our picnic. Dotty wants to go on ahead of us. I guess she thinks they will be a united front that way. Karen, I never dreamed I'd be meeting a suitor so soon, and especially not one who is a grown man!"

"I know, but I don't think the heart has the same boundaries as the mind. This man may be the love of her life. I don't think anyone should stand in the way of true love," Karen said as they walked back toward the house.

As Rachel and Fletcher were riding toward the mill, they caught a glimpse of the young couple. Dotty was standing beside him and talking. She had put on her best dress. The slim man with the red shock of hair was dusty from his day's work at the mill. He was sitting on a log and had his head down with a stick in his hand. He appeared to be drawing something in the dirt. Fletcher slowed the wagon down as they approached. Hearing the wagon wheels on the rough dirt road, the young man looked up and sprang to his feet.

Fletcher looked at Rachel as they arrived at the mill. "Well, here we go. Are you ready to meet your future son-in-law?"

Rachel blanched. "Fletcher, let's not get ahead of ourselves."

He smiled thinly. "You need to prepare yourself, my dear. I think that is where this is headed. I don't think that he'd kept this appointment if he didn't feel something for our daughter. That says a lot for him."

They dismounted from the farm wagon and walked down the path toward the young couple. Dotty came out to meet them, practically dragging the young man with her. "Mom and Daddy, this is Patrick Murphy."

Patrick held out his hand to shake Fletcher's outstretched one. He had a strong grip but clammy palms. It was only natural that the man would be nervous. He also shook Rachel's hand and smiled shyly.

"Patrick, glad we finally got to meet you. Dotty has told us a lot about you," said Fletcher. He watched the young man closely to gauge his reaction. No fear. That was good. Fletcher reasoned, *That can mean the young man has no shame or nothing to be ashamed of.*

Rachel spread out the quilt she'd carried with her. Fletcher helped her remove the food from the picnic basket. Fletcher talked of mining and farming. He asked Patrick about his crop that year. Rachel asked about the man's family. Fletcher asked him about his job at the mill. Patrick seemed to relax a little as he answered their questions.

Fletcher stood when they finished eating their light meal. "Hey, Patrick, why don't you show me around the mill?"

As the men left, Rachel heard Fletcher asking him how long he'd worked at the mill and about his pay. Dotty searched her mom's face.

"What do you think of him, Mom? He's so nice!" Dotty exclaimed.

"I can see why you would like him. He is quite handsome and very polite. I'd like to meet his mother. She seems to have done a good job with her son," Rachel told her daughter.

The two men had been gone a good twenty minutes. Dotty was nervously looking toward the mill. "Mom, do you think Daddy will be ugly to Patrick?"

"Dotty, have you ever known your father to be ugly to anyone? There are man-to-man questions that your father will want to ask him, and he will give him an opportunity to respond," Rachel said.

"No, Mom, but…" she exhaled as she saw the two men exiting the mill. She ran toward them and took Patrick's hand.

"Young lady, your mother and I need to get back to the house. We will see you shortly, right?" Fletcher asked his daughter.

"Yes, Daddy," Dotty told him.

On the ride home, Fletcher told Rachel that Patrick had asked for their daughter's hand in marriage. Fletcher told him yes but that he and her mother required a courtship period of at least six months so they could all get to know each other. Besides, the young man would need to work out the details of their life together. Mostly, he wanted Patrick to understand how precious Dotty was to him and her mother. That set the right tone for the relationship.

Fletcher reached over and took Rachel's hand and watched the tears rolling freely down her cheeks. "Rachel, he told me that until today, he has never even held her hand, so we don't have to worry about our girl being ruined."

About an hour later, Dotty appeared to be floating down the lane to her house. Fletcher and Rachel were sitting on the steps enjoying a cup of coffee in the early evening.

"Patrick told me he loves me and asked me to marry him. He said you gave your permission. Thank you, Daddy!" Dotty hugged her father's neck.

"Did he tell you the rest of our discussion?" Fletcher asked.

"Yes, I know, we have to wait for six months. Don't worry, I'm not going to change my mind, and neither is he," Dotty told them as she went inside.

In the spring of 1935 on a blustery March day, Fletcher gave his oldest daughter's hand in marriage to one Patrick Murphy at the little community church she'd grown up in. Rachel had taken her own wedding dress and fashioned a dress for her daughter with a hand-stitched lacy shawl. Dotty made a beautiful bride. Patrick's mother, Hannah, gave the young couple hers and her husband's wedding bands. Patrick thought that was only for the ceremony, but his mother insisted that they keep them to secure their matrimonial bond. Fletcher almost felt sorry for the young man marrying his bossy young daughter.

It had been very difficult for Rachel to have "the talk" to prepare her daughter for her wedding night. She'd thought she would have years before that discussion was necessary. They would live with Patrick's mother and his brothers. It was a small house, but Patrick had finished the attic space for them. Rachel made them feed sack curtains and gave the newlyweds Dotty's bedroom furniture to get their life together started.

25

Blessings of Family

Rachel watched from the porch as Joseph and Arwood took down an old tree at the edge of the garden. It had leafed out sparsely the year before, and this year, its limbs were bare. She looked at her two fine sons. How was it possible that those strong young men were her babies? They were twenty and eighteen. It was near the end of April of 1935. She'd put a shawl around her shoulders and thought the air still had a bit of a winter nip to it.

She could see the young men wiping sweat from their brow from the exertion. She was extremely proud of her hardworking sons. Times were hard, and living off the land more important than ever. They would dismantle the tree limb by limb, split the logs, chop the wood, and sell it in town to help offset the family's expenses. They were all lucky to be living on this farm with its rich soil. Each year, their labor with the garden fed them and many neighbors for another year.

Rachel knew the country was struggling with the Great Depression. She'd read that many people had their money tied up in banks and businesses that had failed. She heard talk of men taking their lives because they had lost everything and were so ashamed because they couldn't provide for their families. She thanked the Lord that they had all been raised humbly and taught to work the land and to keep their wants and needs simple.

She knew that Papa still owed a little balance on their Sear's house. She and Fletcher helped with the payments when they could. It was hard to hear about friends who had lost their homes and land when banks had to foreclose. She'd seen them with all their possessions packed on wagons traveling to wherever they had family that could take them in.

Her father, Amos, and Fletcher's father, John, were getting older too. This year, Amos would be seventy-four. He made out all right, but Rachel noticed how easily he became winded. Agnes took good care of him and obviously loved him. Agnes never complained. It was charming to see them sitting in church holding hands and winking at one another. In Rachel's heart, she'd feared that she wouldn't be able to accept anyone married to her father other than her own sweet mother, but God bless her mother's memory, she'd grown to love the unpretentious, sweet Agnes.

The children loved to go visit and hear their funny stories. They'd carry their grandparents' fresh vegetables from the garden or a cake Rachel had baked for them. She tried to get her father to see the doctor, but he insisted that he was fine, just tired. He mostly did his smithy work these days, but with the hard times folks were going through, his work was slow.

From her front porch perch, over her steaming cup of coffee, Rachel watched Fletcher's father, John, coming from the barn. He was only sixty-three but moved liked a much older man. Arthritis in his knees and back was taking its toll. John, or Papa as they thought of him, was a good man. They all pitched in and helped him as much as they could. He still put in long days on the farm. It seemed he was in a competition with his sons, trying to show them he could still do his part.

She knew Mama scolded him but to no avail. He was going to do exactly what he set out to do each day, even if it killed him. They all worried about him overdoing it. She hoped he was getting more rest now that he and Mama had their own little place. Lord knows the home they shared with Peter, Karen, and their children could be a madhouse. Rachel loved every minute of it but also welcomed a quiet break to sit on the front porch and put her feet up for a minute or two.

Fletcher had left out early this morning headed to mines. She always got up with him so she could make breakfast and pack his dinner pail for him. Today, he had soup in a canning jar. It was their homemade vegetable soup they'd put up last summer. She packed him a biscuit leftover from last night's supper. He never complained about what she fed him. Rachel thanked the Lord for him every day of her life.

Her coffee cup empty, Rachel rose to get her housework started for the day. This would be a day of sewing. There was always a pile of clothing needing mending, but that could wait. She had drawn up a few new designs and had plans to make her twin daughters a new dress. Rachel had been putting back the colorful feed and flour sacks. The chicken feed sacks had the prettiest patterns. She'd washed them several times already, so the company name had faded away.

"Waste not, want not," was the American way these days. Her husband's and son's patches on their work jeans had patches. When underwear wore out and couldn't be patched anymore, those got made out of feed sacks too! They all had to make do. There wasn't money for luxuries, but they had enough to survive on.

Rachel could look a body over and surmise their size, whip up a pattern and turn out a new piece of clothing fairly quickly. Keeping herself in thread was a challenge. She planned to teach the girls to sew this summer. If she got time today, she wanted to make the new young pastor's two little girls new dresses. They were six and eight, with curly red hair. She had green printed fabric that should work nicely. *Redheads look so pretty in green*, Rachel thought. With her mind awhirl with the work she had before her, Rachel rose from the front porch steps, which had chipped and fading paint, and went inside. Sometimes, you needed a day of work that made your soul feel good too.

Karen was in the kitchen feeding her hungry brood. Andrew, their oldest, had just turned fourteen, and her twin sons, Kellen and Kolten, were now twelve. They adored their older brother. Today, they'd be out in the garden with Papa helping get the crops in the ground. Papa had taught them how to save the seeds from the vegetables. They had rows and rows of starter plants in the barn that they were going to set out. The boys thought there was nothing better than helping their grandfather. He needed and appreciated their help.

Papa worried about Andrew's slightly cocky attitude, which he considered just shy of rudeness. Peter and Karen had many a conversation with Andrew about the importance of being respectful in both his tone and words. He'd always been a good kid with a sharp wit but quick to speak his mind. He tended to be argumentative, which came across to adult family members as disrespectful.

When you had as many people as they did living in one house, you found arguing could make conversations uncomfortable. After all, didn't that usually mean that the person presenting the argument thought his intelligence was superior to others he was talking to? There had been a trip or two out behind the woodshed when Peter thought Andrew had overstepped the good manners' threshold.

Karen tried to quietly coach him on his communications, but she couldn't seem to get through to him. She hoped his younger brothers didn't mimic his behavior. On the positive side, he was a good worker, didn't curse, attended church. If only they could get him to keep his tongue in check.

As everyone busied themselves with all the morning's activities, the day seemed to get steamier and steamier. *For April, the weather is certainly outdoing itself*, Karen thought. She surveyed the work of the men and boys. Peter appeared to be precariously perched on the roof of the barn doing patchwork. Papa and the boys were bent over working the rows, filling them with plants and gently patting the soil around them. *They must feel like their work will never end*, she thought.

Karen knew something about that feeling. Housework certainly had its share of drudgery. She wasn't complaining. She was thrilled to have her little family to take care of. She thought of all those years when it seemed they'd never have a child. She felt tears well up, but there was no sorrow, only a tremendously grateful heart.

She saw Papa stand and take a long thoughtful look at the sky. She looked up and saw darker clouds moving in. A little rain would be a welcome relief. It would water the plants and cool the air. Ruby and Ruth came sailing down the stairs looking bright eyed and bushy tailed.

"Girls, how about going out to the well and drawing a cool pail of water in the bucket and taking it with the dipper out to the menfolk? It's awfully warm today, and they look like they could use a drink," said Aunt Karen. She watched the girls scampering across the yard with the water sloshing about. They were both holding the handle and looking like they might trip up at any minute. *What energy*, Karen thought.

She watched nervously as Peter gingerly came off the roof and down the long handmade ladder. Her twins raced to be the first ones to the water dipper. They took a long drink and went for another one. She looked at Papa as he slowly made his way down the row of tomato plants. His face certainly was red, but then he'd been working in the hot sun all morning. When the boys got their fill, Papa had a drink of water from the cold metal dipper. He pursed his parched lips, letting the water moisten them, then helped himself to another scoop of water.

She saw Peter come up and place his hand on his father's shoulder. Peter looked worried, and his forehead was furrowed in concentration. He was speaking to Papa in what appeared to be a fatherly manner. Papa waved Peter off and passed him the dipper. Peter took a slow methodical drink of the water, watching his father all the while. Papa was headed back to the garden, already correcting the boys and telling them to wait till he got out there with them.

Karen could imagine the conversation between Peter and his father. Peter would be encouraging Papa to rest for a while, go sit under the shade tree or on the porch swing, have a little more water, cool off a bit. And just as plainly, she could picture Papa protesting that he was fine, telling Peter that those boys needed him right by their side so he could show them exactly how to place the tender young sprouts in the soil just so, not too deep, and make sure they properly patted the soil around the delicate stems.

She shook her head and headed back toward the kitchen. Papa had always been stubborn. He loved their boys and wanted to train them up right. When Joseph and Arwood got to the water pail, they had a couple of scoops each and then dumped the rest of the water on their heads letting out a big whoop as the cold water cruised down their necks, soaking their shirts. Peter smiled at Fletcher's boy's shenanigans. He loved those two as much as he loved his own.

Karen had decided to fix a simple fare of canned green beans and potatoes with biscuits for their dinner. She busied herself in the kitchen wishing she had lemons to make lemonade. *Wonder if lemon trees would grow in Virginia?*

Rachel had been cutting patterns and sewing all morning. She had both of her daughters' dresses finished except for the detail work like collars and sleeves and hemming. She was thinking of adding a belt. *How will the dresses look if the tie belt, collars, and sleeves were made with a contrasting color?* she wondered.

She stood and stretched. Her muscles were stiff from sitting in the same position for so long. How long had she been at her sewing anyway? Rachel pondered. Seeing Ruby and Ruth coming through the screen door, she called out to them, "Girls, do me a favor and run over to your mama's house and bring me back a big jar of her tomatoes. Take the wicker basket to put them in. Don't be racing with the tomatoes. You might break the jar," their mother warned them. "Invite Mama to come over and eat dinner with us too."

Rachel smiled at Karen. "Mama never needs an invitation, but she is snug as a bug in her little house. I don't want her to forget about us."

Karen laughed at the thought of Mama ever forgetting them and all her grandchildren. "You know that's highly unlikely, Rach. What are you planning to make for supper with those tomatoes the girls are fetching?"

"I overheard a couple of the older ladies at church talking about fixing tomato dumplings. Doesn't that sound interesting and delicious? I'm going to try my hand at making them. If we have any of those green beans left from dinner, we'll serve them too. The men and boys have been working so hard today, I thought I'd make them a hearty supper. I'm preparing deviled eggs too."

26

A Knock at the Back Door

Mama came over with the twins bringing a jar of her delicious bread and butter pickles and a little streaked meat to go with the green beans. She carried her basket into the kitchen and sat it down on the counter. She was startled by a knock at the back door.

Who could that be? she wondered. Without any hesitation, she pulled the door open and peered outside. Her dream was to someday get her sons a screen door to go on that back door. She knew Papa could easily make one, but she hesitated to create any more work than necessary for him.

She was surprised to see a tall aging man standing on the back steps. His hat was in his hands in a show of respect. He had kind, sad eyes. She studied him. His gangly frame, his hair and beard both needing a trim, his worn-out clothes and the holes in the knees of his trousers gave him away. Mama quickly recognized his sort as a hobo. So many of his type were traveling the land these days. Many people had fallen on hard times. She figured he wanted food; they always did.

When she glanced back into the kitchen, she noticed Karen, Rachel, and the girls had left the kitchen, but she wasn't frightened of the man. She certainly wouldn't invite him into her house, but she'd give him a meal. "Have a seat there on the steps, and I'll get you a bite to eat and give you a glass of cool spring water."

As she was preparing a simple meal, she heard men's voices out back. Nothing ever happened on the back stoop, but today it was becoming a gathering place! When she peeked through the window, she saw Papa and Peter talking with the man. Next thing she knew, they were ushering him into the kitchen. Mama clucked her tongue in disapproval. What were they thinking inviting that hobo into the house like that? He obviously needed a bath, and they didn't know a thing about him. She gave her husband the big eye and an inquiring look.

"Now, Cooper, I believe you met my wife, Hilda," said John.

The man lowered his eyes and said, "Yes, sir, she kindly offered to fix me something to eat."

"Hilda, Cooper said we may call him Coop," said John. "He is a farmer by trade and was one of those unfortunate souls who lost his home and land during the Depression."

Hilda wondered why they needed to call him anything, but she'd play along. "I'm sorry to hear that, Mr. Cooper," said Mama as she sat a biscuit with a piece of streaked meat before him. She noticed he eyed the food hungrily.

"We have encouraged him to stay with us for a while and help with the crops," said Papa. "I explained that we can't pay him anything, but we can let him sleep in the barn and keep his belly full." Papa clapped the man on the back.

The older man smiled weakly as if waiting for the farm woman's response.

"John, quit rambling on and let the poor man eat," said Hilda. "If that's your decision, I'll hold up my end of the bargain." Hilda nodded, signaling the man to sit and have his meal. He tucked into the simple meal like it was a grand feast. He seemed to savor every bite.

John smiled gratefully at his wife over the man's head.

Hilda wondered, *Is John turning into an old fool, or is this his way of admitting he recognizes he can't do it all?* She would talk to Peter, but for now, she didn't see any harm in trying the arrangement. She still didn't like the idea of serving the man at her kitchen table.

As spring turned into summer and summer droned on, Hilda managed to overcome her objection to having Cooper join them for meals. He became a good friend to them all, but especially to John. They loved to hear him tell them stories of surviving off the land and riding the rails in search of better opportunities. However, he would clam up in a hurry if they asked him too many personal questions.

His past seemed a taboo subject. In their innocence, the children would often pose questions about his family. The others would wait anxiously to see if he would respond. He would skillfully skirt the answer and ask them a question in return.

As the sky darkened in the evening, the men and boys would build a "hobo style" fire out in the backyard and gather round it. That was when their hobo storyteller would regale them with his tales. When he wasn't telling stories, he taught the young men how to make "tramp art." Coop explained that hobos made the trinkets to exchange for food or other things they needed.

Sometimes, they would get lucky, and a shopkeeper would buy their handcrafts. Getting in the front door was usually the obstacle to selling their crafts. Using a small block of wood, he hollowed it out into a box and made a lid to fit the box. That wasn't anything especially difficult, but it occupied the young men and took their minds off the farmwork for a time.

Then he demonstrated to them the art of making intricate designs and pictures on the wooden box lids. Using a little coal dust, he accented the carvings, giving them depth. Coop pressed the stain into the exposed pulp. He showed them how to file down the edges of the lid so it fit snugly on the box. Next, he showed them how to carve a small picture frame with a lattice-like design. They began working on gifts for Christmas for their family. It filled them with pride that they could make something so beautiful to give their loved ones.

Everyone got used to having Coop around. They thought of him as a member of their family. He always had a big warm smile to greet them with in the morning. It wasn't long before the autumn leaves began to fly, and the nights became cooler. The wind whistled as winter stood at their door.

Hilda remembered looking out her kitchen window one morning and seeing the first frost on the ground. She pulled her shawl tighter around her shoulders and put another log in the stove. John was making his rounds and feeding the animals. She had bacon and eggs frying for him and Coop. She had run out of flour, so there'd be no biscuits today.

She noticed that John seemed to be moving slower than usual this morning as he headed back toward the house to get his breakfast. His arthritis was surely acting up again. Cold or damp weather always aggravated that ailment. She thought there was something almost sad in his demeanor and step this morning. *Wonder why Coop isn't with him? Probably finishing up a chore.*

Wiping her hands on her apron, Hilda stood on the porch watching him approach.

"What is it, John? You look like you've lost your best friend. Are all the animals okay?"

"Oh sure." He met her eyes, and she saw deep melancholy there. "It's Coop. He's gone, Hilda," her husband told her.

"What did you say? Coop is gone? Well, maybe he had to go into town or something," said Hilda.

"Now, Hilda, you know he doesn't have any money, and when has he ever gone into town by himself?" said John.

"Did he leave a note? That would be the respectable thing to do," said Hilda.

"No, but you know, I'm not even sure he can write. It's not the kind of thing we ever talked about," said John.

"Well, surely he wouldn't just leave without his breakfast or without saying good-bye. Why, he has become like family to us all," said Hilda. She wrung her hands. "You don't think he was sick and didn't want to worry us, do you?"

"No, I think it's the cold weather. He probably felt like he couldn't earn his keep around here in the winter and didn't want to be a burden to us, the dang fool," John lamented.

They all watched for Coop's tall frame and engaging smile as the weeks sped by, and before they knew it, a month had passed. He was gone. They all missed him and felt a little hurt because he didn't say bye. They wondered if they'd ever see him again.

27

Dotty's Big News

Rachel, Karen, and the girls gently unpacked Rachel's delicate glass Christmas ornaments, a gift from her father after her mother's death. As a young girl, she had placed these same ornaments on the tree with her mother. Of course, they had added more ornaments to the special collection, including many that were homemade by various family members.

She always felt her mother's presence and remembered how much she had cherished this Christmas tradition. It was hard to believe so many years had sped by since her mother's death. It got more difficult each year to remember her mother's fine features. What was it about the holidays that refreshed memories?

Rachel's sons had selected the tree and placed it in the living room in front of the big picture window. The younger kids had busied themselves earlier in the day by stringing popcorn for garland. Rachel and Fletcher loved the house being full of family. Dotty and her husband were there, and so were Mama and Papa. Rachel had invited Amos and Agnes, but Agnes had a bad cold and had begged off. She'd encouraged Amos to go without her, but he didn't want to leave her by herself. He told her he wouldn't be able to enjoy himself for worrying about her.

The family gathered around after supper to decorate the tree. The dinner had been a simple one. They had brown beans, onions, sausage gravy and biscuits, and pan-fried potatoes. Papa had joked that if they'd skipped the beans and had eggs, they could've called it breakfast.

Mama brought over blackberry and chocolate chess pies. That would be the end of her sugar rations for a while. She'd been saving them up for just this occasion. They always had their dessert and hot chocolate after the tree was done. Karen would treat them to hot chocolate.

Dotty started not to come because she too hadn't been feeling well for the past week. Patrick had finally persuaded her to see the doctor a few days ago. The doctor assured them that her condition wasn't contagious and to go ahead with her holiday plans.

After dinner, Patrick stood and nervously cleared his throat. He spoke in a too-loud voice and broadcasted, "Dotty and I have an announcement to make. I'm expecting a baby!"

They all laughed, and Patrick looked confused. That was not the reaction he expected.

Dotty looked up at him and said, "Patrick, dear, I think you meant to say *we* are expecting a baby."

Fletcher and Rachel gave their daughter and son-in-law hugs and congratulated them. Mama watched the goings-on and remarked to Fletcher and Rachel, "I guess you two know what this means, don't you? You're about to become grandparents."

Fletcher looked at Rachel and joked, "I guess that's right. I'll be married to Granny."

Their family laughed at the expression on Rachel's face, somewhere between shock and thrill. Ruby and Ruth came over to Rachel's side. "Momma is too beautiful to be a *granny*! We have to think of a better name for her." "How about *Me-Maw*?" suggested Dotty.

"I like that," said Rachel, putting her arms around Dotty's waist. "We are so excited for you both. How are you feeling?"

"The doctor says I'm about three and a half months along. We didn't want to say anything because I've been so sick. We were afraid that we might jinx things if we spoke too soon. I've been nauseated for the past week. I don't know how the baby can get any nourishment because everything I eat keeps coming up. The doctor told us my system should calm down soon," Dotty said weakly.

"Oh, honey, I know that feeling very well," said Rachel. "And your doctor is right. That sick feeling does eventually pass, usually before now. Maybe there's something you're eating that your stomach can't tolerate right now."

Karen hugged her niece and asked Dotty, "What are you hoping for, a boy or a girl?"

Dotty glanced up at her husband. "I think Patrick is hoping for a boy. We haven't had much time to think about being parents yet."

The men teased Patrick some about becoming a first-time dad at the ripe old age of thirty. Patrick said, "I'm not concerned about me. Dotty is so young. I'm worried sick about my wife. Mama has a remedy she has cooked up to help Dotty deal with the morning sickness."

Dotty made a gagging face. "I think I'd rather take my chances with the nausea. I have no idea what she puts in that concoction, I mean *cure*, but it tastes awful!"

Fletcher hadn't stopped beaming since Patrick's announcement about the baby. "This is a wonderful

Christmas surprise. When will your baby arrive?" "In June," said Dotty.

"Perfect, the little one will get a good start before next winter," said Mama.

"Oh, Mama, you make the baby sound like a calf," wailed Dotty.

Papa laughed. "Well, don't worry about Patrick there.

He'll survive this whole ordeal just fine."

Patrick squeezed his young bride's shoulders. "Mother is excited about the idea of having a baby in the house again. She will hardly let Dotty lift a finger. At least we know this baby will be loved."

Everyone pitched in, and soon the tree was beautifully adorned. Mama and Papa did the honors and lit the candles on the branches. Fletcher and Peter extinguished the room's lanterns, and the eyes of the children, young and old alike, filled with wonder and excitement. Papa hugged Mama and produced a little sprig of mistletoe and held it above her head before planting a big sloppy smooch on her cheek.

The young couple stood near the Christmas tree. Rachel noticed that Dotty had her hand instinctively on her stomach as if sharing the moment with their unborn babe. Patrick's arm was around Dotty's shoulders. He made a good husband for their daughter, thought Rachel.

Fletcher has been studying Rachel's face. She glowed from the anticipation of becoming a grandmother. He realized they were standing on the threshold of a whole new adventure for them both. He suspected she was both excited and apprehensive for her young daughter, who still seemed like a child to him. *Hard to imagine our child having a baby*, he mused.

Peter and Karen were snuggling on the sofa. Fletcher felt blessed to be in their warm home surrounded by family.

After dessert, Joseph, Arwood, and all the younger boys quickly disappeared to their rooms while the girls and older folks enjoyed each other's company and a cup of coffee in the living room by the tree. Rachel suspected they were working on some sort of Christmas surprise, but she had no clue what it could be. There was only money for the bare necessities. She'd been sewing something special for each of them from the beautiful feed sacks she'd put back.

Before they knew it, it was Christmas morning. Once again, the family gathered at the home place. After a hearty breakfast of bacon, eggs, and biscuits, they congregated around the Christmas tree once more. The boys begged to go first with their gifts for everyone. They presented the family with the lovely "hobo" boxes Cooper had taught them to make. Rachel's gift from her sons was large, about the size of a jewelry box. It had a snug-fitting lid. They excitedly explained that they had made it to be a button box for her since she loved to sew.

Karen's twins gave her two small matching boxes that had their initials carved on the bottom. Andrew had made her a larger box similar in size to Rachel's, with an intricate diamond pattern carved on the lid.

Rachel gave the girls and ladies lovely homemade ruffled aprons with pockets.

Peter and Karen's twin sons, Kellen and Kolten, were thirteen. They gave them both a small pocketknife. They were thrilled with their gift. Andrew looked a little downcast that he hadn't gotten one too. Peter asked him if he could see that nice wooden box Andrew had made his mother. He took the lid off and admired it. Andrew was looking down at his feet.

"Here, son, give this back to your mother," Peter told him. He purposely had not put the lid on very well. He fumbled handing it off to Andrew. Out fell a genuine Swiss army knife. Peter winked at Andrew. "Now how did that get in there?" he asked. "Wonder whose gift that is?"

"Ah, Dad, quit kidding. It's mine!" Andrew exclaimed. He went over and gave Peter a big hug. "How did you know I wanted one of these knives?"

"Son, do you think your dad is blind? How many times have I seen you over at the store counter looking at the knives they have in there?"

Other little trinkets were gifted among the family, and in no time at all, another Christmas was in the history books.

28

Dotty's Sorrow

The howling March winds made the weather unfit for man or beast. Fresh-fallen snow lay glistening atop another foot of snow that had steadily built up over the past week. The temperatures had been so bitterly cold that no one ventured outside unless they had to. It was the wee hours of the morning, and Fletcher was sleeping soundly. He awoke with a start when he heard someone knocking on their door. His first thought was that Cooper was back. He grabbed his trousers and bounded toward the front door without even getting a shirt on. There stood young Patrick, looking scared to death.

"Patrick, get in here before you freeze to death. What's wrong, son?" Fletcher asked.

"Mother thinks Dotty is losing the baby. We don't know what to do," the big man sobbed.

"Oh God, no. Hold on, let me go wake Rachel and Karen. Karen has some experience helping the midwife. I'll get dressed and go into town to see I can raise either the midwife or the doctor," said Fletcher. "Can you get the women to your place?"

"Yes, yes, please hurry." Tears streamed unashamedly down Patrick's face.

Fletcher hugged his son-in-law. Whatever reservations he'd had about his daughter marrying so young were gone. There was no doubt that this young man loved her with all his heart. "Buck up, Patrick. We don't want you scaring the women any more than necessary. After the initial shock of this news wears off, they will take their cue from you. If you're panicky, it might panic them too."

"Okay, Mr. Broce, I'll try to steel myself," said Patrick, wiping his tears with the back of his bare hands.

"Women know about such things as birthing and babies. I'm going to wake them now. You warm up by the stove and be ready to go when they get out here," said Fletcher.

About two hours later, Fletcher and the doctor arrived at the Murphy house. A sad crew greeted them.

Karen led the doctor to the upstairs bedroom. She explained that the perfectly formed baby had been stillborn. The doctor examined the fetus and agreed with her assessment. "I'm sorry, there's no hope for the baby," he announced. He examined the distraught young mother.

Afterward, using his expert bedside manner, he took her hand in his and stroked the back of it. He explained what had happened and his instructions for her personal care. Rachel pushed the damp hair from her daughter's brow.

Dotty's eyes pleaded with her mother to tell her it wasn't so. Rachel spoke softly to her daughter. "Honey, I know it doesn't help much to hear this, but you are young. Give it some time, then you can try again. We're going to head home and give you and Patrick a little time together to mourn the loss of your first baby." Hugging her daughter, she hid her own tears and heartache.

Mama cried openly when she heard the news of Dotty's miscarriage. Papa said, "We have to have a graveside service. The baby needs a name. Was the baby a boy or girl?"

Fletcher told him it was a little boy. He didn't know if Patrick and Dotty had a name yet.

"I'm making a little casket for him. Fletcher, come on out to the building with me," Papa said.

By the next day, Papa had constructed a tiny wooden casket for the infant. He had carved a delicate little cross on the lid. Mama had been making a baby quilt for the child. She quickly finished it and placed it in the undersized casket to receive the baby.

Patrick and Dotty named the baby Kip Murphy, a short name for a short life. The family gathered around as they buried the infant. Dotty was too weak to attend the simple service. The men sang a song, Fletcher led the prayer, and their pastor said a few words of comfort for the family. Kip

Murphy was laid to rest in the Murphy family cemetery on their land next to his paternal grandfather.

The day was bitterly cold. Rachel thought it was the saddest thing she'd ever seen—that tiny casket, the shallow grave in the frozen ground. She believed every life had a purpose and every child was a tiny miracle. She thought of the babies Karen had lost before she had become Kellen and Kolten's mother. *Did Karen think of those lost children?*

She never spoke of them, and Rachel never asked.

29

Stranger in Town

"Peter, when you take the eggs and greens to town, see if you can find any lemons. If they're too pricey, let them go. We've all been craving lemonade. Lord knows we haven't had any in ages, but that's a small thing," said Karen as she looked at Peter's worn-out work boots. Andrew's didn't look much better, and winter was coming. Well, they'd make do and patch what they could.

"Sure, honey," said Peter. He called out to Rachel, who was sewing away as usual. "Can I pick up anything for you, Rachel?"

"Thanks for asking, Peter. I could use several spools of brown and white thread. Get the largest our money will buy. I also need buttons for the family's shirts. There's a pile of clothes that need mending. My supplies are so low right now, but that's the story of our life these days, isn't it? Ruby, run upstairs and get that dollar I have on the dresser and give it to your Uncle Peter," said Rachel. "That should do it, but put back the brown thread if it's not enough."

"If you're short, I might be able to throw in a dime or two for the thread. You work on our family's clothes too," said Peter. "I have no idea how you and Karen manage with your small household budget. You two ladies are something else."

"Please check with Mama too. I know she was getting low on flour and needs ointment to put on Papa's sore back. She can't slow that man down, so she tries to keep him well oiled." Karen laughed.

"Andrew, go hitch the horse for me. I'd like for you to ride with me. Rachel, I'll stop and check on Amos and Agnes on the way in to see if they need anything," said Peter.

"Ah, Dad, why do I have to go too? I wanted to get in some fishing today. All we do is work, work, work," moaned Andrew in an exasperated tone.

"Son, this isn't up for debate. Please do as I asked you. I want to make several stops on the way in and talk to our neighbors about buying wood from us this winter. My plan is to introduce you to them since you'll be making most of the deliveries. Folks like to know who they're dealing with," Peter patiently explained.

Karen cringed. She appreciated both Peter's patience and firmness with Andrew. Her oldest son could be contrary at times. She watched as Andrew slowly put on his coat and hat. He almost slammed the door on his way outside to do as his dad had instructed. Andrew shut it just hard enough to be able to swear that the wind had caught it. His mother knew it had more to do with temper and temperament than it had to do with any wind.

Karen walked out on the front porch and waved good-bye to her men. It made her heart heavy when Andrew behaved the way he did at times. She was grateful that it wasn't any worse, but still it gave her pause. His teacher complained last year that she suspected Andrew had somewhat of an aggressive attitude toward the other children in the class. She had worried because he didn't have too many friends due to his nature and sometimes sarcastic retorts.

Karen sighed. It seemed she was always having to defend her oldest son. She always tried to follow up any criticism of Andrew with a litany of his positive traits. He was very bright, as evidenced by his high marks in school, nor was he disrespectful to his teachers, and he was strong, handsome, and a hard, if not reluctant, worker. He was great with his younger brothers and cousins. He could be so patient with them. She thought he was especially kind to his grandparents. There were times, however, when he seemed like a pot about to boil over. Maybe he would outgrow whatever he seemed to be going through.

When Peter finally got into town, they headed straight to the store to gather the list of supplies everyone needed. Andrew separated from him and went over to once again lollygag over the knife collection in the locked glasstopped case. *Maybe Mom and Dad could get me a spiffier one for Christmas this year*, he daydreamed. He reasoned, since he was almost sixteen, it was high time he had a hunting knife of his own. What he preferred though was one of those fancy switchblade knives. You pushed a button, and the blade snapped out with lightning speed. He knew his parents would never buy him something like that, but maybe a practical hunting knife wasn't out of the question.

Andrew glanced around to see where his dad was shopping and whether Peter was paying any attention to him. Good, he wasn't. He signaled for the kindly old Mr. Jones to open the glass case for him and let him examine one of those fine switchblade knives. *Man, this little jewel is something else!* thought Andrew. He pushed the button a number of times and marveled at how quickly the blade sprang out. He slashed the air with the blade, imagining it being a sword.

Mr. Jones cleared his throat and held out his hand for Andrew to return the knife to him to put back in the case. No words were spoken between the two; none were needed. Andrew felt the cold metal and weight of the knife in his palm and reluctantly handed it over to the clerk. Mr. Jones locked the case and proceeded to assist another customer. He knew boys would be boys, and it certainly wasn't the first time a young man had wanted to hold a switchblade knife. He smiled to himself, thinking it probably wouldn't be the last time either.

Andrew continued looking at the knife display. He was startled when a rather rough-looking, slightly overweight fellow grabbed him tightly by the arm. "What's your name, son? How old are you?" he gruffly inquired of him.

Andrew felt uncomfortable as the man studied him intently. He glanced toward his dad, hoping this time, he *was* looking his way, but he was still turned away from him. Andrew prayed silently that he would look around. He could smell alcohol on the man's breath, and his cold stare made Andrew's skin crawl. He tried to step back to break the man's grip, but he squeezed his arm harder. Andrew could feel the man's rough fingernails pinching his arm.

Andrew stammered out," I'm Andrew Broce, sir. I'm fifteen."

The man continued to hold on to the young man's arm as he said, "I don't know you, but you are the spitting image of me when I was your age. It's like looking back in time into a mirror. You could be my son, if I had one."

Andrew felt his stomach sicken at the thought of this man being his father, but he didn't say anything.

"Who's your ma?" the man asked bluntly, still looking at him as if he could see right through him and read his mind.

"Karen Broce, and that's my father, Peter Broce, over there. Excuse me, I believe my dad needs my help," Andrew said as he scrambled from the man's viselike clutch. He nearly knocked over a lamp oil display as he made his escape. He heard the man's loud, obnoxious laugh at his expense, and his face reddened.

Maybe I'm not so grown up, thought Andrew.

The commotion caught Peter's attention. He thought Andrew looked shaken. He saw the steely-eyed man standing in the aisle staring after his son. Andrew reached his dad's side in a flash.

"Son, who is that man over there at the counter? Were you talking with him? Was he bothering you?" Peter asked.

Andrew was breathless and slightly embarrassed, although he didn't know why he should feel embarrassed. Maybe what he was feeling, for the first time in his life, was *fear*. None of it made any sense to him. "I don't know, Dad, but I think he's been drinking. I could smell it on him. He acted like he should know me. Told me I reminded him of himself at my age. Look at him, Dad. He's dirty, drunk, unshaven, fat. I don't look anything like him. Everyone says I look like you and Mom."

Peter continued to watch the man. "What else did he say to you, son?"

"He wanted to know my name and who my mother was," said Andrew, still disgusted by the fellow. *The nerve of him thinking we could be related*, he thought.

The man was careful to keep his head turned slightly so Peter couldn't see him plainly, but he appeared to be straining to hear their conversation and watching Peter's interaction with his son. The man must have sensed Peter's interest in him because he headed toward the back of the store. Peter thought the man acted peculiar, but there had been no harm done. "Son, you'll meet all types in this world. I wouldn't worry about him."

Outside, Peter and Andrew loaded the wagon and unhitched the horse. Peter climbed up beside Andrew and took the reins. He glanced over his shoulder as they pulled away and caught sight of that same man leaning in the doorway of the store, watching them drive away. The fellow managed to let the brim of his hat hang down over his face, obscuring his identity in the shadows.

Very odd, thought Peter. *Probably just a nutcase.*

When he had traveled about a block, he gazed behind and was surprised to see the man still looking after them. The hair on the back of Peter's neck stood up suddenly. There *was* something vaguely familiar about the man. He didn't recognize him, but it gave him an uneasy feeling that he couldn't quite shake. He might come back into town tomorrow by himself and see what he could find out about the fellow—quietly, of course.

The stranger watched the wagon until it was out of sight. He saw the young boy turn around and look back at him once. He'd quickly swung back around when he realized he was being watched.

Wonder why he was so skittish? Yes, this might be something for him to investigate further. He performed calculations in his head. He could be his son, but that wasn't his mother's name. It was confusing, but he would get to the bottom of it. He always did his best thinking when he'd been drinking, he cackled to himself.

Going back into the store, he proceeded over to the counter to talk the older gentleman who had waited on the man and his son. He asked him to tell him about the customers he'd waited on before he walked up.

The storekeeper didn't answer at first as he studied the man before him. It was obvious to him from the man's red eyes and slightly slurred speech that he'd been drinking. It was still early in the day. The clerk hesitated to respond. His gut told him to not be too forthcoming. Something didn't feel right. "May I ask why you're asking about those customers?" the older man asked.

The man became angry and belligerent, raising his voice and attracting the attention of other customers in the store. He cursed under his breath and belched loudly. He leaned toward the clerk ominously. "Since when did it become a sin to make a neighborly inquiry about someone?" he sneered. "Maybe I'm looking for work. Why is that any of your business?"

The older gentleman became flustered and in backing away from the unsavory character, inadvertently knocked over the bell on the counter. The fellow on the other side laughed uproariously at the old coot's nervousness.

Mr. Tilley came out of the stockroom when he heard the bell clang. "Mr. Jones, is everything all right? You look a little pale."

Flustered, Mr. Jones cleared his throat, which had suddenly become very dry, and explained that the customer standing before him had questions about the family that had just left the store.

"Well, who was it, Mr. Jones?" asked Tilley.

"It was that nice young man who brings us eggs and greens, Peter Broce, and his oldest son, Andrew," Mr. Jones practically whispered to his boss.

Mr. Tilley addressed himself to the shabbily attired man standing at the counter. "What is it that you want to know?"

The man could feel everyone's eyes on him. They were all quietly watching the goings-on, pretending to busy themselves with this or that at the store. Anyone of them would be willing to spring to the storeowner or Mr. Jones's defense if necessary. People looked after one another around here, and this man looked like a threat to them. He was decidedly uncouth from what they'd witnessed of his interaction.

"I might want to call on them to see if they could use any help on their farm. Can you tell me how to get to their place?" he asked in the most cordial manner he could muster, fooling no one.

Mr. Tilley cleared his throat and felt a reluctance to give the man too many specifics but realized that maybe telling him something would get him out of his store so he'd stop disturbing his help and customers. He was glad that the store was mostly full of men today. Many days, it was filled with ladies, and that would've been awkward. "If I'm not mistaken, they live down in the Prices Fork area somewhere. I've never actually been to their farm. Sorry, I can't be any more helpful than that."

The man was still cursing under his breath, recognizing that he was getting the runaround. He turned to the other store customers milling around and asked, "Anyone else know where they live?"

He looked at their retreating backs as they all shook their heads and muttered in various ways that they couldn't help him. "Wouldn't help him" would have been a more honest response.

They certainly seem to be protective of that family. Must mean they have money or influence or both.

Everyone in the store felt like this character was up to no good. They would keep an eye on him. They all believed in giving a fellow a chance, but there was something almost sinister about this man.

30

Sixth Sense

To the onlookers' dismay, the man headed back inside the store. He asked anyone who would listen if they knew where he could borrow or rent a horse for a few days. Someone suggested he try the blacksmith shop there in town and pointed him in the general direction. He hurried out, and the men watched him walk quickly toward the shop.

"What do you think of that character, Slim?" asked Mr. Tilley.

Slim said, "I don't rightly know what to make of him. He certainly seems to be an oddball. Who arrives in a new town and shows himself like he has? Surely, he must know that no one is going to go out of their way to help him when he displays such an arrogant attitude?"

"I know what you mean. I didn't much care for the way he spoke to Mr. Jones either. It ruffled the old man up so much, he had to go in the back and get himself a cold drink. I told him to sit for a spell till he was ready to come back to his post," said Bert Tilley.

"Mr. Jones can be a little on the sensitive side. From what I heard, this stranger didn't make any friends today. In fact, he seems to have stirred up a great deal of ill will. I've got a bad feeling about him. Wonder why he chose to take such an interest in the boy and his family? I saw him grab the boy by the arm, scared him to death, I'd say," said Slim.

"Yes, I agree. We'll all have to keep an eye on him. He certainly seems to be up to no good," said Tilley.

Peter and Andrew made a stop at Amos and Agnes's house to drop off their supplies. They asked about Amos. Agnes said he'd decided to go in and tidy up around the blacksmith shop. "I've never known him to not tidy up before he leaves for the day. If you ask me, I think the old boy just needed to get out of the house for a bit," said Agnes.

Peter smiled broadly at the affable Agnes. "You're probably right. Us men have got to be doing something. It's in our blood!" he told her.

Once again, they started down the road. Peter had the sensation of being watched or followed. He looked over his shoulder and saw a horseback rider some distance back. Peter thought, *There is always someone coming or going on this busy Prices Fork Road.* That prickly feeling he'd experienced made him feel a trifle foolish.

"What is it, Dad?" Andrew queried.

"Oh, nothing, son. We'll take Mama's grocery package to her before we go home. I want to talk to Papa about the fence mending we need to do. If he's not feeling up to it, we'll get Joseph and Arwood to help us. He likes to be asked, so that's what we're doing," said Peter.

"I'm starved. Wonder what Mom is making us for supper tonight?" said Andrew.

"Andrew Broce, you're always hungry. Papa came by early this morning and dropped off a couple of chickens he'd killed. I heard your mom talk about making us chicken and dumplings for supper," said Peter.

Andrew's stomach growled, and they both laughed. His mother was a good cook. She and Rachel took turns about it. It wasn't that Rachel wasn't a good cook, but she liked to experiment with new recipes. Most turned out all right, but occasionally she'd hit a sour note. Mom made her tried and true recipes that she knew her family loved.

About thirty minutes earlier, the stranger had arrived at the blacksmith shop on foot. He told the old gentleman working there that he needed to rent a horse and saddle so he could ride out to area farms and hopefully find some work.

Amos observed the seedy-looking man whose hands didn't suggest that they had hit a lick of hard work in his life. He hoped he had cash upfront because it wasn't his policy to grant credit to strangers. He could overlook the man's appearance. Many folks were struggling now in this bad economy. Because he hadn't seen the man around, Amos asked him where he hailed from.

The man's whole attitude changed, and he eyed Amos menacingly and grumbled something under his breath about "town folks." Amos's hearing wasn't what it used to be so he didn't catch all the words the fellow said, but there was no mistaking the man's bad attitude. He assumed the man had fallen on hard times and wasn't handling it very well. Amos decided to give him the benefit of the doubt and let him rent his own horse. He could always catch a ride home with one of the farmers going past his place.

The stranger seemed in a hurry to get on his way. He quickly counted out coins for the amount Amos had quoted him and promised to have the horse back in a couple days. Amos brought the horse around for him.

The man bounded into the saddle and was off before Amos could even tell him the horse's name. Amos was left standing in the dust.

What was that fellow really up to? Amos wondered. He hoped it wouldn't be the last time he saw his horse and saddle. He felt somewhat guilty for thinking that way. He didn't have a good reason not to trust the man, but still…

Karen was sitting on the swing. She waved at Peter and Andrew when they drove by the house on the way to Papa and Mama's place just around the curve. She watched Rachel and her twins, Ruby and Ruth, playing a new game the girls had heard about called hopscotch. If someone didn't know better, they might think Rachel was a child too because of her petite stature. It looked like they were having a lot of fun. All three were laughing and hopping on the squares after they managed to toss their smooth little rocks in the right spot. Karen loved seeing them all happy like that. She got up, dusted off her apron, and walked inside to check on their supper.

Rachel and the girls hadn't noticed Peter and Andrew ride by in the horse-drawn wagon. They were trying to keep an eye out for Fletcher coming home from work. They were determined to draw him into their little game of hopscotch. Rachel warned them that Daddy might not cooperate with them. She smiled to herself thinking of her big, tall husband jumping around on the little squares.

Suddenly, Rachel froze. She felt an inexplicable chill run down her spine. She wasn't superstitious, but she had a strong feeling of being watched. She heard the boys playing ball in the backyard and listened to their laughter and good-natured taunts to each other. She looked toward the garden. Papa had left, heading home a little earlier. Karen was inside.

Her sons were in the house getting ready to call on lady friends tonight. Joseph was still sweet on Ada, and Arwood liked one of her friends. She whirled around and looked down the long lane to their house half expecting to see Fletcher walking down to the house, or even Peter and Andrew returning. What she saw made her skin prickle.

There was a man mounted on a horse silently watching her and the girls. Rachel shielded her eyes from the sun to see if she could make out the man's features. He immediately ducked under the low tree branches, out of view. She felt the sensation of pure evil exuding from the solitary figure. Rachel might be wrong, but it looked like he was on her dad's old horse, Joe. She only caught a glimpse of the steed, so she couldn't be sure. There was something foreboding about the scenario. She suddenly felt very distressed and fearful. She caught hold of the girls' arms and told them to get inside the house right away.

She knew she was probably being foolish, but she couldn't brush off the awful feeling that was twisting her stomach into a tighter and tighter knot. The girls protested at first but became concerned when they saw their mom's ashen face.

"What's wrong, Momma," asked Ruby.

"There's no time to explain. Get inside right now. It's probably nothing."

The girls looked around but didn't see a thing.

"Momma, you're scaring us," said Ruth.

She wished Peter and Andrew and Fletcher were already home. What was she thinking? Her sons were grown men too. She didn't want to act rashly and get them overly excited. When they got inside, Rachel went to the window and peered out. The man was gone! Had she imagined him there? She didn't believe that for a minute.

A few minutes later, she heard the sound of the wagon and horse coming down the lane. Oh, what a relief it was to have Peter and Andrew back. What had taken Fletcher so long today? He may have stopped off at Mama and Papa's. He did that sometimes.

Rachel jumped when Karen came up behind her and looked out the window with her and said, "I thought I heard the men coming back."

"Rachel, I'm sorry I startled you. You look like you've seen a ghost! What's wrong, honey?" Karen asked.

"I'm fine. I thought I saw someone on my dad's horse out at the road looking down towards the house," she told Karen.

That was it, thought Rachel. *I imagined in my heart that the man at the end of the lane was that dreadful man who attacked me on the ship. That makes no sense. He's in prison. Surely, it couldn't be him.* But how time flew. That was over fifteen years ago. Now that she had that suspicion, she didn't dare say anything to Fletcher, Peter, her father, or Papa about it. She remembered Fletcher and Peter's raw anger and Papa's quiet outrage toward the man. There was no telling what any one of them might do.

She certainly didn't want to say anything to Karen and get her upset. *Is Andrew in any danger? Was it that man?* Her mind raced with possible negative outcomes. Were their lives about to change? Hopefully, she was being overdramatic. She needed to compose herself before the men came into the house. That would be a challenge because she had never been able to hide her true feelings from Fletcher. He knew her too well.

31

Close Encounters

Fletcher always rode back from the mines with the same group of men He was the last to be dropped off each day before the wagon driver headed to his own house. Today, the man said, "Hey, Fletch, I've got to make a stop before I get to your place. It might take a while, so do you mind hiking the last little bit? I hate to hold you up while I'm over there jawing, but I promised I'd stop by today."

"No problem, Paul. That'll give me a chance to stretch my sore legs and muscles," said Fletcher as he scrambled from the wagon with amazing agility. "See you tomorrow, man."

"Sure will, regular as clockwork too," Paul told him.

Fletcher was ambling along looking at his nearly worn-out work boots. He thought, *There won't be any money to replace them anytime soon. These would have to last.* Lost in his reflections, he was jolted back to reality by the sound of horse hooves coming his way. It perplexed him to look up and see Amos's old horse, Joe, approaching him, but Amos wasn't riding him. There was a scowling stranger on his back.

Fletcher strained to make out the man's features. He looked like a rather rough sort from his dress and the unpleasant look on his face. He looked like he was angry at the world.

Fletcher's first thought was, *What is this stranger doing on Amos's horse, and where is Amos? Has the man stolen it? Has he harmed Amos?*

As they drew closer and closer, Fletcher felt himself tense up. His body was ready to do battle if necessary. The rider slowed and then stopped when he got within about ten feet of Fletcher. He didn't speak, just stared at Fletcher.

Fletcher walked over and took the horse by the bridle, studying him to be sure it was Joe. The horse whinnied in recognition. "Hey, Old Joe, what are you doing running around with this here stranger?"

He diverted his attention to the horseman to study him also. Giving the man a level look, he spoke to him. "I recognize this horse. He belongs to my father-in-law. You a friend of his?" asked Fletcher.

"I don't know who your father-in-law is. I rented this horse over at the blacksmith shop from some old fellow. Excuse me, but I didn't bother to ask him his name. He seemed more than willing to let me rent Old Joe here for a few coins. I told him I'd have his horse back in a couple of days. That concluded our business," the man said, acting very put-upon. *What is with all the questions from everyone you meet in this town*, he thought.

"I haven't seen you around these parts," said Fletcher.

"I get that a lot, from nearly everyone I meet," said the man.

"I didn't catch your name," said Fletcher.

"That's because I didn't give it," snarled the man. "I'm getting a little fed up with all the nosy questions from everyone in this hick town. I rented the horse to ride around and see if I could find a job in this area. Do you know of anyone looking for help on their farm?"

His sour disposition didn't make Fletcher feel especially inclined to help him. He hesitantly told him, "As you can imagine, times are hard. Most are barely making a living and struggle to feed their own families. I've heard of one man over in the Norris Run area who said he was looking for farm help."

"How do I find this man?" the stranger asked.

Fletcher considered for a moment whether he should send the man to that farmer. He decided. *Well, it won't do any harm. That man can make up his own mind about whether or not he wants to hire this fellow. He might be a blessing in disguise for the poor man.*

The man impatiently watched Fletcher deliberating. To the stranger's amazement, Fletcher responded, "I'll tell you how to get to his farm."

The man listened intently to Fletcher's directions. "How about if I tell him you sent me?" he asked Fletcher.

"No, I don't know you, so I can hardly give you a recommendation," Fletcher told him.

Cursing under his breath, the man glared at Fletcher. "I see how that works. That's okay, I'm used to making my own way in this world," he said as he rode off.

Fletcher was speechless watching the man's retreating back. He thought, *That fellow has a chip on his shoulder and seems to be daring someone to knock it off.* He was quick to ask for information that served his purpose but offered no personal information in return. What or who was he hiding from?

He'd thought of that particular farmer because the man's wife had died the previous year. He had a big farm and didn't have any sons. He had two daughters who weren't much help to him, Fletcher had heard. *The farmer isn't known to be all that friendly either, so maybe those two will get along famously. Who knows?*

Fletcher reached his father's house and stopped in to talk with him and visit with his mother for a moment. Mama told him he had just missed Peter and Andrew. "I'll catch up with them later," said Fletcher.

His mother pulled a big pan of biscuits out of the oven. They were piping hot and smelled wonderful. It was like inhaling biscuit heaven! He helped himself to one on the way out the door. She pretended to smack his hand but was secretly pleased that he still liked his old mother's cooking. She shooed him out the door and told him he'd better get to his own home for supper. She told him Karen was making her famous chicken and dumplings tonight. Fletcher's mouth watered.

Fletcher strode across the fields between their two houses. He loved this land. It boasted good rich soil for growing their food, mountains to hunt in, a generous pond for the animals, a deep well for their water, and a bold little mountain stream running through it. He smiled, remembering his sons gigging for crawdads when they were younger. They used them to catch bigger fish at the river. Last year, Mama taught Rachel and Karen how to salt fish to preserve and can it, but mostly they feasted on fresh fish, nature's bounty, whenever they could.

Peter and Fletcher had rigged up an outdoor grill using stone from this very field. That allowed the ladies to cook outside and not heat up the kitchen so much in the milder months. *Wonder why food tastes so much better when cooked and eaten outside?* Fletcher speculated. Rachel had a fancy name for it when they ate outside. She called it dining al fresco. The boys teased her about that. She was always reading and coming up with something.

Getting to the house, Fletcher stuck his head in the door to speak to everyone before heading around back to wash up. Ruth and Ruby were helping their mother set the table.

They had both been pretty girls and were quickly, too quickly, turning into lovely young ladies, Fletcher thought. They had Rachel's sweet, gentle nature and dainty features. Ruth had a bit of a temper, but Ruby could soothe her sister's ruffled feathers with a touch or sometimes by speaking softly to her. Fletcher smiled. She might have gotten that temper from her father. He could get fired up too at times.

His eyes met Rachel's. She gave him a weak smile and quickly turned away. *Uh-oh, what is going on?*

Karen seemed fine. Her twin boys were playing quietly. He didn't see his sons, but that wasn't anything unusual. They were courting heavily these days. He kept wondering when Joseph would ask Ada to marry him. There hadn't been any other girl for him for years.

Now that Arwood was another story. Fletcher smiled. He was a regular flirt, and the girls all seemed to adore his good looks, engaging smile, and quick wit. All that thick curly brown hair probably didn't hurt either. Peter's son, Andrew, was a handsome young man, but he hadn't caught the lovebug yet.

That will change soon enough, thought Fletcher.

Fletcher dropped his dinner pail off by the front door and proceeded around to the washhouse to clean a little of the coal dust off of himself before supper. When he emerged, he saw Peter sitting on the back stoop, whittling and looking lost in his thoughts. His good-natured brother looked so serious tonight.

"What are you up to, brother?" Fletcher asked.

"Oh, nothing. Had something a little odd happen in town today that is still working on me, I guess." He recounted Andrew's encounter with the stranger at the store and the bad feeling Peter had about it all. Nothing specific that he could put his finger on.

"What did he look like?" asked Fletcher.

Peter described what he could recall about the man who seemed to go out of his way to keep his face in the shadows. "Andrew saw him more up close and could better identify him."

Fletcher looked surprised. "I think I saw that same man riding Amos's old horse, Joe. It gave me a start to see someone on that horse besides Amos."

"You mean he was down this way?" said Peter uncomfortably. Fletcher could see his brother's agitation level ratcheting up a notch or two.

"He said he rented the horse for a couple of days from an old man at the blacksmith shop and was riding around looking for work. He was a right surly type. I suspect he's going to have a hard time getting anyone to take him on," said Fletcher.

Peter was on his feet and pacing. "I don't like this, Fletcher. What else did he say?"

"Nothing much. I told him about a fellow over on Norris Run that might be able to use him," said Fletcher.

"What kind of impression did you have of him, Fletcher?" asked Peter.

"Well, first off, I thought it was suspicious that he never told me who he was. I'm certain I've never seen him before," said Fletcher. "How about you? Do you recognize him from anywhere?"

"That's just it. There's something about him that is vaguely familiar, but I don't know why," said Peter. "I'm going to make it my business to go back into town tomorrow and ask around about him."

"Do you think that's a good idea, Peter? It's not like you to go asking for trouble, and I suspect that's what this man is," said Fletcher.

"I don't know," Peter told his brother honestly. "I'm not going looking for trouble. I do know I'd like to learn more about him."

"Well, brother, let's give it a rest for tonight and go enjoy that good supper your wife prepared for us. By the way, do you know what's wrong with Rachel? I thought she was acting a little strange when I stuck my head in the door," said Fletcher.

"I noticed her sitting in the parlor kind of staring off into space, but I guess I was so preoccupied with my own thoughts that I didn't pay much attention. Sorry, Fletcher," said Peter.

"You know how moody women can be sometimes. It's probably nothing," said Fletcher.

They all enjoyed Karen's delicious supper. Fletcher asked his daughters if they would clean up the kitchen so he and their mother could take a little stroll. The girls giggled and thought that was so romantic of their dad.

Ruby said, "That's a good idea, Dad. Momma was upset this afternoon and made us all come in the house."

Ruth piped up, "Yes, she did. We wanted to wait on you so we could teach you how to play hopscotch with us, but Momma said she saw someone watching us. We didn't see anyone, though."

"Interesting. Don't you girls worry. She just wants to keep you safe. Momma and I will talk about it later. I'm sure it was nothing," Fletcher reassured his daughters.

Something is definitely off, thought Fletcher. First, his own experience with the man, the man had met Amos, possibly stalked his wife and daughters, confronted Andrew, and avoided Peter. He and Peter would talk more tomorrow when he got home from work to see if Peter had learned anything new in town. But now it was time to spend a little time with Rachel. That was nearly impossible in this busy household.

Rachel agreed to go walking with him and surprised him by asking if they could walk in the woods or by the creek that ran through their own land. "Sure, Rachel. The girls are going to take care of the kitchen cleanup for their Aunt Karen," said Fletcher. "They're good children. I'm very proud of them."

Rachel agreed. They left hand in hand out the back of the house. "Any reason you don't want to walk down the road like we usually do?" asked Fletcher.

His question caught her off guard. "No, Fletcher. We have such a pretty place here. I thought it would be nice to stay on our own land," said Rachel quietly.

They walked along without talking much at first. *It is pleasant just being in each other's company and relaxing too*, thought Fletcher. It was nice having Rachel's hand in his. When they were out of sight of the house, he pulled her into his arms and kissed her lips. She responded to his embrace. God, how he loved this woman!

He continued to hold her close and looked deep into her eyes. She looked away. "Okay, let's have it. What's bothering my girl?" asked Fletcher. He turned her face back toward his and lifted her chin so he could see her eyes once again.

Her lips trembled. "Fletcher, it's nothing I want to talk about."

"Would it have anything to do with that man you saw up at the road today?" Fletcher asked.

Rachel gasped. "Fletcher, how do you know about that?"

"Our daughters told me. Don't be mad at them. They're worried about you, and so am I," said Fletcher.

The tears started slowly at first and developed into big gulping sobs that shook her body. Fletcher pulled her close and let her cry. She needed to release all that bottled-up fear and emotion. When she seemed spent, he said, "Now tell me what you saw and what frightened you," said Fletcher patiently.

"I sensed, rather than saw, someone watching me," Rachel stated. "I turned around, but the sun was in my eyes, and I couldn't make out who it was. All I could tell was that it was a man on a horse at the end of the lane. You're going to think this strange, but it looked like Dad's horse." "Anything else, Rachel?" Fletcher asked.

"He didn't wave or call out like one of our neighbors would have or make any effort to come down the lane but instead he seemed to try to hide under the limbs of the trees by the road," said Rachel.

"How long do you think he'd been there?" asked Fletcher.

"I don't know. I hurried the girls into the house. From inside, I looked out the front window, and he was gone. I almost wondered if I had imagined him," said Rachel. She searched Fletcher's face to see if he believed her.

"I can tell you that you did not imagine a man on your dad's horse. I saw him myself when I was walking up the road towards Mama and Papa's house. Paul had to drop me off a little below there," said Fletcher.

"Did you speak to him, Fletcher? Who was it?" She felt like she was in shock. Her pulse raced, but her mind seemed to be processing Fletcher's words in slow motion as if in a dream.

"That's the curious thing. He never introduced himself to me. I can tell you, he wasn't a very pleasant man. That was my first impression. He said he was looking for work. I'm hoping that the reason he didn't come down the lane was because he could see only womenfolk there and didn't want to startle you," Fletcher told her.

"But how did he get Daddy's horse?" asked Rachel.

"I wondered the same thing and was prepared to confront him about that. I have never known Amos to loan out Old Joe, especially not to someone he didn't know," said Fletcher. "The man told me that he'd rented the horse for a couple of days. Maybe your dad could use the extra money. Who can't these days? That may have made him take a chance on this stranger."

"Did you believe him, Fletcher?" asked Rachel.

"Yes. I didn't especially care for his manners—or lack of manners, I should say. I told him about the fellow over in Norris Run who has that big farm. He lost his wife last year. I heard he's got two daughters, a young one around twelve or thirteen and an older one around sixteen. They aren't much help to him because the younger one has to look after the older sister, who has a problem," said Fletcher.

"Fletcher, you probably think I was foolish to feel threatened by him," said Rachel.

He put his arms around her again and told her, "No, Rachel, I don't. I believe we should always trust our instincts. That doesn't mean we shouldn't gather all the facts we can, but that feeling is God-given and is designed to alert us to possible danger."

They started back toward the house. Rachel felt much better. She hoped she hadn't scared her daughters to death. Her husband was a special man, and she always felt safe when he was around.

32

Taking Advantage

The stranger rode out toward the farm on Norris Run Thursday evening after talking with Fletcher. It didn't take him long to get there. He looked around but didn't see the farmer anywhere in sight. What he did see was one fine-looking slice of young womanhood. She was out in the yard picking flowers.

He looked around again to see if her younger sister was around. Seeing no one, he sauntered down the road. He put on his brightest smile and got down from the horse. When he approached the young woman, she smiled shyly and lowered her eyes.

"Now aren't you just the prettiest little thing?" he teased her. "Where is everyone else?"

The sixteen-year-old girl said, "Working."

He moved a little closer to her and asked, "Do you think it would be okay for me to get a drink of water and maybe a sandwich? I've been on the road for a while, and I'm hungry and thirsty."

She shrugged her shoulders and smiled sweetly at him. She started walking toward the house, and he followed her, all the while looking around to see if he saw anyone coming. Once they were inside, out of view, he turned her around and pulled her toward him. It startled her at first. He laughed and said, "I bet you've never been kissed by a man."

The girl shook her head no. He began to kiss and tickle her as someone would a child. She laughed and ran into the kitchen thinking it was a game. He followed her and continued his persistent game of kissing and tickling, but then his hands began exploring ever so slowly. He touched her breast, and she pulled away, but he laughed and coaxed her back into his arms, telling her how beautiful she was.

He said, "I'd better go before your daddy and sister get home. I want you to do something for me. Tonight, when everyone is in bed asleep, I want you to be quiet as a mouse, slip out of the house, and come meet me at the road. I'll take you down to the river and show you what it looks like in moonlight. How about that?" She nodded her head.

"Now don't tell anybody. This will be our little secret."

She grinned at him. He made her tummy feel all funny inside. She watched him leave. Then she realized he forgot to get a sandwich and a glass of water. She laughed to herself about the funny stranger. She'd never had a secret before. She wouldn't tell Daddy or Nancy. They never let her go anywhere.

He rode away thinking this town might be all right after all. That girl didn't seem especially bright, but she was beautiful. He could tell she had never been with a man either. They would have a little fun tonight. No harm done as he saw it.

The girl was sitting on the front steps watching up the road when her sister Nancy came into the front yard. Nancy had been helping her poppa put up hay in the back field all afternoon and was so tired. She got back a little early so she could start supper. Poppa was going to work a little longer tonight while the weather was pretty.

"Sarah, you're a mess. What have you been doing all day? Your hair is all tangled. I combed it this morning. Where's your hair clip? Your blouse is unbuttoned too. Oh no, it looks like you've lost a button."

Sarah smiled sweetly at her sister, who was always fussing over her. She wished she could tell her about the river so she could go with her tonight, but she had to keep the secret. *He said don't tell anybody.*

"Come on inside and let's get you changed and your hair combed before Poppa gets in," said Nancy.

When the stranger reached town, he was feeling pretty pleased. It was getting late, so he decided to treat himself to a hotel room at that fancy Preston Hotel. He could use a bath. He'd wash up and go over to the café for supper. He reached inside his pants pocket and pulled out his flask. It was mighty low on rum, he thought as he drank the last of it.

As the disheveled man walked into the Preston Hotel, the front desk clerk gave him the once-over, looking him up and down. He certainly didn't measure up to their typical higher class clientele.

"I'd like to pay for two nights," he told the gentleman. The clerk was thankful and relieved that since business had been slow, he wouldn't have to field too many complaints about this chap. He'd already decided to give him a room on the first floor near the back entry.

By rote, the clerk asked, "Will you need any assistance with your bags, sir?"

The man let out a loud derisive laugh that could be heard all over the lobby of the fine establishment. "Do I look like I have a huge wardrobe? For your information, I own one change of clothes. I have that right here in my saddlebag," the stranger retorted.

"Very well, sir. You will be in room 108. It's at the end of the corridor on the right. There is a back entry for your convenience," said the clerk.

The man glared at the clerk but didn't offer any further comment. *He thinks he's being clever advising me indirectly to use the back door so his other esteemed guests won't be bothered by me. My money spends as good as anyone else's. I may give him a little comeuppance when I check out.*

The clerk became nervous beneath the man's fiery gaze. He busied himself with a stack of paperwork on the back counter. He heard the man finally shuffle off. He watched as the annoying guest made his way to his assigned room for the next two nights. *Heaven help us all*, he prayed.

About an hour and a half later, the man appeared in the lobby once more. This time, he did look somewhat more presentable. His hair was washed and combed but still damp. He had shaved and was wearing cleaner but still dowdy attire. The glassy eyes told the clerk the man had already began his evening with a drink or two. *There is something disquieting about the fellow*, he thought. *Oh well, two nights here, then he'll be someone else's problem.*

The man went across the street to the Café, where he feasted on pork chops, salty fried potatoes with onions, and a cup of coffee. He tried to flirt with the matronly waitress. She recognized his sort, was courteous and prompt with her service but, otherwise, didn't give him the time of day.

After he paid his check, he asked the man at the register if he knew where he might get a bottle of that mountain moonshine he'd heard some fellows talking about. The cashier took his money. He put his dinner check upside down on the nail driven into a wooden base. "Meet me around back of the restaurant in fifteen minutes," he told him. "It's $1.50 for a pint."

After the man left, the cashier removed his apron, told the waitress that he was going to take a smoke break, and left the restaurant. He walked down the street a couple of blocks and entered a building there. He emerged five minutes later with a pint of applejack in a mason jar. It only cost $1, but the half dollar was his tip for taking a chance on getting caught distributing illegal alcohol.

He met the man in the alley and made the exchange. "If you tell anyone you got this from me, I'll deny it. Who do you think they'll believe? Me or a complete stranger?"

It was dark when the man reached the Norris Run farm. He looked for the girl and didn't see her anywhere. Shoot, she might not show up, but it was a gamble he was willing to take. He remembered how her eyes had lit up when he mentioned taking her to see the river in the moonlight. He dismounted the horse and tied him to a tree. He waited quietly at the road. He decided to have a smoke while he waited.

As he sat there working on his second cigarette, he heard a sound. He put out the butt and leaped to his feet. Peering down the lane, he saw the girl coming up by the trees, apparently wearing nothing but a white cotton nightgown, with her long hair loose and flowing down her back. She kept looking over her shoulder and then started running softly up the hill. She laughed when she saw him.

He put his finger to his lips to shush her, like one would do with a child. He got up in the saddle and helped her up behind him. They quickly galloped off toward the river. At the riverbank, he helped her down from the horse. He told her he'd brought some apple juice for her. She took a big gulp and began coughing and sputtering. It burned her throat.

She handed it back to him, shaking her head no.

"Wait, you're doing it all wrong," he teased. "Hold your nose and drink it slowly, really slowly. I bet you can't drink half of this jar."

The girl tried again. It *was* easier the way he told her, but it still felt so hot in her throat. She didn't want any more of that apple juice. The hot liquid seemed to be snaking through her bloodstream. They sat down on the grassy bank of the water. She leaned back. Her head seemed to be spinning, and the stars looked kind of fuzzy.

He took the jar from her hands. "I think I'll have a drink too," he said as he took a couple of healthy swigs.

They sat looking at the water. It truly was beautiful in the moonlight. He began to nuzzle the side of her neck. She liked his hot breath on her neck, and he smelled better than he had this afternoon.

"Was everyone asleep when you left?" he asked as he ran his fingers up and down her soft arms.

"Yes, they were tired. They worked hard, and it was hot today," she said, her speech slurring slightly.

"Let's have a little more of this apple juice," he suggested. "You haven't finished your half yet, and I bought this especially for you."

She sat up and reluctantly drank the rest of the jar of moonshine. This man was being so nice to her, she thought. His arm was around her, and he kept telling her what pretty legs she had. She was getting very sleepy. She felt him pulling up her gown.

He began kissing her very hard. His hand was squeezing her breast. He began touching her all over, even *down there*. She tried to protest and push his hand away, but he was very strong. She had that funny feeling in her stomach again. This time, she felt like she was going to be sick, but she was so sleepy.

She must have dozed off. She didn't know what he was doing now, but suddenly, he was hurting her. Again, she tried to push him away. He was breathing hard and dropped his weight on her and was trying to kiss her mouth again.

She turned her head. The pain was too much. She screamed out. He smashed her in the face. She lay unconscious for what seemed like a long time. When she came to, the man was standing over her and pulling up his pants. She was in an almost dreamlike state, more akin to a nightmare. She watched as he got up on his horse. In the moonlight, she could see blood all over her gown. Her body hurt.

Sarah started crying and asking him why he had hurt her. She thought he was a nice man. He grinned evilly at her and rode off, leaving her all alone with her pain. She didn't know what to do or how to get home. Poppa and Nancy were going to be so mad at her. The night air was chilly. Her eyes became heavy, and the tears kept flowing.

33

Lost Innocence

It was about four thirty in the morning when Nancy woke up. They had a busy day ahead of them, so she'd better get up, start Poppa's breakfast, and put his morning coffee on the stove to brew. She missed her momma so much. A lot of responsibility had fallen on her young shoulders when her mother died last year. She loved her sister but had to help her with everything, including getting dressed. She had to keep an eye on Sarah constantly so she wouldn't hurt herself.

Nancy opened her sister's bedroom door to look in on her. Hopefully, she was still sleeping. She wasn't there! Nancy recalled helping her change into her nightgown and getting her into bed last night. Maybe she woke up early and went downstairs. That wasn't like her, though. Sarah normally slept until late into the morning.

Nancy ran down the stairs. She could hear her poppa stirring around in his room. She didn't see her sister anywhere. She went outside in her bare feet and nightgown. She looked all around the yard. Feeling panicked, she ran back inside the house. "Poppa, Poppa," she screamed, "I can't find Sarah!"

He hurried out of his room. Sarah had to be close by. She'd never run off before. "Calm down, Nancy. We'll find her."

They searched in the root cellar by lantern light, looked in the barn and in the other buildings. They called out her name. There were a lot of acres of land around them, but Sarah had never had any interest in the land. Her limited world existed between the yard and the house.

Now even Poppa had become worried. *Where can Sarah be at this hour? What possessed her to leave her room in the middle of the night in her nightgown? When did she leave?* So many questions and no answers. He'd been up fairly late last night, but both he and Nancy were sound sleepers.

"Nancy, saddle up a couple of horses. We'll find her. I'll head out towards the river, and you go the other way. She's always talking about that blame river. I don't think she could've gotten far barefoot in her nightgown," said Poppa.

He looked at Nancy and noticed that she was crying. She was so very young and such a huge help to him. "Here, here now." He put his arm around her shoulders to comfort her. "I'm not blaming you. Let's not worry. We'll have her back here in no time. Now hurry and get dressed while I get the horses."

Nancy rode for about a half an hour and turned back toward the farm. She saw other neighbors starting to stir about. She didn't want to tell them anything about Sarah. They probably wondered why she was out riding so early in the morning. When she got home, she didn't see Poppa, so she headed toward the river to help him search. As she neared the river, she heard her Poppa shouting for her. She saw his horse tied up at a tree.

She followed the sound of his voice.

Nothing prepared her for seeing her sister lying there so still. She almost fell from her horse in her haste to get to her sister's side. "Oh, Poppa, is she alive?" Nancy cried.

"She's alive but badly hurt. It looks like she's been beaten…and worse, I'm afraid. I'm going to stay with her. I need you to go back to the farm and get the smaller wagon and hitch it up. Bring it back here to me so I can put her in it and get into town to see the doctor. We need to get a hold of the sheriff too," Poppa told her.

Nancy had only seen her father cry one time, and that was last year at her mother's funeral. She watched as big tears cruised unbidden down the big man's face.

"I'll hurry, Poppa!" Nancy said as she expertly mounted her horse and sped off. She prayed her sister would be all right. She cried and couldn't fight the guilty feelings that threatened to drown her. *It was my job to take care of Sarah*, Nancy keened.

When her momma was on her deathbed, she told Nancy that she needed her to take care of her sister. That was her momma's dying wish, and Nancy had already failed. She was inconsolable.

Nancy arrived at the farmhouse. She quickly ran inside and grabbed old quilts to put in the wagon. She prayed Sarah would live. They had always sheltered and babied her. It broke her young heart to see her sister lying there so still and seriously injured.

Poppa gazed down at his daughter through his tears. Although his heart was grieving for her and all that she'd been through, his blood was boiling. Someone was going to pay for this! Had someone entered his house and taken her? Was she wandering down the road, and the wrong sort grabbed her? Who would do such a thing? He couldn't imagine any of their neighbors capable of such an evil thing.

Everyone knew Sarah had a problem. It was obvious to anyone who spoke to her. She had such a sweet, trusting nature, and mentally, she was about five years old. That's what the doctor had told them when she was small. Hot tears burned his cheeks. He never dreamed that he wouldn't always be able to keep her safe.

He recalled that she was all aflutter last night at supper. He thought it was because he and Nancy had left her alone at the house for a couple of hours while they worked. Sometimes, it couldn't be helped. It had never been a problem before.

He heard Nancy coming back with the wagon. When he stood up, he noticed the light glinting off something near Sarah's head. He picked up a mason jar and sniffed it. Moonshine! Had she drunk any of it? The jar lid was off, and it was empty. He put the lid on and wrapped it in his bandana to give to the sheriff as evidence.

As a father, he wanted to protect Nancy's innocence too. She didn't need to know all the sordid details of what had happened to her sister. He hadn't seen any reason since his wife's death to talk with his daughters about relations with a man. He would simply explain to Nancy that her sister had been brutally attacked.

Nancy got down from the wagon and spread the covers in the back of the wagon. She'd even brought a pillow for Sarah's head. She watched as Poppa gently lifted Sarah onto the wagon. Nancy heard her sister moan. It was good to hear her make any sound. Nancy offered to help her Poppa, but he said Sarah was light as a feather. When he lifted her, they noticed a big knot on the back of her head that was bleeding. Nancy could see that her sister had been struck in the face, which was bruised and swollen.

"Honey, I want you to take my horse and ride ahead to let the doctor know I'm on my way with your sister. I want to go slowly so I don't jostle her. You saw that big place on the back of her head? We don't know how badly she's hurt yet," said Poppa. He instructed her to go by the police station after stopping at the doctor's office to have them contact the sheriff's office since they lived out in the county. He wanted them to come by the doctor's office to talk to him so he wouldn't have to leave her sister's side.

She did as she was told but wished she could ride in the wagon to comfort her sister and herself.

The night clerk at the hotel noticed the slipshod, dirty, and slightly drunk man entered the lobby. He couldn't help but notice the blood on the man's pants, and even on his shirt.

He called out to him, "Sir, are you okay? Should I call the police? Do you need a doctor?"

The stranger's face turned dark, and he began cursing loudly. It was about two thirty in the morning. The clerk was afraid he was going to wake the other guests. "Sir, please lower your voice. Our other guests are sleeping. Do you need any assistance getting to your room? You are a guest here, right?"

"I don't need any of your help. You need to mind your own business if you know what's good for you," he threatened.

The clerk's face reddened, and he felt a chill go up his spine. Perhaps he should call the police. There was no telling what this fellow had been up to that night. He watched him stagger down the hallway, pausing to bang on a door or two of other guests.

What a scoundrel! Luckily the few guests they had were near the front of the hotel, but that man didn't know that.

The clerk was content to let him sleep it off. He watched which room the man went into after much fumbling with his room key. The clerk quietly went down the hallway and placed a "Do not disturb" sign on the doorknob so the maid wouldn't enter the room to clean it early the next morning. She would check with the desk first, and he could apprise her of the situation.

34

Looking for Trouble

It was Friday morning. Peter was a determined man today. He had a busy morning planned working on the fencing he'd talked with Papa about earlier. Next, he was going to get all the boys and younger men involved in the project. After their midday meal, they should have a good start and need very little supervision from him. That's when he'd slip away and head into town to see what he could learn about that character. It was late September but as hot as blazes in the fields.

He wouldn't be able to clean up much without arousing Karen's suspicion about why he was on his way back to town so soon. He'd slept fitfully last night. He certainly hoped he hadn't been talking in his sleep. He couldn't figure why that man would have an interest in his son, Andrew.

Andrew was getting older and seemed to question everything. He and Karen had never even discussed telling him that he was adopted. They had always been one big happy family. He didn't want anything to change that. There was no telling how that news might affect Andrew. He'd been their first baby, and they loved him with all their hearts. Maybe they would never have to tell him about the adoption.

But that fellow asking Andrew questions and watching him like he had seemed to rub salt into a wound. Peter felt guilty about not telling Andrew. It was hard to know what the right thing to do was.

Now he would have to come up with a good excuse to go back to town since he'd been there yesterday. They could hardly afford to spend any more money. Then it hit him. He could say he wanted to check on Amos because Agnes had said he had straightening up to do at the blacksmith shop. Of course, that would have to wait until he had a chance to investigate the stranger. He would definitely stop by on his way back through and lend Amos a hand if he needed it. He'd be glad to help him anyway he could.

The morning flew by, and Peter left out as planned. Everything went smoothly with Karen. She was preoccupied with giving Rachel and her girls haircuts.

The stranger woke up with a splitting headache from his evening of revelry. The moonshine the cashier had supplied him with the evening before packed a punch. He barely remembered the night before except for that delightful little romantic encounter. *I won't forget that anytime soon*, he thought, smiling to himself. He was proud of himself for being the girl's *first*.

He looked at his clothes. They were a mess. He decided to put on his earlier set of clothes. He set about trying to wash out the soiled garments. Some bloodstains wouldn't wash out but did fade somewhat. He hung the wet clothes to dry over an ornate chair in the hotel room, unconcerned that they were dripping on the fine hardwood floors.

Feeling hungry, he headed over to the Café, where he'd eaten the night before. Seating himself at the counter, he ordered a bowl of soup with soda crackers and a cup of coffee. The waitress served him a hot cup of coffee while his food was being prepared. He could feel the strongly brewed beverage coursing through his veins, energizing him. He put his head down and tucked into the steaming bowl of soup that was sat before him.

A whiff of perfume floated through the air when a very attractive middle-aged lady came through the front door. She had somewhat of a hard look about her caused in part by the almost theatrical makeup she was wearing. Her lips and cheeks were brightly painted, and her eyelashes looked practically like spiders. The neckline of her dress was a tad too low, revealing her lack of modesty. To the stranger, she almost appeared to be a lady of the evening. She settled herself at a table and surveyed her surroundings. Most of the men present didn't seem to pay any attention to her. They continued their conversations or silently consumed their meals. She looked somewhat dejected and ordered a milkshake while she waited for her husband to join her.

When the stranger turned around, taking in the sight of her, she was fussing around with her hair. She flashed him a flirty smile. She suspected her husband, David, might be a while at the hardware store, so it might be interesting to talk to this stranger.

The man smiled back. He asked the waitress for a refill on his coffee and decided to go over to her table and chat. He had paid for two nights at the hotel, so no need letting it go to waste.

The other men in the restaurant exchanged knowing looks as they watched the man make his way toward her table. He immediately struck up a conversation. To Anna Leigh's credit, she told the man she was waiting for her husband. However, it wasn't long before the two were talking and laughing like old friends. One of the men in the restaurant made the remark to another man that there was no accounting for taste—his or hers. They noticed his hand was touching her arm when the door opened and her husband, David, strolled into the restaurant.

Everyone in town knew David had a temper. They'd seen many a fight about his wife over the years. He was as strong as an ox and suspicious of anyone he thought looked her way. If a person had any sense, he'd ignore David's flirtatious wife and keep his distance.

David's nostrils seemed to flare as he slowly approached the table where the two sat. The man and David's wife were talking so animatedly that they didn't notice him until he was standing before the table.

David was furious. "Who do you think you are coming in here, a complete stranger, and trying to make time with my wife?" he asked through clenched teeth.

The man looked over at Anna Leigh, shrugged, and laughed. That was the last thing he did before David jerked him out of his chair and shoved him out of his way. Like a charging bull, the fellow came right back at David. Tables and chairs went flying. The patrons scattered to avoid the melee. The cashier ran out the door to get the police before the two men tore up the place.

David was clearly the stronger of the two brawlers, but the stranger fought like a street thug. When David had cornered him and was ready to deliver the knockout punch, the stranger came up with a switchblade flashing. He held it out to the side, ready to attack the younger man.

Peter opened the Café's door at that very moment. His eyes quickly took in the violent scene. The stranger's back was to him. Peter grabbed the man's wrist that was holding the switchblade. He managed to whack the knife out of the man's hand. The man was making a dive to retrieve it from under a table. With a lunge, David hit the man with one powerful blow and knocked him out cold.

The town police arrived just as the stranger hit the floor. David picked up the knife and closed it before handing it to the police. "I had to defend myself against this," he told them.

"Someone get him up. Give me a glass of water," the town cop demanded from the waitress. He promptly threw it in the man's face. He came to with much cursing and sputtering. He tried to get to his feet to do battle once again.

"Where's my blade, you dirty thieves," he yelled.

"You've got more to worry about than your knife right now, buddy. I have taken it as evidence," said the sternlooking police officer. He looked at the other two men involved in the fight. "I'm taking all three of you to jail so we can sort all this out." Looking at the restaurant owner, he said, "Mac, figure out what these bruisers owe you for the broken furniture and dishes, plus any other damage they've caused."

Peter wasn't used to be treated like a common criminal. *What possessed me to get involved in that fray?* he questioned himself. He went along peaceably and was prepared to tell what had happened. He felt like he'd saved David's life. He was fairly certain the fight had started over David's wife. He decided he wouldn't put up with her for one minute but realized David must love her.

The three men were sitting at the precinct waiting for their interview by the police officers. Peter had an opportunity to study the man's profile. The violent fight scene brought to memory another fight he'd engaged in a long time ago—in fact, about sixteen years ago.

He felt nauseated when the realization dawned on him. That disgusting lowlife was Andrew's biological father! The sick feeling gave way to an overwhelming anger. *How dare he show his face in my hometown asking questions about our son! Does he think he has any rights where Andrew is concerned after what he's done?*

Peter felt like he was at the boiling point. There was something else at play too—the fear of losing Andrew, having their family secret revealed, and ruining Rachel's reputation. He fought hard to compose himself for the interview. It would be important to carefully choose his words. Evidently, the stranger didn't recognize him as the man who'd nearly beat him to death over a decade before, probably because the man had been so drunk at the time.

They came and collected the stranger first to hear his version of the events. Peter was sure it would be quite the fantastical tale that man would concoct for his own benefit. He could imagine him describing himself as being *ganged up* on by the other two men and having to fight for his life.

David looked over at Peter and said, "Thanks Peter. I didn't see him pull that knife. I'm glad you saw it and stepped in. I'm sorry to drag you into all this mess. Anna Leigh's going to be the death of me. Shoot, she almost was today."

Peter told the younger man, "David, you're getting too old to keep getting into fights all the time."

"I know, man. Anna Leigh makes me crazy. She knows I love her. I give her plenty of attention, but she's always trolling, it seems. I think getting into these ruckuses keeps me from killing her. You know we've been married nearly ten years. When is she ever going to settle down?" David groaned.

The stranger had become so belligerent while being questioned, they'd stuck him in a jail cell so he could calm down. They then interviewed the other two men. David and the stranger were both given a summons to appear in court. David's independent testimony had saved Peter the same fate. Peter was dismissed with a warning to stay out of trouble. That alone was enough to truly humble the good man. He recalled telling Fletcher he wasn't looking for trouble when he came to town.

Before Peter left the station, the Cafe cashier brought in the tally for the damage at the restaurant. David and the stranger were each fined $30 for the replacement cost. The charges were certified with the magistrate, and a court date set for the following month.

Peter's shoulders slumped as he left the police station. He'd come to town with questions, but he didn't like the answers he gotten. The man apparently didn't recognize Peter. *That, at least, is something,* thought Peter, *a missing puzzle piece for the stranger, but how long before he puts it all together?* Peter was torn about sharing any of the information he'd gleaned with Karen. He reasoned there was no reason to get her upset yet. Maybe this would blow over. He knew Fletcher would be asking questions tonight about what he'd learned today. That sick feeling returned.

Peter stopped by to see Amos at the blacksmith shop on his way out of town. This morning, he couldn't wait to get to town, and now he couldn't wait to leave. Amos was helping a customer. When they concluded their business, Peter had a man-to-man chat with him about the scuffle at the Café and his involvement. He didn't want Rachel's father and his friend to hear about it secondhand. He swore Amos to secrecy. No need to get the women of the family upset by the day's events.

Amos agreed. He put a fatherly arm around Peter's shoulders. He could tell the man felt miserable about it all. Hearing all that made Amos concerned about getting his horse back. "I didn't see your horse," said Peter. "I heard folks say the man was staying at the Preston Hotel. He probably has Old Joe tied up there. I'll keep an eye out for him."

The men walked outdoors and stood there talking in the bright afternoon sunlight. They saw the Norris Run farmer coming down the road very slowly with his wagon and horses. "Those are mighty fine horses," remarked Amos, studying the animals. As he neared, they noticed that someone was lying in the back of the wagon. It looked like the man's older daughter lying there! The men nodded their heads at the farmer as he passed by. He curtly nodded back.

"Must've been an accident," remarked Amos. "I hope the girl will be all right."

The farmer's eyes looked sad, but there was something else, thought Peter. *Anger? Yes, that was it. He looked mad as a wet hornet!* He wondered what had happened but would never think to intrude. Peter said his goodbyes and got on the road home.

Amos went inside and finished the work he had on the table. As he was closing up shop, something unusual happened. He was surprised to see a couple of the local police stopping at his place of employment.

"Hello, Amos. There has been an attack on a young girl from down Norris Run way. Someone meeting the description she gave us was said to have been seen on a horse that we've been told belongs to you," the officer explained.

Amos's heart sank. That girl was known to have mental challenges. *Who would do such a thing?* He recalled again the bad feeling he'd had about the man using his horse. "I'm sorry to hear that awful news. Yes, I rented out Joe to a stranger a couple of days ago. I was hoping he would bring him back this evening before I closed, as promised, but I haven't seen him."

"Stealing a horse might be the least of his troubles," the young officer told Amos. His partner wrote down the description that Amos gave of the man. It was much more detailed than the girl's, but that was understandable given the circumstances and her mental issues.

The younger officer volunteered, "The bad news is we believe we had him in custody this morning for a brawl at the Café downtown and let him go. Well, let us know if you see him. We want to talk to him again."

"My son-in-law's brother, Peter Broce, was by here a little while ago. He told me about that unfortunate fight. When I told him that I was worried about Old Joe, he said someone in town had mentioned the man was staying at the Preston Hotel," offered Amos. "I was going to go by there and see if I saw my horse."

"He's a pretty rough character, Amos. Why don't you let us look into it for you so you can head on home? Don't think you want to tangle with him. He pulled a knife on someone earlier today and might have been involved in that other incident," the older police officer told him.

Amos agreed. He'd never been a ruffian and didn't want to start now in his seventies.

When the law arrived at the hotel, they instructed the desk clerk to admit them to the man's room. He nervously jiggled the skeleton house key in the lock. When the door unlocked, they had him step aside as they entered the hotel room. The clerk could see past them and observed the messy room. It was hard to believe one man who was only there for the two days could by so sloppy. He didn't miss the water puddle on the floor under the man's laundry.

"That'll be all. We'll let you know when we're through here," the officers told the clerk and waited for him to leave. They scrutinized the damp clothes hanging over the hotel chair and noticed the bloodstains the man had tried to wash out. Blood had a way of seeping into the very fiber of clothing and was difficult to remove.

They gathered the items and looked about the room for any other evidence. Finding none, they had the hotel employee lock the room. "Don't clean this room until we tell you to. We may have to come back here. Send someone to get us the minute the man returns. Don't confront him. We believe he's dangerous."

The jittery desk clerk gulped. He certainly wouldn't be putting himself on the line with that character. This was not good for business either. Should he have alerted the manager about the man? He'd better do it now or it might be his hide or his job. He couldn't afford to lose his job. He wished he'd never seen the man before.

When the men left the hotel, they headed down to the Norris Run farm to let the anxious father know what they'd found out so far.

35

Decisions

Peter's mind was swirling with the day's events. Suddenly, he began to see a pattern emerging from the chaos. What he realized hit him hard, like a sucker punch. The man in town *was* the same one who had attacked Rachel on the ship. He felt his knees buckle.

What bizarre twist of fate would land that person in their little town? Had it been purposeful on the stranger's part? Had he sought her out? Why was he here? Did he plan to harm Rachel as an act of vengeance for the time he had spent locked up for his crime against her? Had he somehow learned about the existence of a child from that violent union? The unanswered questions were tying Peter's stomach in knots.

Memories of that night came flooding back into Peter's consciousness. He wouldn't ever forget that fight, when he had pulled the man away from Rachel. He'd never been in a real fight before that night, just schoolyard skirmishes. Even though the man was obviously drunk, he'd been a worthy opponent in terms of physicality. But what had shocked Peter was his own bloodthirstiness. He'd wanted to kill the man. The combination of indignation, anger, and protectiveness had overridden any thoughts Peter had about self-preservation. He remembered feeling fearless. Afterward, the raw, animalistic emotions had frightened him because he realized *anyone* could become a murderer given the proper motivation. Peter shook his head as if to expel the disheartening thoughts.

Peter's thoughts moved to his younger brother, Fletcher. He recalled Fletcher's conversation with the man on the road. Fletcher had sent the man to the Norris Run farm to look for work. He wasn't to blame. He didn't know who the man was. Next, the farmer's daughter was brutally attacked. There was no doubt in Peter's mind that the stranger had committed the shameful act.

He was conflicted about telling the police what he now knew about this character's previous criminal activity, but he simply couldn't reveal what he knew. Too many people would be hurt. He had to hope that justice would prevail and that this man would have to account for what he'd done. He knew that in America, there was a presumption of innocence until a court could prove otherwise. What if the man never paid for his crime? Peter knew it was wrong, but right now, he couldn't worry about that. He couldn't risk putting Rachel and his family in a vulnerable position. They had too much to lose.

Peter felt duty bound to tell his brother so Fletcher could keep Rachel safe. None of them wanted Rachel to ever be victimized again. Then of course, there was the potential impact on Rachel if she learned this man had followed her to Virginia. She'd dangled on a dangerous precipice between terror and depression after the man assaulted her, and especially when she learned of the ensuing pregnancy. It had taken much time, but she had moved on with her life. This man currently held no power over her happiness and sense of well-being. She must think of that terrible night from time to time, but she never spoke of it.

There was also his father to consider. He had shared in the powerless and painful feeling because the two of them hadn't kept Rachel safe on the journey to this new land. He certainly didn't plan to alert his father to his suspicions about the man. It wouldn't serve any useful purpose and would be upsetting to him. Peter wished he knew what the stranger's intentions were.

Then lastly, and perhaps this should have been his first consideration, there was Karen to consider. They had so much to lose if this man's true identity and sordid past was revealed. He had to admit that Andrew could drive them both crazy at times, but they couldn't love him any more than they did right now. Not having birthed him didn't make him any less their child. Through Andrew, they had first experienced the joys and challenges of parenthood. This man's story could destroy the bond of love and trust between them.

Peter felt himself wishing that David's powerful blow during his fight with the stranger would've put the man out of his misery for good. He bowed his head. *Forgive me, Lord, but turning the other cheek and giving that man control over our destiny seems like the exact opposite of what we should do.*

Peter found himself wondering how many other women had become victims of this evil man.

Peter had to make tough decisions about what to tell whom or if he should keep the information to himself. By the time he reached his house, he was mentally exhausted and felt the worst possible kind of sickness—heartsickness. After supper, he'd try to get Fletcher off to himself for a talk. Even though Fletcher was the younger of the two brothers, Peter thought his brother possessed a wisdom beyond his years. He respected his opinion. Between them, they'd sort all this out.

The stranger considered leaving town; however, he felt like he had options. That farmer down in Norris Run had no idea that he was the one who'd had his way with his daughter. Obviously, she wasn't the sharpest knife in the drawer. Heck, she might not even recognize him. It had been dark when they were alone at the river. She may not even remember him being in her house teasing her earlier in the day. Her father and sister had never seen him. Now if only he could get a job with them, he'd do his best to stay away from the girl, but he certainly couldn't make any promises.

Then there was that charming lady he'd met at the Café. Sure, she was married to that hotheaded man, but they might be able to spend a little time together. He sensed that she wasn't happy in her marriage. Maybe that fellow she was married to didn't know how to take care of a lady like her. One of the men at the store told him where she and her husband lived. He also warned him he'd better stay away from her if he knew what was good for him. He'd take that as a challenge.

He mused. Then there was that matter of figuring out the connection between that girl on the ship and that young man he'd met at the store. He knew deep in his bones that he was indeed his son. He couldn't explain it. He just knew. *What are they trying to pull on the good folks of this town?* He laughed mirthlessly. Could be he wouldn't have to work anywhere this winter if he could persuade them to pay for his silence.

Yes, this little town might prove interesting after all. He'd picked up a pound of cheese and some soda crackers at the store. That would be supper tonight. He should be back in his room before it got too late. He'd paid for another night, so he needed to make the best of it. He planned a route that would take him by all the parties of interest tonight.

Of course, he still had that old fella's horse, but it wasn't like he'd left town with it. He was going to be a little late getting it back to him, maybe tomorrow morning after he had a little time to consider his next move. He'd spent most of the afternoon riding down in the Luster's Gate community. It had been a right rough road down there, but the views were well worth the trouble. He'd gotten back a little later than planned but still managed to get by the Café and secure another pint of that good home brew. The sun was setting as he steered his horse toward New Town, the black folks' community on the edge of town near Prices Fork road. People were sitting on their steps to escape their hot houses. As he sauntered through, some got up and went back inside.

I must be pretty scary looking to have that effect on people who don't even know me.

A little boy crossing the road to get to his home let out a distress yelp and scrambled to get out of the way of the stranger on the horse. The man's mean laugh rang out. When he looked the direction the boy was headed, he saw a tall muscular man standing in the yard glaring at him. "Get in the house, son," the man told his offspring. He watched the stranger until he was out of sight. That stranger looked like trouble. His wife nervously watched her husband from the edge of the door. "Samuel, come on in the house. We don't want no trouble," she begged him.

Fletcher and Peter told their wives they were going to get in a little night fishing. The other males in the family begged to go along. Peter told them no because he and Fletcher had a few matters they needed to talk over. Karen's eyebrows flew up, alert that something must be amiss. She walked out on the porch with Peter while Fletcher was getting ready to leave. "Peter Broce, what is going on? Why are you being so mysterious?" she demanded.

"Karen, I'll tell you what I can later, I promise, but now is not the time. Everything is fine. I need to talk to Fletcher so we can figure something out," Peter told his anxious wife.

"Peter, if it involves our family, I need to know," Karen insisted.

"In good time, Karen. Now go on back inside before everyone else starts to wonder if something's wrong. I promise we won't be too long. I will tell you this, Fletcher isn't going to like what I have to tell him. That's why I want to get him away from here for a while, so Rachel won't worry at his reaction."

About that time, Fletcher came out the front door, smiling. He looked forward to spending a little time with his brother. He thought Peter needed to get something off his chest.

When the men returned a couple hours later, Karen had put all the children to bed. Peter was her rock, and she knew something was bothering him. It had to be pretty serious for him to lock her out the way he had. When he got to their bedroom, he was surprised to see Karen still waiting up for him.

"Karen, I thought you'd be asleep by now."

"Peter, do you think I don't know when something is bothering you? Please talk to me. I have entirely too much imagination to be left guessing. I couldn't sleep if I wanted to."

Peter rubbed his bristly chin. Karen noticed how tired he looked.

"You're right. This whole thing with the farmer over on Norris Run's disturbed daughter getting attacked, the stranger that frightened Rachel, probably the same stranger who spoke so roughly to our son, Andrew at the store, my fight at the Café with the same stranger…it has all been eating at me."

"Who is that man, Peter, and what does he have to do with our family?"

Peter cleared his throat and took a deep breath, exhaling slowly. "I believe he is the man who raped Rachel and who is the father of our son, Andrew."

Karen gasped, and her eyes filled with hot, burning tears. "Why do you think that?"

"His face has haunted me since the first time I saw him at the store. I can't be sure of anything, but what if he somehow is here looking for Rachel and our son? I had to talk to Fletcher about my fears so he can protect Rachel." "But, but—what about Andrew? Could we lose him to that man after all these years? How could he prove Andrew is his flesh and blood? Oh, Peter, how could this be happening to us all?"

Peter held his sobbing wife in his arms. "I've tried to protect you from my fears too, Karen. I didn't withhold information to shut you out. I want to be wrong about this whole thing, believe me, I do."

"Peter, I can't believe or accept it."

"I know, Karen. You and I have a decision to make. Do you think we should tell Andrew about the adoption?"

"Peter, how can we, without telling him about how it came about, how his mother was raped, and that Rachel is his mother? How could we possibly expect him to understand?"

"He's not a child anymore. He's practically grown, but I have the same concerns you do. We love him, and I don't see how knowing this information will make him a better person or help him in any way."

"We can't tell him. He will think we don't love him. He will wonder why Rachel and Fletcher didn't want him."

"I agree. For now, let's keep this information to ourselves. Rachel doesn't know that we suspect that stranger is the man who attacked her. Can we keep it that way for her sake too?"

Karen numbly nodded her agreement.

"I'm afraid there's something else I need to tell you about, Karen. You've heard Fletcher and me speak of the farmer over on Norris Run with the two daughters he's raising by himself after his wife passed away?"

"Yes, as I recall, the oldest girl isn't quite right. I heard folks say she is beautiful, but has the mind of a young child."

"That's the one. A man attacked the oldest daughter and left her for dead. Somehow, he lured her from her home, and I hear her father and sister found her at the river."

"Oh dear God, I can't believe it, Peter! What is this world coming to?"

"I've never worried much about you ladies being here by yourselves while we're off working. I think it would be a good idea to be more cautious until they catch that man. Talk to Mama and Rachel and make sure you don't travel alone or answer the door to strangers. I would hate to think of anything happening to any of you. I don't mean to panic you, but I want you all to be safe."

"Don't worry, Peter, I'll tell them. I hope it doesn't trigger any bad memories for Rachel. Her twin daughters are beautiful young girls, and it would kill Rachel if anyone bothered them. You remember how she reacted with Dotty dating Patrick before they met him? I'm going to talk to them about us ladies going over to see if we can help nurse his daughter back to health. Maybe we could prepare some meals and offer our friendship to the girls."

"Well, don't get your hopes up. He has never been the friendly sort, and with what has happened, he might not welcome any interference from the outside."

"Nonsense. I bet he's feeling overwhelmed. Maybe we could offer to watch his daughter while he's working."

"You can try. Karen, I'm beat. I don't know how I'll get to sleep with so much on my mind tonight."

Karen looked at her husband, took his face in her hands, and kissed his cheeks. "Thank you for telling me, Peter. The Lord will give us the strength we need to get through this rocky patch. Let's try to get some sleep. Tomorrow's going to be a long day."

At Anna Leigh's house, things were more than a little tense. Her husband, David, had always been a hothead, but today, she thought he had carried things too far. A public brawl over an innocent flirtation.

For heaven's sake, she'd only been talking to that man in a public place with plenty of people around. It wasn't like she'd slipped off with the mysterious stranger. There had been no call for David losing his temper and making such a fool of himself. She berated him all afternoon for his lack of control. The man was insanely jealous.

You would think after all these years of marriage, he'd realize her teasing was harmless—well, for the most part. What he didn't know wouldn't hurt him. She smiled secretly to herself.

They had a quiet supper but not in a good way. David choked down a quick bite and stormed out of the house in anger. She noticed he'd left with his rifle and hunting gear. *Good, maybe he could walk off some of his misery.* He'd hardly spoken to her since they got back to the house. Anna Leigh preferred silence to his usual rant of accusations, which were so tiresome. *Well, I certainly won't bother waiting up for him tonight.* He'd calm down in a day or two. He always did.

Anna Leigh turned her musings to the man in the diner. He was charming despite being crudely dressed. There was something very worldly about him. She thought his slightly graying hair made him quite distinguished looking. And he certainly had a silver tongue. She'd enjoy his flattery. Under different circumstances, you just never knew. They might've hit it off.

She and David had never been able to conceive children. She suspected he resented her for that. She was inwardly relieved. She certainly didn't feel any inclination toward motherhood. There was no point in ruining her figure to bring another brat into the world. She'd seen that happen to many of her female friends. They had let themselves go once they became mothers. But not Fletcher Broce's wife! After birthing all those children, she looked like she got younger every year and still had that fabulous figure. *If something happened to Rachel, I might still have a chance with Fletcher*, she thought.

Teaming up, the town police worked with the county sheriff's office to search for the stranger the young girl claimed had attacked her. They methodically went from neighborhood to neighborhood. It seemed they'd just missed him. He seemed to be really getting around. Luckily, he didn't appear to realize they were looking for him because he obviously wasn't making any effort to conceal his location.

They were quickly losing daylight and decided to call it a day. They agreed to meet up at the sheriff's office early the next morning and head toward the New Town community on the edge of town since that was where he was last spotted. He reportedly was a heavy drinker, so they half expected to find him on the side of the road sleeping it off.

Amos arose at dawn the next morning. He and Agnes sat on their back porch and watched the sun rise on a clear day. They'd already partaken of a simple breakfast, a buttered biscuit and a strong cup of coffee. Agnes told him she planned to help the church ladies clean the church today. Amos told her he intended to go by the blacksmith shop to take care of some work that had come in the previous day just as he was closing up.

Noting the sad look in his eyes, Agnes reached over and patted his rugged hand. She knew he feared he'd never see his beloved horse, Old Joe, again. "Amos, you're not going to believe this, but last night I prayed that your horse would come back to you. Now just as clearly as I can see you sitting here beside me, the Lord gave me a vision of him walking up to you at the blacksmith shop just as pretty as you please. Now you try to have a little faith," she said, kissing him gently on the cheek. She heard the wagon pulling up out front. "I have to go. There's the Joneses here to pick me up." She pulled her shawl around her shoulders and smiled brightly at her husband.

"I hope you're right, dear Agnes," Amos told her, his damp eyes shining.

Amos quietly hitched his neighbor's young steed to his wagon. He was grateful to have use of the horse, but it was a bit too high-spirited for his liking. "Whoa, boy, settle down," he coaxed in a soft but firm voice. "Easy, easy, that's a good fellow."

When he got to the shop, it was around a quarter to seven in the morning. *The day's a-wasting*, he thought. He unhitched the lively horse and placed him in the little corral behind the shop. Going inside, he got the fire started and laid out his work for the day. Soon, he'd be able to heat the metal to make it malleable. It got hot in the shop in a hurry. Opening the side door to let in a little breeze, he heard something. It was a familiar nicker from a horse. He raced out the door and to his amazement, there stood Old Joe. The horse looked a little worse for the wear but, to Amos, was a heavenly sight!

With grateful tears streaming down his wizened cheeks, Amos dropped to his arthritic knees. "Thank you, Lord, for answering Agnes's prayer. I hope you will forgive me for not wanting to bother you with my prayers to have my old horse returned to me."

Amos marveled at the fact that his horse had appeared just as Agnes had envisioned. Would miracles never cease? Feeling extremely blessed, he took his old friend by the reins and led him around to the corral. He removed the bridle and saddle. Old Joe studied his master momentarily and then headed straight to the water trough. He lapped up the liquid thirstily. Amos put out some extra hay for both the horses. He patted his horse and wondered about the stranger who'd had his horse this week. Wiping the tears from his cheeks, he walked around the building with a lighter heart. Having his horse back felt like an enormous burden had been lifted from his shoulders.

Amos looked up as he heard men's voices and the sound of many horses approaching the shop. This was an interesting morning. When he rounded the corner, he noticed about six lawmen on horseback. The horses snorted. They were rested and anxious to get on with their job. Amos waved the men over.

"Good morning, sir. How can I help you?" the sheriff asked.

"You're not going to believe this, but my horse showed up this morning. He still had on his saddle and bridle but no rider. There's a saddlebag in here that must've belonged to that stranger you were asking about. I haven't opened it." "Marcus, get the saddlebag and inspect its contents. Well, this is something. But you didn't see that man we're looking for, did you?" the sheriff asked.

"No, sir, but I'm relieved to have my horse back," Amos told him. Amos handed the young deputy the saddlebag. It felt empty. The man opened it and shook out some crumbs and a faded, wrinkled handkerchief.

"Take that with you," the sheriff told his employee. Looking at Amos, he said, "If that man happens by here, please tell him it's urgent that I talk to him to clear up a little matter."

"I certainly will. Looks like you have a posse with you. I hope you find him today," said Amos.

"We hope so too. We've been by the hotel, and he didn't return to his room last night. Everything is just the way he left it yesterday," said the sheriff. "At this point, we need to interview him to see whether we can eliminate him as a suspect in a crime. He tipped his hat to Amos, and the men rode off down Prices Fork Road, the hooves of their horses kicking up dust on the rutted dirt road.

Amos stood there watching after them. He wondered what had spooked Old Joe. It wasn't like his horse to wander off. How far had he raced to get back to the shop? What direction had he come from? Hopefully, they'd have that man in custody soon and get some answers. He went back into the shop and worked steadily for several hours.

His work was almost complete. Needing a little break, Amos walked out front into the bright sunlight. He stretched his arms above his head, then removing his handkerchief, he wiped his sweaty brow. He rotated his head side to side to loosen up the aching muscles. Just a little longer and he'd be done for the day. Amos planned to spend a little time in their garden this afternoon, but right now, a nap sounded like a good option. It had been an exciting morning. Their garden was small, but it produced enough for Agnes and him. He was glad to have Old Joe back home. He couldn't help but smile as he finished up his work. Amos felt like an enormous burden had been lifted from his shoulders.

Just as he was turning to go back into the shop, he heard a commotion. Peering down the road, he saw the lawmen returning. As they got closer, he heard their excited voices. He noticed they had a wagon with them now. They must've commandeered it for official business. When they got closer, Amos could see that a man's body was in the back. Was he injured or dead? Was it the stranger or someone else? As hot as the day was, a chill ran through Amos. As they came closer, he could see that a blanket covered the man's face. Not a good sign. Had the lawmen killed him or found him dead?

They surprised him by pulling over at his shop. The men became very still. "Is that the man you were looking for?" asked Amos.

The sheriff nodded affirmatively.

"Did he resist arrest?" Amos asked.

No one responded. The silence was deafening and made Amos uncomfortable. He realized his question might have made him appear to be prying into official police business.

"We're going to need you to come down to the station to answer some questions," the sheriff told him. The other men studied Amos's face.

"Certainly, I'll come down. I don't know how much good I can do you. I haven't seen the man since he rented my horse," Amos told them. "I'll lock up and get my horse so I can follow you downtown."

What a strange turn of events, thought Amos. *Surely, I'm not a suspect.* He guessed they had to talk to everyone who had interacted with the man.

As the procession reached town, the wagon driver and a couple of the officers turned toward the coroner's office. At the police station, the lawmen told Amos to wait in the lobby. He took one of the hard wooden chairs and rested patiently until they were ready for him.

Shortly, they took him back to one of the offices and began to question him. Did he own a knife? Where was his knife? Amos removed it from his pocket and handed it over to them. Did he notice whether the stranger had a knife when he picked up the horse? Did he kill the man over the horse? Did he know anyone who had a beef with the man? Amos responded to question after question, answering honestly.

Eventually, they told him he could leave, but they might need to talk with him again. Amos was stupefied that they considered him a suspect. He appreciated that they had a job to do, but he couldn't help but feel annoyed. He didn't even know how the man had been killed. From the nature of the questions, he assumed the man had been stabbed.

He wondered what had happened and why the man had been murdered. Had it been self-defense? Amos tried to cease his speculation. His mind went to two most likely suspects, David and the farmer whose daughter had been attacked.

Meanwhile, Anna Leigh watched as her husband returned home, changed his clothes, and proceeded to go out behind their house. He hadn't met her eyes and didn't speak to her. She watched as he burned the clothes he had worn the night before. He stood and waited until there was nothing but ashes left. He took a stick and scattered the ashes. Getting some water from the well, he doused the fire. He glanced back at the house in her direction. She stepped away from the window hoping he hadn't seen her standing there. A chill ran down her spine. Why had he burned up his clothing? What had he been up to? She made a decision then and there not to ask him any questions about the matter. He certainly was acting strangely, and frankly, it frightened her for some unknown reason. Despite his hot head, David had never been violent toward her, but she didn't know what he was capable of.

Mountain Justice?

The sheriff and his deputies knocked on the doors of David, Peter, and the Norris Run farmer nearly simultaneously. All three men were brought in for questioning. The farmer was reluctant to leave his daughters by themselves. The officers accompanied him while he took them to stay with their grandmother on McCoy Road.

Each man was put in a separate room and questioned for hours about their whereabouts on the evening the stranger was murdered. They were all near the location the body was found. All had motive but also had plausible answers. Peter and Fletcher were at the river fishing between 8:00 p.m. and 11:00 p.m. David reported he had been hiking in the mountains until the wee hours of the morning. He was in the woods alone. He told them he had a lot on his mind, sat down to think, and fell asleep there. He swore he awoke stiff and sore and then went home to his wife.

When they interviewed the farmer, he was quick to say that if that man was the one who had hurt his daughter, he could've killed him with his bare hands if he'd had an opportunity. He told the deputies that he would never leave his daughters alone, especially after what had happened to his oldest daughter.

The deputies discussed their interviews and prepared written reports for the sheriff's review. In his estimation, his most likely suspect was David, with his infamous temper, jealous rages, and tendency toward violence where his wife's flirtations were concerned. David had no witnesses as to his location during the night in question. His wife had confirmed that he'd stormed out saying he was going hunting.

His next most likely suspect would be the farmer with the teenage daughter who'd been assaulted. That would be enough to make any man's blood boil, but had it pushed him to murder? The farmer had no record of violence; however, he had been passionate about wanting justice for his daughter's attacker. He certainly had motive, but how would he know that the man was the culprit?

Peter Broce was his least likely suspect, but he had been involved in the fight at the Café. His brother had been with him and could vouch for his location during the probable time of death. He didn't appear to have any motive other than coming to the defense of an acquaintance.

For the time being, each of the men were considered simply persons of interest. The sheriff pinned his hopes on getting some tip, even anonymously, from someone who lived in the area where the crime had occurred and might have witnessed something or someone out of the ordinary.

The stranger had been stabbed in the gut with what appeared to be his own switchblade knife. Had it been an act of self-defense? Had the stranger pulled a knife on someone else as he had at the Café earlier that day? Perhaps a stronger or bigger man who'd outmaneuvered him? His body had been found at the edge of the woods near Nutter's Store. When the deputies came up on the body, they'd assumed the man was drunk and had passed out there. When his officers tried to rouse the motionless man, they noted the blood and evidence of a struggle. There was a strong smell of alcohol and a broken mason jar lay on the ground near the man's head.

What events had led up to the man's death? They gathered what evidence they could find. Officers had been sent back to the hotel to gather the rest of the man's personal effects. They hoped for a break in the case and for an eyewitness to come forward.

The men had taken the body directly to the coroner's office to determine the cause of death. If experience and judgment had taught them anything, the stab wound was going to be the answer. The man had bruising, but then he had been in a fight the day before. The sheriff received the coroner's report the next day. It stated that the cause of death was a stab to the abdomen accompanied by internal bleeding. He saw evidence of bruising from the previous struggle and more recent wounds that appeared to be defensive in nature.

A murder was high excitement in the small town. The newspapers created an air of mystery around the unwelcome stranger and his untimely demise. They attempted to interview the suspects, but all refused to talk with the reporters. It was learned that the stranger's name was Emanuel P. Sturgis. An anonymous envelope filled with cash arrived at the funeral home. The man who assisted the undertaker said he saw a woman walking quickly down the sidewalk. She wore a cape and he couldn't identify her. He couldn't even be sure it was she who had dropped off the envelope. She'd glanced over her shoulder once while he was standing there and he thought she wore heavy makeup, but of course, he wasn't a judge of women's cosmetics. His wife didn't wear makeup. The typewritten instructions indicated that the stranger was to be given a proper burial. The note and the envelope was turned over to the sheriff. Was that someone's guilty conscience? Times were tough with the little community still reeling from the Great Depression. Who would possibly be concerned about the burial of an apparent rapist? The sheriff and his deputies were at the funeral to observe the attendees and search for a possible suspect. Only reporters, the preacher, and the funeral home personnel were present. After the funeral, the hubbub died down, and things quickly returned to normal.

Was the deceased the man who had attacked the farmer's daughter? Her doctor advised that she not be called on to identify the man as her attacker due to her fragile mental state. They would possibly never know the truth.

With a name and a previous address located in the man's effects, the sheriff was able to make discreet inquiries. He learned of the man's arrest record, his ten-year prison sentence for the apparent rape of a young lady on a ship. The victim was said to be of German descent, but for some reason, her name was omitted from the records. The arrest documents had been signed by the ship's captain and the onboard physician.

Strange, the sheriff thought.

Of course, there were a number of Germans who had settled in the Blacksburg and Montgomery County area. If he had the resources, it might be worthwhile to obtain the ship's records from nearly sixteen years ago and attempt to identify the young lady. That might put him that much closer to learning the identity of the killer. *If I'm ever in New York, I might just look into those records.* It was unlikely that he would ever get an opportunity to travel that far. It was also a real stretch to think his previous conviction had anything to do with the current murder case, but made it fairly likely he was guilty of assaulting the young girl with the crime being of a similar nature as his previous conviction.

He heard talk around town of it being a clear case of "mountain justice." The sheriff wasn't sure about all that. The fellow seemed to make enemies at every turn and could not be cleared of the assault of the teenage girl from

Norris Run. The best he could figure is that the Sturgis fellow had messed with the wrong person. It was most likely a man since the deceased was reportedly physically strong.

He placed the police reports and the evidence collected in a box in the file room. For some time, the case haunted him as the box attracted more and more dust. The sheriff loathed the expression "mountain justice," which in his mind amounted to nothing more than lawlessness. It angered him to think of folks romanticizing murder and disregarding proper legal process. It was beyond his comprehension.

37

The Prodigal Hobo

On a lovely spring day, Rachel had raised the window and was washing the glass when she heard a man whistling a familiar tune. Pulling back the curtain, she gazed out. To her surprise and delight, Cooper was coming down the lane. He looked basically the same, but his hair might be a little whiter. She ran to the side window and called out to Papa, who was hard at work in the garden already this morning. He didn't look up. He probably couldn't hear her. She ran down the steps, out the back door, and across the lawn. Just as Papa turned around to talk to her, he spotted Cooper standing expectantly at the edge of the garden.

A slow smile started spreading across Papa's face until it was a broad grin. His eyes widened as if taking in an incredible sight. He straightened and got his feet under him. The two old friends started walking toward each other in the garden path. One moved almost as slowly as the other, not from reluctance but from aging joints. Cooper's smile mirrored Papa's.

Papa patted him on the back. "Cooper, what a sight you are for my sore eyes. We figured we'd never see you again. Are you just passing through?"

"Probably, they say a rolling stone gathers no moss," said Cooper.

"Well, I could use a break myself. Come on in the house and have a cup of coffee with me. I had my breakfast earlier this morning, but I'm sure this young lady can whip up something to warm your belly," said Papa as he beamed at Rachel.

"I certainly can. I think I still have some biscuits I can warm up and serve with our homemade jelly or a little bacon this morning. How's that sound?" said Rachel.

Cooper's stomach growled loudly in acceptance.

"I think you have your answer, Rachel." Papa laughed.

"Well, give me a few minutes. You two wash up and then meet me in the kitchen," said Rachel. Walking toward the house, she glanced over her shoulder. The two men had sat down in a couple of chairs out by the garden. She could see Papa pointing out the various plantings to his friend. Was it the bright sunlight or the friendship of kindred spirits that made their faces glow?

She called out to the two men to let them know breakfast was ready. When they got to the kitchen, she surprised Cooper with a hearty breakfast of bacon and eggs to go with his biscuit. Rachel gave Papa another biscuit and served both of them a steaming cup of coffee. She knew Papa had no use for lukewarm coffee. He wanted it to practically burn the roof of his mouth.

Rachel began to tidy the kitchen once more. Cooper dove into the delicious breakfast she'd prepared for him. She looked at Papa, who merely winked at her. He was relishing watching the prodigal hobo enjoying his meal. He finished every bite and might have licked the plate if they weren't watching. He hadn't eaten in two days but would never tell them that.

"Bring your coffee and come on out on the stoop. We'll rest and chat for a bit," said Papa.

Cooper rose from the chair. He humbly thanked Rachel for his meal.

"You're welcome. Good to see you again. We missed you," said Rachel. "The children will be excited to see you when they get home from school today."

The two men sat on the back porch steps with their coffee. They beheld the beautiful Appalachian Mountains. From their vantage point, they could see the sun glinting on the big pond out behind the barn. Bees were buzzing about the flower beds.

Through the open window, Rachel heard Papa say, "Where has your journey taken you, my friend?"

"I slipped down south to work in the orchards and earn a little money. I tried to make it back this way last spring but had a health problem crop up," said Cooper.

"Sorry to hear that. Nothing serious, I hope?" said Papa.

"Well, to tell you the truth, it almost took me away from here. I wasn't prepared to meet my Maker but thought I might last year. It started as a bit of a sour stomach for a spell, then I would get sharp pains in between my shoulder blades. I thought maybe it was my heart acting up," Cooper told him.

"Were you near a town or on the rails?" asked Papa.

"You know I don't have money for any doctor, so I just kept traveling on hoping whatever was going on would pass. Just happenstance really, but I managed to collapse at the edge of town near a small house. The man who lived there was a retired doctor," said Cooper.

"That was the good Lord watching over you Coop, yes, sir," said Papa.

"I know you're right about that. He and his kindly wife managed to get me into their house, and I nearly passed out on their sofa." Cooper's eyes had a faraway look in them, remembering the awful pain.

"What was causing all that pain?" asked Papa.

"The good doctor poked and prodded on me, took my temperature, listened to my heart, and checked my blood pressure and my pulse. I don't know what all he did, but he suddenly looked right worried," said Cooper.

Papa leaned in anxious to hear more about his friend's ailment.

"Then he told his wife to go next door and get their son to hurry into town and bring the new young doctor back.

To tell him to be prepared to perform surgery," said Cooper. "I told them I couldn't afford any medical treatment."

"The suspense is killing me, Cooper. You always were a great storyteller, but get on with it, man," said Papa anxiously.

"Well, it seems my gallbladder had turned against me. The young doctor arrived and confirmed the older doctor's suspicions. They got me undressed, which was right embarrassing, if you know what I mean. They put one of the doctor's nightshirts on me, cleansed the area, and gave me a shot of something that knocked me out cold," said Cooper.

"They didn't take you to the doctor's office? They did surgery right there on the sofa?" asked Papa.

"Yes, sir, they did," said Cooper. "I woke up in excruciating pain. They gave me another shot of something that made it ease up some. They said I was lucky to be alive because that organ was so diseased."

"Where did you recuperate? Surely you didn't go back on the road right after that happened to you?" asked Papa.

"You're not going to believe this, but they put me up there the entire summer until I got back on my feet. They were some of the best Christian people I ever met—besides your own family, I mean."

"We had a rough winter last year weatherwise and otherwise," Papa said. He told him about his granddaughter Dotty losing her baby.

"I'm sorry to hear that. Hope this will be a better year for your family. I decided to stay south last year once summer was over and try to pick up a little work in the orchards," said Cooper. "It was tough on this old body after that surgery."

"You know, we watched for you and wondered about you. Our family remembered you in our prayers. There's just one thing, though. Why did you go away without telling anyone good-bye?" asked Papa, letting his guard down a bit.

Cooper hung his head and after a moment, cleared his throat. "I'm sorry about that. It was selfish of me really. I tell you the truth, your family was so good to me. I was tempted to stay, but winter was coming. I felt like I'd worn out my welcome."

"You're back now, and all that is forgotten. Glad you're feeling better and had such excellent care. You're welcome to work with us again. Same terms as before," said Papa.

"That's good, and I'm obliged to you," said Cooper.

"Do you need to rest for a while before you get started? I'm done lollygagging. I've got to get back to the garden," said Papa.

"Not sure what lollygagging is, but I'm ready to help you in the garden," said Cooper.

They returned their coffee cups to the empty kitchen and set out across the yard like a couple of brothers or best friends, walking, talking, and laughing. From the upstairs window, Rachel watched them and smiled. If she didn't know better, she'd say Papa had a little more pep in his step today.

38

A New Job Opportunity

After supper, Peter, Fletcher, Papa, Cooper, Joseph, Arwood, and Andrew gathered around the blazing fire pit the men had built out between the house and the barn. It had rained most of that late April day. The women were making plans to teach the younger girls how to make lye soap the next day. Dotty was joining them. They were all in the house trying to get their housework caught up so they'd be ready to start early in the morning.

The men thought it best if they cleared out of the house before the women got them caught up in housework. They had put in a full day on the farm and were looking forward to a little relaxation. Papa had joked that with those women, it was best to be out of sight, out of mind.

They all picked a spot to sit on the long logs lying around the fire pit. It felt good to stretch out their long legs and watch the flames reaching for the sky. Peter had always worked side by side with his dad, first on the family's farm in Germany and now here in Virginia. His next words shocked everyone sitting there. "I'm thinking about getting a job," he told them.

Clearing his throat, Papa reminded him, "Son, you've already got a job right here with us."

"I know, Dad, but I thought with Cooper back that I'd go help with that dam everyone's talking about over in Pulaski. Last time I was down at the river fishing, I spoke with some of the fellows who live in Parrott. They said there were going to be plenty of jobs. They hope to have it built in a few years," Peter told him.

"What do you know about building a dam, Peter?" Papa asked.

"Nothing really, but I hear they can use lots of manual laborers. The pay is $25 a month too. We could sure use that to help with some of the work that needs done around the farm," Peter told him.

Joseph's and Arwood's eyes met. Joseph said, "Can Arwood and me get in on that too?" he asked his uncle.

"Now hold on, boys," said Papa. "If all of you run off to work on that there dam, who's going to help us here? Cooper and I both are nothing but a couple of brokendown farmhands, at best. There's no way we can keep this farm running without all the help we get from you three."

"Dad, the work on the dam is day work. We'd be home every evening and of course, be able to help on the weekends here on the farm too. It doesn't have to be either-or," said Peter as he attempted to soothe his dad's fears.

"It's a lot of money, Papa," Joseph said. "I'd like to save a little bit of mine if I can get on there, but the rest I'd give to Dad and Mom to help with expenses."

"I'm willing to do the same thing, Papa," said Arwood.

"Dad, Kellen and Kolten are fourteen, and Andrew's turned sixteen. If Karen doesn't object to pulling them from school, they could be a big help. The school year is practically over anyway," said Peter. "Andrew, how do you feel about that?"

Andrew let out a big whoop of celebration. "Yes, please get me out of school early. That teacher is killing me with homework. I can't do anything to please her."

"What do you think, Dad? Will that work?" asked Peter.

Papa cut his eyes over to Fletcher. "Son, you're awfully quiet. What do you think of this state of affairs?"

"Peter mentioned it to me earlier today. To be honest, I had the same reservations you did. I hadn't talked to Joseph and Arwood, so this is news to me too, but they're grown men. They can make their own decisions. We're also family and have to make decisions that are beneficial to the family. The reason we've survived this blasted Depression is because of this rich soil, the sweat of our brow, and the little bit I've brought home from the mines. I wouldn't want us to forget that," said Fletcher.

"Fletcher, you left out something—*by the grace of God*," said Papa.

Peter hung his head, disappointed. He'd always felt guilty that he wasn't able to bring in a paycheck to help out. He'd seen this as his opportunity to do just that. He got to his feet. "It's okay, Dad, don't worry about it. I just thought it might give us some extra cash to take care of things here on the farm. There's tools we need. The home place is getting rundown, it could use a good coat of paint. I saw this as a chance to contribute more."

Papa studied his oldest son. He saw something there he'd never noticed before. He couldn't quite describe it, like a yearning. "Now see here, Peter. Don't get yourself riled up over this. Give me a chance to chew on it a bit. I might see the whole matter differently when I've had a chance to sleep on it."

The two younger Broce boys, Kellen and Kolten, joined them and asked Cooper if he'd show them how to use their new pocketknives they'd gotten for Christmas. They wanted to learn how to carve a horse and a rooster. Cooper admired their new knives and sent them scampering off to find a piece of wood to work on. The interruption broke the tension, and the men settled in to talking about their day and plans for the next day.

39

Working on the Claytor Dam

As Peter, Joseph, and Arwood rode home in a horsedrawn wagon with a number of other men, they marveled at the big plans a foreman had shared earlier in the day for the Claytor Dam. It was mind-boggling to imagine how all their manual labor was so painstakingly orchestrated to bring about the big picture, which would emerge in a couple of years. This was 1937, and the work was expected to be wrapped up in 1939.

When finished, the land they were working on would be flooded, and a new lake, which would be over twentyone miles long, would miraculously appear. He said it would cover nearly forty-five hundred acres of land. The whole purpose of the dam was to generate electricity. This would be the power company's biggest electrical plant and hopefully would produce over seventy megawatts of electrical power. Times were changing, and it was a moneymaking proposition for the electric company but, in turn, would give a broader range of citizen's access to electricity in their homes. That would simplify their lives and bring them into the modern age.

Peter mused on that term—*simplify*. How could his family possibly live any simpler than they did right now? They grew their own food, had livestock, made their own soap and most of their clothing, and rarely had a meal that wasn't prepared by a family member's hands. They purchased the oil that was used in their lamps and lanterns. It was difficult to fathom the impact that having electricity would have on their daily life. He imagined it would be one of those things that once you had it, you wondered how you survived without it.

It was the end of the month, and it felt good having that extra twenty-five dollars in his pocket. After three months of work, they'd managed to save each paycheck, giving them all a tidy sum. Between working all day on the dam project and into the evening on the farm, they were all exhausted.

215

No one had any time to go anywhere to spend their money. It relieved Peter to see that his young nephews were just as worn-out as he was at the end of the day. He thought it was just him.

The thing that surprised Peter the most was how much he missed working full-time on the family farm. Admittedly, he had become bored with the day in, day out monotony of farm life. He'd seized on the opportunity to stretch his wings. He'd find himself thinking of that work when he was at the dam job. He figured that was probably natural because the farmwork was so familiar and the new job, at times, so puzzling. People were definitely creatures of habit.

Being away from home so much also gave him fresh eyes to see how much his parents had aged, especially his dad. True, Papa still had plenty of gumption to want to get up and go, but that steam didn't seem to carry him as far as it had at one time. He'd taken to carrying a bucket out in the fields with him. Many a time, he'd flip it upside down and sit for a spell to catch his breath. Mama noticed this too and fussed over her husband. It did her no good because John Broce was going to do what he wanted to. Peter had heard him consoling Mama and reminding her he wasn't as young as he used to be but could still put in a good day's work. Such talk left his mother clicking her tongue. Maybe that kept her from protesting more.

When Peter handed the money over to Karen, he told her, "I heard today that just in Virginia, six out of ten people have no visible means to support themselves. We are truly blessed to have this farm and outside jobs for at least four members of the family."

Karen hugged her husband and ran her fingers through his sandy hair. "I know, dear, but I still miss you. I used to take for granted being able to look up from my work and see you working around the farm. It always gave me such a peaceful feeling."

"Are the boys helping as much as we'd hoped?" Peter asked.

"Oh yes, Peter. They seem to like the new responsibility we've heaped on their shoulders. They don't hardly have time to pick on each other anymore. They're tired at the end of the day," said Karen.

"Well, good, it'll help them appreciate the value of putting in a real day's work. There's a pride that comes with that which can't be described with words. It's like looking over the job you just finished and feeling your heart swell just a little," said Peter.

"They're good boys. Am I sensing a wistfulness from you?" asked Karen.

"Maybe a little." Peter smiled. "The work we're doing is meaningful and exciting in the long run, but sometimes, I can't envision how the little things we're doing day after day contribute to the big picture," said Peter.

"I can see how that would be frustrating," said Karen.

"But bottom line, I'm thankful for the work and the little nest egg we're building against future storms," said Peter.

"I know, dear. You'd better wash up. I think Rachel and Mama have whipped up a hearty supper for everyone," said Karen. "I heard something about a pork roast, gravy, mashed potatoes, and greens. There might even be a cake of corn bread, if you're lucky."

"I feel lucky." Peter grinned at his wife. As she smiled back, the evening sun shone on her face. He noticed the little lines at her eyes and lips that only made her even more beautiful to him. *What a wonderful wife I have*, he thought.

Later at supper, Arwood remarked about some of the sights he'd seen while working at the dam such as the airplanes that flew overhead. "Man, those biplanes are loud when they zoom in. Seems like they're right above our heads. I overheard someone say they're taking pictures of the work we're doing,"

Papa listened intently. Young Arwood's eyes lit up when he talked about the planes. His voice became animated. It was easy to see the excitement those airplanes stirred up in him.

"Arwood, it sounds like you might like to try your hand at flying one of those birds yourself, or is it the picture taking that excites you?" Papa asked.

"Shoot, I don't want to take any pictures. I would like to see those pictures, though. Can you imagine how things down here must look from up there?" said Arwood.

Rachel cleared her throat at the mild oath at their supper table. *Shoot* wasn't the worst thing a young man might come up with, but she could already see the influence of her sons being around people outside the family.

"Sorry, Mom," said the blushing Arwood.

"If you can't be a good influence on the men working around you, at the very least, don't let them be a bad influence on you, son," his mother told him.

Mama smiled. *Rachel is tough on her children, but it never hurts to have high expectations for their behavior*, she thought.

Papa winked at her. They were both so proud of their family. "How can I ever learn to fly an airplane?" wondered Arwood aloud.

"I've heard of them being used by some of the bigger farming operations to spread fertilizer or insecticides," said Fletcher. "Might be something to ask around about, but who is going to let you fly their plane?"

"Exactly!" said Arwood with a dreamy look in his eyes.

Peter said, "At the job site, you see these carloads of men in dress shirts and pants racing around with binoculars and rolled-up papers. I guess those are the diagrams for the dam completion. Sometimes, they take some photographs too."

Joseph said, "We have foremen who tell us what to do, how to do it, and where to do it."

Everyone laughed. "Just like home, right, guys?" asked Fletcher. They all nodded in agreement.

Peter said, "Yes, but sometimes all that observation and talk filters back down to our level, with the boss man barking out orders that usually involves us having to redo something or head off in another direction if something isn't progressing exactly like those engineers think it should."

"Yes, that's tough. We're used to having Papa, Mama, or one of you get after us about something, but it's something else to have a stranger yelling or cursing at you because he doesn't think you're doing something right or fast enough," said Joseph.

Papa piped up, "They're paying you men good money, and they want an honest day's work."

Fletcher looked concerned. "You boys are giving them their money's worth, aren't you, sons?

Uncle Peter quickly came to their defense. "Fletcher, you would be proud of your two sons. They are two of the hardest-working men at the job site. They're always respectful regardless of how they are spoken to."

Fletcher said, "Just like in the mines, you have to learn to not take criticism personally, but it's hard not to. I understand that very well. You're working for a paycheck, so the man that is in charge makes the rules."

Joseph spoke up, "Thanks, Uncle Peter. Dad, it's easy to spot the fellows who aren't pulling their weight. They make a good show of working when the boss man is around but slack off when he is out of sight."

"Some of them aren't as crafty as they think, boys. I've seen the boss pay a few of them and tell them not to bother coming back next week. I feel sorry for their families, but it's not fair to rest of us who are trying to put forth our best effort," said Peter. "The thing I think about is that we are a part of something that will be here long after we're gone. You might say we're making history."

Something else Peter had observed was some of the other workers hitting the bottle on their dinner break. He tried to steer his young nephews away from them. One had even offered Joseph a sip of his mountain dew. To Joseph's credit, he'd politely refused and continued with the simple meal his mother had packed. The mason jar of water she packed them both from their own well was quite refreshing enough for him. Peter didn't think it appropriate to discuss that subject with the ladies present. Maybe he'd share that at one of the men's campfire talks.

Arwood's eyes were big, and he was taking it all in but didn't partake or talk about what he saw at work. The young men were learning more than dam construction. They were all getting a quick lesson in human nature, as well. Peter hadn't thought much about how sheltered their life had been there on the farm—that is, until he saw firsthand other peoples and their values, or lack thereof.

Peter heard one of the men in the drinking group talking about how rough his family with five children was having it. He prayed silently that the man didn't lose his job because of the drinking while at work. It seemed there was always someone new showing up looking to be hired. The power plant folks could afford to be choosy.

Papa said, "When you men started talking about taking that job, I know I was skeptical about how we'd manage all the work here on the farm. I want you to know that I have three fine young farmhands as my able assistants."

"Thanks, sons. Your mother gave me a good report on you today too when I asked her how you were doing. We're proud of every one of you. Keep it up!" said Peter.

"I still can't figure how they can get work done so quickly that would've taken me most of the day. But I sure do appreciate Andrew, Kellen, and Kolten. Cooper is a big help too, and of course, I appreciate all of your help in the evening when you get home. I think we're going to be all right," said Papa.

40

A Lost Community, Mahanaim

Peter delighted in learning some of the local history surrounding the Claytor Dam property. The men loved to share stories while they worked. He was actually the quiet one in the family, but he couldn't keep these stories to himself. He knew his family enjoyed hearing the tales. Sometimes, it was difficult to separate fact, fiction, and embellishment, but he just told the stories as they were recounted to him.

One old-timer told him how the community got its present name of Dunkard's Bottom. It seems a religious group had settled the land back in the mid 1700s. They were hoping to convert the savage Indian natives and others to the Christian faith. The men told Peter that the Dunkards were from Germany, like Peter's own family. He said they were called Dunkers because they believed in dunking the converts' heads under water when they baptized them.

They called their community Mahanaim. They constructed a series of small houses to live in. They hired Italian tradesmen to build limestone chimneys on each house. Everyone admired the craftsmanship of their work. It was said that the Dunkards were gentle people interested only in promoting their religion.

But those were violent times, with the French and Indian Wars going on. The Dunkard settlement was attacked. People were killed and their leaders, the two Eckerlin brothers, taken prisoner.

As Peter shared this story one night over supper, Mama listened closely. That settlement name resonated in her mind. She couldn't quit thinking about it. She told Papa later that night that she thought she'd read something in the Bible about a place called Mahanaim. After he'd gone to bed, she pulled out her Bible and began to search for the name. In the very first book of the Bible in the Old Testament, she found what she was looking for in Genesis 32:1–

2. She read, "And Jacob went on his way, and the angels of God met him. And when Jacob saw them, he said, this is God's host: and he called the name of that place Mahanaim."

That was it. Her heart grieved for the poor, peaceful Dunkards. They couldn't possibly have envisioned either the violence that met their mission work in Virginia or the fact that someday the land they lived and worked on would be flooded, just as its namesake had been in biblical times. That matter settled, Mama's mind was at rest. She went to bed. That would be interesting to share with her family tomorrow night.

When Peter's and Fletcher's sons got home the next evening, he talked of a time a little later when a man named William Christian, who was a military commander who fought the Indians, had married the sister of the famous patriot Patrick Henry. He bought the fertile bottomland and brought his family there to live. He built a large house for his family. He used the wooden Dunkard houses as quarters for his slaves, who worked on the plantation. He and his family moved to a new western territory in Kentucky, where he continued to fight the Indians until his death in battle.

In the early 1800s, a local family, the Cloyds, bought the land. For over one hundred years, they owned what everyone around thought was the best farmland in the area. They added a couple of brick mansions and a family cemetery with a stone wall surrounding it.

Later, when the power company negotiated purchasing the land, the family was given the option to move the bodies from the graves along with any tombstones or monuments. Peter didn't know if anyone had been moved from the cemetery.

Something else he found out was that the local government could take someone's land for the public good. They still had to compensate the landowner, but they might not get as much as they would if they sold it themselves. It sounded like the power company had threatened to do just that if the last owner hadn't agreed to settle with them.

Papa spoke up, "You mean if the county or state decides they want our farm for some public use, we have to sell?"

"That's how it sounds to me. They call it eminent domain," said Peter.

"Well, that doesn't seem fair to me. A man shouldn't have to sell his land if he doesn't want to!" said an outraged Papa.

"I wouldn't think something like that happens very often, but I don't like the idea either," said Fletcher.

"You know times were hard. It might have been a blessing in disguise when the opportunity came along to sell that land to the power company," said Rachel.

"Well, you can't fault that family for trying to get as much as they could for it," said Mama.

"I think that's sad to know that if you don't reach an agreement about whether to sell or for how much, your land can still be taken," said Karen.

"I agree, Karen. I can't get over thinking about all those family graves left there. It doesn't seem right," said Mama.

They sipped their coffee and grew quiet. Each person seemed to be grappling with their own personal feelings about the process Peter described. None of them had any legal training, but felt for the family whose land had been sold. It was easy to put yourself in their shoes and to speculate about how you would feel in that circumstance.

Papa broke the silence. "Those folks had to make a big sacrifice for the rest of us to have electric power in our homes. When it is available and if we can afford it, I'd like to see both of these houses wired up for that electricity."

Mama started to speak. She opened her mouth but closed it again. *I don't like the idea of spending money on luxuries, but I think my old man might be right this time.*

41

Floodgates

On a hot August evening in 1940, Fletcher and Rachel sat on the front porch swing. Everyone else in their big extended family had taken off tonight to do one thing or another. The last three years had been a blur of busyness, joy, and sorrow for their family. Rachel rested her head on Fletcher's shoulder feeling overwhelmed by it all. Nostalgia and bittersweet memories engulfed them both like a fog.

The past few years had ushered in so much change for their family. Change had been sprinkled with both joy and grief. They were still getting used to their new reality. For one thing, they'd both lost their fathers, their oldest son had gotten married, they became grandparents twice over, and they had seen their youngest son leave home to pursue a career in aeronautics. Their son might be studying flight, but to them, their life was in a constant tailspin. Fletcher had left his mining job to help out more on the farm. That had been a difficult decision for them both but necessary under the circumstances. Cooper left in the fall of 1937. He later wrote John and Hilda to let them know he had met a nice lady in Georgia and gotten married. They would never forget Cooper, nor him them. They missed him dearly, but were happy for him at the same time.

In the spring of 1938, Joseph had married his childhood sweetheart, Ada. Her parents, Clyde and Clarisse, were dear friends of the family. After a short formal engagement of just four months, they had a simple church wedding. The young couple found a small house down the road from the home place to rent until they could afford to buy it. When Fletcher and Rachel went with them to see the house, it tore at their hearts. It was in horrible condition, just like their first home had been. They remembered the long hours of labor that went into making it a home. And similarly, it sat on a beautiful piece of land with a musical brook out the back door. The mountain rose prominently behind the home, and it had a nice front yard.

It took all the parents' willpower not to rush in with suggestions on how to improve it. They told the newlyweds to let them know if they needed any help. Ada's eyes were full of love, and they could see how enthralled she was with both her husband and the new home.

By the end of summer, the place began to take shape. Rachel taught Ada to sew, and her daughter-in-law was so proud of her homemade curtains for the windows. Hilda had given them a crocheted bedspread as a wedding gift. She made them a quilt for Christmas that year. It pleased Mama to no end that Ada had expressed an interest in learning to quilt.

Karen, along with Rachel's girls, had helped clean their little home from top to bottom before they moved in. Peter's sons, Kolten and Kellen, under Mama's direction, dug up and transplanted some perennial flowers from Mama and Papa's place around the little house. When Ada mentioned wanting a chicken coop so she could bring over her chickens from her former home, Joseph and Arwood built her one. Fletcher and Peter helped patch the roof with materials they had on hand.

Papa didn't like the idea that the young couple didn't have a written agreement about the rent and future purchase. He paid a lawyer in town to draw up the paperwork. The landlord seemed reluctant to sign the official-looking document but had relented at last.

Peter, Joseph, and Arwood had worked on the Claytor Dam until its completion in 1939. Then when they got home, they all helped Papa on the farm. Rachel suspected that Papa secretly resented the men looking for outside employment even though he understood why it was necessary. He never vocalized his feelings, but everyone noticed that he pushed himself harder than usual.

In late October 1938, while the teenage boys were in school and the other men at work, Papa insisted on going into the woods to chop some trees and get started on their wood supply for the winter. Mama insisted that he wait until the other men of the family could go with him, but he wouldn't hear of it. He'd hitched up his wagon after breakfast.

Mama packed him a lunch and begged him to not stay too long. It had rained that week. The ground was still muddy, and the temperatures had gotten right chilly. He had a chest cold already.

He put another log in the stove as he prepared to leave. "Now, Hilda, quit worrying so much. I'm a lot tougher than you think. I want to get a start on this job. I'm not going to sit around the house when there's work to be done."

"John, you know I love you, but you're an old fool! I know you're still feeling poorly from that cold. I heard you tossing and turning last night, so you didn't get a proper night's rest. We have a big stack of wood out back already. You don't have to get this done today," Mama nagged.

"Now you just save your breath. I'll be fine," Papa said as he kissed her on the forehead, trying to console his sweet wife. He left her wringing her hands on her apron.

Mama kept herself busy that morning, all the while hoping to see him riding up after a few hours or so. She walked over to Fletcher and Peter's house. The boys were just getting home from school. John had been up there in the woods practically all day. She asked the boys to go check on their grandpa. Meanwhile, she walked back over to her house to start supper. She was relieved to see the boys driving Papa's wagon back about an hour later. She went about her work in the kitchen, glad to know John was on his way home.

Fletcher had just gotten home from the mines and was covered in coal dust. He spoke to the boys and then jumped up in the back of the wagon. He ran into the house. Karen and Rachel came running outside and climbed into the back of the wagon. Papa was lying there clutching his chest in pain. His color didn't look good, and his skin felt clammy. Fletcher sent Andrew into town to get the doctor. He sent the ladies over to get Mama.

His father tried to speak but couldn't seem to get his words out. He managed to ask for Fletcher's mother. Fletcher told him to rest and explained that Rachel and Karen had gone to get Mama. That seemed to calm him somewhat. The boys brought out a couple of blankets and put them around their grandpa to keep him warm. Fletcher looked up and saw Mama running across the field with the two younger ladies trying to keep up. Her face was tearstreaked. She was screaming John's name.

"I told him not to go, but he wouldn't listen. How is he, Fletcher?" Her eyes searched her son's face.

"He looks bad, Momma. Brace yourself. He asked for you. We've sent for the doctor. I'm afraid to move him," said Fletcher lamely as he helped his mother into the wagon.

She put her head on her husband's chest while he weakly patted her head. He struggled to speak. "Hilda, Hilda…I want you to know that I love you, old girl," he started. "John, you hold on. The doctor is on his way," Mama screeched.

She started when she heard horses in the drive. It was Peter's and Fletcher's sons coming home from work. They helped lift and carry him into the house out of the damp air. They had just got him settled it seemed when the doctor appeared at the door. He asked them to leave so he could examine the patient. Shortly, he came into the parlor, where everyone was waiting expectantly.

He went over to John's wife and put his arm around her shoulder. "Mrs. Broce, your husband has had a heart attack. It's a bad one. I've given him something for the pain and have tried to make him comfortable. He is resting. He is too weak to try to take to the hospital. I'm afraid he doesn't have much time left."

Mama cried out and looked as if she might pass out. Her sons rushed to her side to support their mother. They eased her into a chair. Rachel hugged her and let her cry into her shoulder. Karen sent Andrew to the kitchen to get their mama a glass of water.

The doctor looked uncomfortable. "If I had to guess, he might have a few hours left, at best. I suggest you do what you can to comfort him and let him know how much his family loves him. I can see that he is well loved by you all. I'm leaving now but will be available if you think you need me tonight." He asked Fletcher and Peter to walk him out. He saw the pained look on their faces as he gave them instructions.

On a sunny day in early November, they buried the man they all treasured. They knew that their lives would be forever altered by his absence. Mama had been inconsolable. She couldn't stand to stay in the little house by herself without her husband. They moved her back into her old bedroom in the big house. Fletcher, Rachel, and their twin girls moved into the little Sear's house. Arwood wanted to remain with his male cousins.

Dotty and Patrick had a beautiful, healthy baby girl right after Thanksgiving that year. She had brilliant blue eyes and her mother's red hair. They named her Johnsie after her great grandfather.

Christmas was bittersweet that year. They all dearly missed Papa but were happy to share their love with the newest Broce child. Mama was smitten by Papa's little namesake and poured her affection into the great grandbaby.

Joseph and Ada announced at Christmas that they were expecting their first child. So far, Ada hadn't had any morning sickness. Joseph couldn't suppress his happiness at becoming a father. When the men were outside later, Arwood teased his brother, "We worried about you two in that drafty little house this winter. Guess you figured out a way to keep warm." He laughed, and Joseph's face turned red. He could take the ribbing.

Joseph said, "Just wait, some little filly will settle you down someday."

Arwood insisted he enjoyed playing the field, that there were too many lovely girls to choose just one for his attention. Joseph rolled his eyes and chuckled at his fickle brother.

When gardening season started that next spring of 1939, Fletcher gave his notice at the mines. His family needed him full-time on the farm. He had plans to cultivate even more of his land and sell more produce to area grocers. He was willing to deliver to several surrounding counties if their harvest was plentiful.

Rachel knew they needed him on the farm but worried about their finances. They had taken over the payments on the Sear's house. She told Fletcher that if they got in a bind, she'd be willing to find a job since their girls were practically grown. Fletcher had been appalled at the thought of his wife working outside the home. It never came to that. Fletcher's farming enterprise was a huge success. They had to hire some help to keep up but still turned a nice profit. Fletcher's knowledge of farming and his head for marketing were the key to their success. They managed to pay off the Sears mortgage, which had been a big relief to Mama. Fletcher also poured cash back into the farm by updating their equipment and building another larger barn. He promised Rachel he'd build her a bigger house if their success continued. She told him she was happy right where they were.

On a hot summer afternoon, Ada gave birth to a handsome baby boy. She insisted that he be named for his father, so Joseph Broce Jr. was presented to the family. He was a robust little fellow with his dad's hazel eyes. Joseph Sr. had been such an easy baby, and in that respect, Joseph Jr. was nothing like his dad. They all insisted he must've cried the first year of his life. The midwife seemed to think his mother's milk didn't agree with him as they battled colic followed quickly by teething woes. As he approached his first birthday, overnight he seemed to settle down, and his parents began to enjoy a good night's sleep once more. He had a full head of curly blond hair and big brown eyes.

Rachel and Fletcher delighted in having the two grandchildren spend the night at their house. Their fifteen years-old aunts, Ruth and Ruby, spoiled them. They thought they had the most beautiful niece and nephew ever born. The toddlers loved the girls. They nicknamed Joseph "Joey." Often, the girls took them over to see Mama at the big house so she could enjoy them too.

The Claytor Dam was nearly complete. The men got fewer and fewer hours as the project came to a close. It was a blessing to the family to have the menfolk back to help with the farm production. Fletcher had expanded their business to selling ham, bacon, eggs, and cheese. He dreamed of a day when he could open his own country store to sell their fresh produce, but for now, he had all the customers he could handle. He picked out a homesite up in the woods to build Rachel a dream house. It had spectacular mountain views. The pasture land was too precious to put another house there. They talked with the neighbors whose land adjoined theirs about selling their land to the Broce family so they could expand their farm. The couple was older, plus their children had grown, married, and moved away. Fletcher sweetened the deal by agreeing to let them continue to live in their house during their lifetime. They talked it over with their children and reached an agreement. That transaction increased their land holdings to 150 acres and almost doubled their available farmland.

In 1940, life was good. They'd moved into their new home. From the wide front porch, they could enjoy a panoramic view of their family's farm. Arwood had moved back in with them and taken over the large attic bedroom. The girls had a bedroom of their own for the first time in their life. Dotty and Patrick had announced they were expecting another child.

Mama seemed to have come to terms with her husband's death. That didn't mean she didn't think about Papa every day, but her pain was gently easing. Rachel credited the new grandbabies and all the increased farm activity. Mama had a good head for business and would sit up talking with Fletcher and Peter late into the evening about their plans for the land. She was proud of her boys. She told them their father would've been proud of them too.

A few months later, Arwood surprised them all by announcing that he was signing up for the United States Army Air Corps. He was ordered to report to Langley Air Force Base in Hampton, Virginia, by June 1, 1940, to begin his flight school training. He hadn't said much more about his desire to fly planes, but evidently it had never left him. They had the Claytor Dam project to thank for his exposure to airplanes. He was a twenty-four-year-old man and ready to spread his wings. They gave him their blessing and saw him off on the train, all the while feeling like a piece of their heart was leaving. He was excited about the grand adventure. They were worried to death about him flying airplanes but at the same time proud of him for wanting to serve his country.

A month after he left, they were awakened early one morning by a loud knock at their door. When Fletcher opened the door, there stood Ada's brother, Ambrose. Rachel was getting out of bed and searching for her robe. Fletcher stepped out on the porch with Ambrose.

"What is it, son? What brings you out at this hour? What time is it anyway, around six?" Fletcher said, rubbing his eyes. It was Sunday morning, his morning to sleep in a little.

"It's Amos, Rachel's father. He must've died in his sleep last night. Grandma Agnes could be heard screaming by the neighbors. When they arrived to check on her, he was already gone. I thought you'd want to know, so I came right over," Ambrose told him.

Fletcher patted him on the shoulder and thanked him for coming. Ambrose hurried down the steps and left to get back to his grandmother.

Fletcher's wife opened the front door, rubbing her eyes. "Who was that, Fletcher?" she asked.

"Rachel, come sit with me on the swing," Fletcher said as he guided her by her elbow in that direction.

Rachel pulled away, with tears welling in her eyes. "Fletcher, what's happened? Who was that? I didn't get a close look at the man."

"It was Ada's brother, Ambrose," Fletcher told her.

"What's wrong? Is it Ada with her new baby? Are Joseph or Joey sick?" Rachel rapidly fired questions at him.

"No, Rachel, they are fine, probably still in bed asleep," Fletcher told her.

"Then why was he here so early?" she asked, all the while shaking her head no as it dawned on her why he might have come at that ungodly hour.

"It's your father, Rachel. He died peacefully in his sleep last night," Fletcher said as he took her in his arms.

"I don't understand. Dad hasn't even been sick, and he hasn't worked in years either. We just saw him at church last Sunday. He looked good." Her voice broke. "I don't understand."

"I know, dear, I'm so sorry," Fletcher said as he held her and felt her trembling. "You were blessed to have him for so long. He was eighty years old. You know he had a bad heart.

I guess that's what got him."

"When can I go see him? I want to go right now," said Rachel, her heart breaking.

"Let's put on some coffee and give his Agnes a little time with him. I understand she is taking it hard," said Fletcher.

"Well, of course, she is his wife," said Rachel.

They buried her father in the cemetery beside the church he loved. Agnes had been a good wife to him.

She had made his final years happy ones. She planned to move back in with her daughter and Clyde. She didn't feel like she could handle the small house by herself. They had always just rented it. Rachel was always kind to the grieving stepmother and thankful for the love they shared. She'd held her own grief in during the funeral but found it coming out at the most inopportune times as memories of her father were all around her.

Their trip down memory lane had left her exhausted. She and Fletcher made plans to go into Blacksburg and see what was playing at the theater. It had been a long time since they had an evening to themselves. Life had been at times too exciting and at others, too exhausting. Together, they would face whatever tomorrow might bring their way.

Printed by Libri Plureos GmbH in Hamburg, Germany